Praise for *Her Amish Wedding Quilt*

"Griggs builds a cozy world readers will happily settle into, and skillful characterization makes her hero and heroine leap off the page. Fans of Amish romance won't be able to resist this sweet treat."

—*Publishers Weekly*

"An amazing read...This is the first Amish-themed book that I seriously could not put down."

—Only by Grace Reviews

"A darling Amish tale with cute kittens, artistic quilt designs, fine furniture, a caring craftsman, a merry matchmaker, and Christmas cheer."

—The Avid Reader

"A thoroughly charming matchmaking romance, of friendship, faith, and family...A highly engaging read with fun plot twists, and well-developed protagonists."

—Labor Not in Vain

"A really sweet Amish romance and one I highly recommend."

—Splashes of Joy

ALSO BY WINNIE GRIGGS

Hope's Haven

Her Amish Wedding Quilt

Her Amish Springtime Miracle

Winnie Griggs

A Hope's Haven Novel

FOREVER

New York Boston

Forever
Hachette Book Group
1290 Avenue of the Americas, New York, NY 10104
read-forever.com
twitter.com/readforeverpub

First Edition: May 2022

Forever is an imprint of Grand Central Publishing. The Forever name and logo are trademarks of Hachette Book Group, Inc.

The publisher is not responsible for websites (or their content) that are not owned by the publisher.

The Hachette Speakers Bureau provides a wide range of authors for speaking events. To find out more, go to www.hachettespeakersbureau.com or call (866) 376-6591.

ISBN: 9781538735824 (mass market), 9781538735817 (ebook)

Printed in the United States of America

OPM

10 9 8 7 6 5 4 3 2 1

To my large, exuberant, wonderful family who are always such cheerleaders for me and my work, you have no idea how much I love you all and appreciate your love and support.

To my sweet friend Becki, who patiently answered my numerous questions about how things work when a baby is abandoned.

And to my editors Junessa and Leah, who were super patient and whose notes helped me to make this book so much better.

Her Amish Springtime Miracle

Prologue

Hannah Eicher inhaled deeply as she took a sheet pan of sugar cookies from the oven. She loved the aroma of fresh baked goods, but the scent of sugar cookies was her favorite. The sweet smell put her right back into her childhood, baking cookies with *Mamm*. Sugar cookies were the first thing *Mamm* taught her to bake, and they were also the first thing *Mamm* had let her bake by herself. The memory of those special times with her mother normally had the power to lift Hannah's spirits.

But not tonight.

She would give a lot to have *Mamm* to talk to right now.

Hannah fumbled as she went to set the pan down and jumped back as it hit the floor. She winced at the clatter—*Daed* and her older *shveshtah*, Martha, had already retired for the evening.

Fortunately, none of the cookies touched the floor, so except for two that broke they were still usable. She placed the pan on the counter, then leaned over the sink with her head bowed.

Not impossible but highly unlikely.

Even after three weeks, the doctor's words had the power to put knots in her chest, to clog her throat with a tangled ball of emotion. All her hopes and dreams for a large *familye* had shredded in an instant. Timothy breaking off their courtship hadn't made things easier. Not that she blamed him. He deserved a woman who would be a proper *fraa* for him, one who could give him children.

She'd thought she was coping, moving toward acceptance. She'd even made it through all the orders for Mother's Day desserts this week without breaking down.

But then yesterday she'd spotted a young couple, strangers to her, holding hands while the woman had her free hand resting on her obviously pregnant midsection, and suddenly Hannah felt as if she couldn't breathe. With barely a word to her co-worker, she'd fled the bakery and stood, bent nearly double, out back by the horse shed, sobbing uncontrollably.

Her fists clenched. Gotte, *why have You allowed this to happen? Is this the future You have for me, to be a spinster, relegated to the sidelines of my* familye*?*

Hannah took a deep breath, trying to push away the bitterness, to change her prayer to something reflecting faith and humility. She had to pull from the very depths of her being to do it.

Gotte, *it isn't my place to question Your will, but I'm weak. Please help me remember You are a loving Father who cares for His* kinner. *I beseech You for a miracle, but above all give me a sense of peace to face whatever future is in Your will for me.*

Trying to shake off her melancholy mood, Hannah

straightened and closed the oven door. She should have taken care of the order at her bakery before she left for the afternoon—this oven just wasn't made to handle large-scale baking. And Sweet Kneads was receiving more and more special orders these days.

Not that she was working on special orders. These cookies were for her weekly deliveries to shut-ins.

Grabbing a spatula, she gently pried each cookie from the baking sheet and set it on a large platter to finish cooling.

Then she turned to the small loaves of bread she'd baked earlier. A quick touch test verified they'd had enough time to cool, so she quickly wrapped them in plastic wrap and placed one in each of the seven cloth-lined baskets that already contained Martha's contribution of some home-made jam and cheese. Once she added the cookies, all that would be left would be for her friend Alma to add jars of her chicken soup when Hannah stopped by her place in the morning.

It was nearly eleven o'clock when Hannah straightened, swiping the back of her hand across her forehead as she surveyed her work by the glow of the gas lamps. Placing her hands on her hips as she arched her back, she decided she was well pleased with the night's results.

It was tempting to leave the cleanup for morning, but she pushed that thought aside as she pictured the sour face Martha would make if this sight greeted her tomorrow. And Martha was *always* the first one up in the morning.

As she worked, the comforting aroma of the sugar cookies lingered, providing a pleasant counterpoint to the astringent smell of the cleaning soap.

Finally hanging the dishrag above the sink, she stifled a

yawn. Hopefully she'd tired herself out enough that she'd sleep better tonight than she had these last few weeks.

She reached up to turn down the lamp, then paused when she heard a dog outside. That was Skip's I've-got-something-cornered bark. What had him all stirred up tonight? Had he spotted some critter prowling around the barn? It wasn't unusual for animals of one sort or another to look for a cozy place to shelter, especially with the cool-for-May temperatures they'd had the last few nights.

She chewed her lower lip. Should she go check it out?

Before she could decide, *Daed*'s door opened with that creak he hadn't gotten around to fixing yet. A moment later he stepped into the kitchen, his hunting rifle under his arm.

"*Ach*, Hannah, up late again I see."

"I'm just finishing for the night. Did Skip's barking wake you?"

"*Jah.* It's probably nothing, but if I don't check, Skip will keep at it all night." He reached for the flashlight they kept on the hutch.

Hannah followed him to the door. "I'll go with you. You may need me to hold on to Skip if he has an animal cornered."

Daed opened the door, and they walked side by side through the darkness. Hannah rubbed her arms, trying to ward off the cool night air. The three-quarter moon provided enough light for them to pick their way without the flashlight. Skip's barking was coming from the hay barn. If a stray animal was looking for a place to bed down, burrowing into the hay would be ideal.

As they neared the barn door, her *daed* switched on the flashlight and handed it to her. "Take this and shine it inside. Be careful." He raised his rifle. "It's probably just a stray cat, but there's no point in taking chances."

Hannah nodded and pointed the flashlight straight ahead.

Skip ran out to greet them, then rushed back inside to bark at whatever had invaded his domain.

Her *daed* moved ahead of her, his rifle at the ready. The interloper wasn't immediately visible, but based on Skip's position, it was right behind a stack of square bales halfway down the left side.

Was that a whimper? Hannah frowned in concern. Was the animal injured? Had Skip hurt it?

Her *daed* marched forward without hesitation, and Hannah hurried after, trying to keep the flashlight focused a few feet ahead of him.

As soon as he got in viewing distance of whatever was behind the hay bales, he stiffened and halted in his tracks.

What was it? Hannah followed and then she, too, halted at the unexpected sight.

An infant carrier, complete with infant, was nestled in a bed of hay.

Hannah rushed forward and dropped to her knees, gathering the pink-swaddled bundle into her arms, crooning soft nothings as she patted the *boppli*'s back.

The weight of the child in her arms was comfortable, precious, *right*.

"Where did this *boppli* come from?"

Her *daed*'s question barely registered as she continued to marvel at what she knew deep inside was the answer to her anguished prayers.

His next words, however, made more of an impression.

"There's a note." He reached past her and plucked it up. "*Ach*, it's addressed to you."

"To me?" She shifted the *boppli* in her arms so she could read the note.

In the distance, a motor vehicle's engine started up. Whoever had left this precious bundle had apparently stayed close by long enough to make sure someone found the infant.

Hannah looked down at the note.

Dear Hannah,

You don't know me very well, but you were very kind to me once when I needed a friend, and I appreciated it more than you will ever know.

My baby's father abandoned us before this beautiful little girl was born, and I'm unable to care for her on my own. I have no one I can turn to for help, so I'm asking you to take in my precious baby and love her as if she were your own. She comes from Amish roots, and I want her to be raised within the community of Plain people rather than by the English.

The only other thing I ask is that if you ever speak of me to her, please let her know that I loved her very much and truly believe my leaving her with you is what is best for her.

Hannah turned the note over, but the other side was blank—no name, no birth date, nothing other than that the baby was from an Amish family.

Was the mother an Amish girl who'd left the community for a young man only to be abandoned by him eventually? Hannah had heard of it happening before.

Regardless, she felt only gratitude that she'd been

entrusted with this precious gift. She would pray for the *boppli*'s parents every day. Just as she would thank *Gotte*.

She had prayed for a miracle, but to her shame she realized that her faith had been lacking. She hadn't truly believed those prayers would be answered.

But *Gotte* was good. He'd shown her such amazing grace in setting in motion the events that delivered this *boppli* into her care.

She would do everything in her power to cherish this beautiful, living, breathing miracle.

Chapter 1

One year later

Mike Colder pulled his truck into the parking lot of Rosie's Diner and turned off the engine, cutting off the country singer on the radio mid-lyric.

He sat there unmoving, staring straight ahead. The fatigue of the eight-hour drive that had followed a long day of physical labor pressed down like talons on his shoulders, rubbed grit in his eyes and wrapped a cloud of fog around his tired mind. When he'd decided last night to make this trip, he'd barely paused long enough to pack his bag and let his boss know he was taking a few weeks of his accrued vacation. He'd driven without stopping except once to refill his gas tank.

But he wasn't exactly sure where to start his search now that he was finally here.

Here in Hope's Haven, Ohio.

Here in the hometown he'd left behind as a child twenty-two years ago.

Here in the community that had turned their backs on

him and his father, just when they'd needed their support the most.

In fact, based on what his dad told him all those years ago, he half expected a group of bearded men in black *mutza* suits and straw hats to approach, hook their thumbs through their suspenders and demand that he leave.

But of course no one here knew who he was—at least not yet.

He rolled his shoulders and arched his neck, trying to ease the stiffness from his muscles and the fog from his brain. He needed a cup of coffee and something to eat. It was only ten forty-five, still early for lunch. But that day-old pastry he'd grabbed at the gas station three hours back was long gone. And already there were several vehicles, both buggies and cars, in the diner's parking lot, which boded well for the quality of the food.

The diner, located just inside the city limits, hadn't been in existence back when he'd lived here. It was one reason he'd selected this place to stop—no chance of being assaulted by unwanted memories.

Mike stepped out of his truck and immediately felt the difference in temperature. It had to be at least fifteen degrees cooler than the seventy-two he'd left behind him in Missouri. There were also light gusts of wind stirring the branches of nearby ornamental bushes.

He stuffed his hands in his pockets as he hustled toward the diner entrance. A spring wreath hung on the door, and right below it was an aged sign that listed the diner's business hours—the designation for Sunday indicated that this was an English-run establishment. Good.

Mike stepped inside and paused next to the podium where a placard requested customers wait to be seated.

While he complied, he studied the room. Years of experience as a paramedic had made swift assessments of his surroundings almost second nature.

The venue itself was set up like a typical diner. There was a counter with stools near the kitchen, a number of tables, both intimate and family-sized, and a row of booths along the windowed wall facing the street. The decor included an assortment of pie plates, both vintage and decorative, displayed on the walls.

About a fourth of the tables and booths were occupied. They were mostly English with a few Amish as well. As he scanned the room, his gaze paused at a table near the back where an Amish couple were seated. He was about to move on when the woman looked up.

Mamm!

In the space of one breath to the next he realized his mistake. His pulse resumed its normal rhythm and his hands unclenched. Of course it wasn't her—his mother had died twenty-two years ago, just before he and his dad moved away. In fact, he'd always believed that was part of the reason they'd left—too many painful memories here for his dad.

But for just that split second when she'd first looked up, he was a little boy again, basking in his mother's smile. It was only a trick of the light, of course. Couple that with the way she gestured and the lines of her profile, it had all played with his mind. He could see now that she was nothing like his mother, or what he could remember of her.

It seemed, whether he wanted them or not, the memories from his childhood were determined to make themselves felt. And as the past few moments demonstrated, many of those memories were good ones. Because they were the memories of a child, before his eyes had been opened by how deep betrayal could cut.

He pulled himself together as a young Amish woman carrying a menu stepped forward to greet him.

"*Wilkom* to Rosie's," she said with a smile. "Would you prefer a booth or a table?"

When he indicated he'd like a booth, she led him to the one nearest the door.

The fact that his waitress was a young Amish woman surprised him. He'd thought, other than cottage industries, Amish women rarely worked outside the home.

As he slid into his seat, he noticed that the waitress's name tag read Patience. She handed him a menu and placed a water glass in front of him. "What can I get you to drink while you decide on your order?"

"I'll take a cup of coffee please." He didn't bother to study the menu. "Is there something you'd recommend?" He'd found you rarely went wrong by taking the staff recommendations.

"Any of the lunch specials are *gut*, but my favorite is the chicken potpie."

Mike smiled as he waved a hand to indicate the room's decor. "Pies seem to be a theme here."

She returned his grin. "For sure and certain. Our cook makes a wonderful *gut* crust that's hard to beat."

He handed the menu back to her. "You've convinced me. The chicken potpie it is."

She jotted down his selection and retrieved the menu. "*Gut* choice. I'll turn in your order and be right back with your coffee."

Once she'd bustled off toward the kitchen, Mike leaned back and stared at the water glass, watching the condensation droplets sullenly slide to the bottom.

Yesterday he'd figured it was time to go through the last few boxes of his stepmother's and sister Madison's things. After all, the car accident that took their lives had happened just before Valentine's Day and it was now late April. When he'd come across Madison's diary, he'd given in to the temptation to read it. The very first line, though, had tilted his world on its axis.

I think I might be pregnant, and I've never been so scared in my life.

The words had hit him like a gut punch. When he'd finished reading her diary, he realized he'd have to go back on his vow to never return to Hope's Haven.

"Here you go." Patience set a dish in front of him, pulling Mike's thoughts back to the present.

As soon as he pierced the crust of the potpie with his fork, the aromatic steam billowed up, reminding him just how hungry he was. The first bite proved that the dish definitely lived up to Patience's recommendation. He took his time over the meal, savoring each forkful and putting off the moment when he'd have to decide on his next move.

But he finished his meal in what seemed no time at all.

He signaled Patience he was ready for his bill and while he waited, his attention turned to a new customer entering the diner, a young Amish woman with rosy cheeks and bright, curious eyes. Though he couldn't say exactly what it was, something about her caught and held his attention.

As she moved to the counter, her gaze casually scanned the room. When it connected with his, however, her steps faltered for just a second.

Mike had heard others talk about the instant connection they felt when exchanging glances with someone for the first time, but he'd always scoffed at such notions. Real connections were based on getting to know the other person, not in fleeting looks.

But for the first time he knew what they meant.

Something in that look drew him in, made him want to learn all about her. She seemed at once familiar, as if he'd known her forever, and foreign, like a rare creature apart from anything he'd ever seen before.

And by the way her eyes widened ever so slightly, he could tell she felt something too.

But for all that flashover of feelings, the connection was gone in an instant. She ducked her head shyly, then gave Patience a friendly wave as she reached the counter. Apparently she was here to pick up a take-out order.

He watched her chat with the cashier, her smile infectious, her hand gestures animated. Her gaze didn't stray his way again.

He tried not to be too obvious about his interest, studying her from the corner of his eye, until Patience returned with his ticket. Handing her his credit card, he leaned back and resolutely turned his thoughts back to his reason for making this trip.

He still had trouble accepting the revelations he'd found in Madison's diary. Part of him wondered if his little sister had merely been outlining a piece of fiction.

How could his sweet, carefree, barely nineteen-year-old sister have carried a baby to term without him or his stepmom being any the wiser? And to then have abandoned the child...

He scrubbed a hand over his jaw. The entry that had stabbed at him the most was when she'd written that she planned to anonymously leave the baby in Hope's Haven because she knew that, even if Mike were to discover her secret, he would never look for the infant there.

Well, in that she'd been wrong.

Knowing his nephew was out here was one of the few things that could draw him back. Because family was important. Especially when you thought you had none.

Not only did he intend to find the boy and claim him as his nephew, but he would do everything in his power to make sure the boy wouldn't be raised among these people.

The people who had turned their backs on him and his father just when they'd needed them most.

Pushing those thoughts aside, Mike surreptitiously focused again on the Amish woman with the ready smile and intriguing brown eyes. As he watched, she gathered up the bags with her order and moved away from the counter. Then she paused to speak to an older Amish gentleman who was eating alone.

Patience returned with his credit card and receipt, momentarily blocking his view.

Which was probably just as well. He had no business letting himself get distracted from his quest right now.

Mike placed a tip on the table and stood to go. But he hadn't taken so much as a step toward the door when he heard a sharp cry of concern.

"Carl, *was is letz*?"

Chapter 2

The panicked note in the Amish woman's voice jerked Mike's attention back to her. It took only a heartbeat to realize the man she'd been speaking to was choking, and less time than that for his training to kick in.

Mike rushed forward. As he passed a table with an English woman and kids, he issued a "Call nine-one-one" command without pausing. "Tell them we have an elderly man choking on something."

As soon as he reached the man's side, Mike pulled the chair away from the table. He spoke to the woman standing nearby in a calm but authoritative voice as he continued to work. "Your friend is choking, and I'm standing him up so I can help him."

Mike placed a hand on the man's chest and bent him over at the waist. As he administered five quick blows between the man's shoulder blades with the heel of his hand, he noticed that the woman had taken the man's hand, no doubt to comfort him.

When the blows didn't clear the problem, Mike shifted position to stand behind him and delivered abdominal thrusts in the Heimlich maneuver. On the third thrust, a chunk of food forcibly dislodged, and the man was able to finally draw a deep, shuddering breath.

Mike helped him sit, then stooped beside him to perform a quick exam, or the best exam he could do without getting his go bag from his truck. He glanced up at the woman still holding the man's hand. As if sensing his scrutiny, she met his gaze and again he felt that jolt of connection.

The wail of approaching sirens brought him back to the issue at hand. "What's his name?" he asked as he turned back to the choking victim.

"Carl."

"Hello, Carl. My name is Mike. Your throat will probably be a bit sore for a little while, but you should be able to breathe fine now. I suggest you let the guys who are arriving in the emergency vehicle check you out." He offered a reassuring smile. "They came all this way, after all."

"I don't know how I'll ever thank you. You saved my life, for sure and certain." Carl held out his hand.

Mike stood and exchanged a quick handshake. "No need for thanks. I was just in the right place at the right time."

Then he put his hand on Carl's shoulder as the man attempted to rise. "Keep your seat. Here comes the cavalry now." He glanced up and for a moment his gaze again locked with that of the Amish woman. That spark of connection and curiosity was still there. What was it about this woman?

Then the door opened and two EMTs rushed in.

Mike introduced himself to the new arrivals and explained what had happened. Then he stepped back and let them take over.

In the hubbub of the next few minutes, Mike slipped away, only pausing to exchange business cards with one of the EMTs in case they had follow-up questions. The adrenaline still zipped through his veins, leaving him with an edgy feeling that would take some time to dissipate. This was the kind of thing that he'd trained for, that made the long hours and emotional and physical effort worth it. If only all his assignments had happy endings like this one.

Unfortunately that wasn't the case.

Mike stuffed his hands in his pockets. He needed to decide what his next move would be.

But instead he found himself thinking of the woman he'd been drawn to in the diner. She'd smelled faintly of cinnamon and vanilla, scents that evoked warmth and hominess.

He'd glanced her way one last time before making his exit, and he couldn't deny that he'd found the respectful admiration in her expression flattering.

He forced his thoughts away from the woman inside— after all, he probably wouldn't see her again. The EMTs would be coming out of the diner shortly and he didn't want to be found just hanging around.

So where did he go from here? He'd intended to ask the waitress to recommend a local hotel or bed-and-breakfast but had forgotten in all the excitement. Oh, well, he'd just look it up on his phone.

But first he thought he'd check out the establishment across the highway, the one with the sign that proclaimed it to be The Amish Marketplace.

He hadn't taken more than a few steps in that direction when the door opened behind him and someone called out a breathless "Excuse me." Turning, he saw the Amish woman who'd occupied his thoughts a moment ago.

He couldn't help the little jolt of pleasure at seeing her coming after him.

* * *

Hannah had been strangely reluctant to let the compassionate stranger walk out of Rosie's without speaking to him one more time. For all she knew, he was just passing through town, never to return. The thought left her feeling as if her life would be the poorer for not seeing him again.

He'd turned at her hail and now waited for her to catch up to him. "Yes? Is there something I can do for you?"

She hadn't really thought about what she would say to him, so she latched on to the first topic that came to her mind. "I just wanted to say *danke* again for helping Carl the way you did. You saved his life for certain sure."

The wind had picked up, whipping the strings of her *kapp*. She tossed her head to move them out of her face. "My name is Hannah Eicher, and Carl, that man you just saved, is a *gut* friend of my *daed*'s."

"Well, Hannah Eicher, I'm Mike Colder, and there's no need for thanks. I'm glad I could help."

She liked the way the skin crinkled at the corners of his lips and eyes when he grinned. Something about him seemed so familiar, but she was certain she'd never met him before.

He turned back toward the highway crossing, obviously ready to continue whatever business he had here, but she was still reluctant to let him move on. "Are you a doctor?" she asked, reclaiming his attention. "Or just a *gut* Samaritan?"

"Neither. I'm a paramedic." He tilted his head. "Do you know what that is?"

It wasn't the first time she'd encountered an *Englischer* who thought the Amish were uninformed. "I do. But you're new to town, ain't so? Will you be staying here in Hope's Haven for a while?"

He shrugged. "I'm not sure yet. It depends how long it takes me to carry out my business."

She shifted the bags of food to her other hand, deciding she'd pushed the boundaries of polite curiosity far enough. Time to quit prying. Besides, she'd just thought of a business reason to seek him out.

But before she could speak up, he gestured toward her bags. "Do you need some help with those?"

"*Danke*, but I'm not going far. Just across the highway to the marketplace."

He raised a brow at that. "Making deliveries?"

She smiled. "In a way. I run one of the shops inside, the Sweet Kneads Bakery and Candy Store. This is lunch for myself and my co-workers."

"I see." He sounded surprised. Then he changed the subject. "Mind if I tag along? I was planning to pay a visit to the marketplace."

"*Nee*, you are most *wilkom*. All of the shops inside are worth visiting." Then she met his gaze with what she hoped was a convincing smile. "I actually have a favor to ask of you."

"Oh?"

She sensed his guard going up and hurried to explain. "A couple of weeks ago a customer in one of the shops suffered a heart attack. Thankfully the emergency responders arrived quickly, and things turned out well. But it was a close call. Some of the shop owners, myself included, discussed the idea of having some basic first aid training in case something like that should happen again."

"Knowledge is always a good thing."

That was a diplomatic, noncommittal response, but she pushed on. "Since I have the bakery, the procedures you just used to help Carl would be particularly useful for me to learn."

"Are you asking me to teach you what to do when you're faced with someone who's choking?"

She couldn't tell if he was being serious or not. "*Jah.* Or at least help me figure out how to get that kind of training. If you don't mind and can spare the time while you're in Hope's Haven, that is."

They'd reached the highway crossing by then, and their conversation paused while they waited for the light to change.

When he spoke up again, he seemed to be choosing his words carefully. "Surely your local emergency response team would be willing to work with you on this."

She felt the warmth climb in her cheeks. "Of course. It was impulsive and unthinking of me to put you on the spot. You're obviously a visitor and I shouldn't try to trespass on your time."

He waved aside her words. "I tell you what I can do. One of the medics and I exchanged business cards. I'll talk to him and let him know you're interested in getting some training. Because you're right. If the team is on another call or runs into traffic issues, they may not be able to respond as quickly as needed."

She'd definitely put him on the spot. "You're very kind to offer. But you mustn't feel obligated."

"It's no problem. I often do this kind of training or give talks on the subject back home. And I wouldn't mind getting a chance to talk shop with the local crew."

"And where is home, if you don't mind my asking?" There she went being nosy again. She wasn't usually so direct. What was it about this man?

"Drifton, Missouri."

"*Ach*, you're a long way from home." What sort of business would have brought him all this way?

They stepped inside the marketplace, and she turned to take her bags back from him. "This is my bakery," she said, nodding toward the first shop on their right. "Why don't you come in and let me give you a pastry to take with you."

He lifted a hand as he shook his head. "That's not necessary."

"Not necessary, but I'd like to do it all the same. Consider it a welcome to Hope's Haven gift."

She saw a flicker of something unexpected in his expression, but it was gone before she could identify it, replaced by a smile. "Do you by any chance have chocolate whoopie pies?"

His demeanor was that of a schoolboy looking for a treat. "*Jah*. Follow me, and I'll package some up for you."

He looked around, no doubt taking notice of the line and crowded tables. "It appears your place is popular."

"I'm blessed to have a number of loyal customers." She scanned the glass-fronted display cases beneath the tall counter and took quick inventory. The stock of snitz pies and snickerdoodles was low. However, the pecan bars and blueberry pies weren't selling as well as she'd expected. The honey wheat buns and potato bread seemed to be selling well, but they were over-inventoried on oatmeal bread. Everything else was at acceptable levels for this time of day.

She'd have to make a note to adjust her offerings tomorrow.

Ada Mullet, who took care of all the candy making, glanced up from her position behind the counter. Hannah greeted her by lifting the bags, indicating she had their lunches. Maisie Stoll, the seventeen-year-old who worked mornings, was busy answering questions for a customer and only glanced up for a moment before going back to what she was doing.

Then, with a head-tilt motion for Mike to follow, Hannah hurried around the counter and behind the partition wall that separated the main portion of the shop from the kitchen.

Mike leaned a shoulder against the refrigerator. "I feel special, being invited behind the curtain so to speak."

She smiled at that. It was true she rarely had visitors in her kitchen, but she felt this was an acceptable exception. She quickly packaged up six whoopie pies and handed them to him. "Here you go. I hope you enjoy them."

"Thanks, my mouth is already watering." Then he straightened. "I'll get out of your way now and let you get to your paying customers. I'll stop back by on Monday with whatever info I dig up on the first aid training."

"*Danke.* And if you have the time, I hope you'll visit the other shops in the marketplace. I assure you all of the offerings are of the highest quality."

"Perhaps another day." He paused a moment, as if

considering something. "Is there a hotel or bed-and-breakfast around here you'd recommend?"

"Of course." She led him to the coffee counter and picked up one of the tourist brochures to hand him. "This will give you directions to the local lodgings. I understand Blueberry Inn is very comfortable."

He scanned the list, and his eyes lit up in recognition. "The Graber Farms Bed and Breakfast is still in business?"

"*Jah.*" Then she frowned in question. "You're familiar with it?"

He shifted, as if uncomfortable. "I visited there as a child."

Her curiosity was piqued, but she merely smiled. "Well then, welcome back to Hope's Haven."

"Thank you." He lifted the bag he was holding. "And thanks again for the pies." And with that he made his exit.

Hannah moved back to the kitchen and washed her hands, still thinking about the paramedic. There was something about him, a guardedness below his polite exterior that made her want to learn more about what had happened to erect that wall.

Then she shook her head. She'd only just met the man—it was probably her imagination. Or perhaps it was his way with strangers. Especially pushy strangers, she thought wryly.

She picked up a tray of cupcakes she'd made earlier and moved around to the front. "Maisie, why don't you eat lunch first today? The meals are on the counter next to the oven."

Maisie nodded and moved to the kitchen. A moment later she was headed out of the bakery with her lunch bag in hand. Hannah watched her sit on one of the benches in the mall lobby, and shortly after she was joined by Hiram Detweiler, a young man from the woodworking shop across the way. Was there a romance blooming between them?

Before she could pursue that thought, she caught Ada giving her a sly glance.

"Who was that handsome *Englischer* you walked in with?" her friend asked.

Hannah ignored Ada's arch tone and answered matter-of-factly. "His name's Mike Colder, and he just arrived in Hope's Haven. I met him at Rosie's."

But of course Ada didn't leave it at that. "And what did he do to rate such special treatment?"

"He's a paramedic who saved Carl Amstutz from choking to death."

Ada's hand flew to her throat. "*Ach du lieva*, is Carl all right?"

"He is now, thanks to Mike."

"That's *gut*." Then Ada gave her a mock-pout. "How come nothing exciting happens when I pick up our lunch?"

"Because you usually ask me to do it."

Ada laughed. "Well, perhaps I'll start going myself more often."

Hannah smiled in response, but she shook her head at her friend's teasing. True, she found herself attracted to the newcomer, but she barely knew him. And regardless, it could never lead to anything more than friendship.

Even if he hadn't been an *Englischer*, she wasn't fit to be a *fraa* for any man.

Chapter 3

By three o'clock that afternoon, Hannah was ready to leave Sweet Kneads in Ada's capable hands along with Iris Plank and Eva Moser, two young girls who helped in the afternoons.

As she turned the horse and buggy onto the highway, she thought again about the *Englischer* who'd stepped in to save Carl. Truth to tell she'd taken note of the man when she first walked in the diner. He was a stranger, someone she hadn't seen in town before, which was always interesting. But more than that there was a bruised look about him, as if he wasn't just physically tired but soul-weary, as if he'd suffered some great loss that had marked him. It had made her want to comfort him.

Later, when he'd realized Carl was in distress, he'd immediately come to attention, transforming into a sharp, confident professional. He hadn't hesitated, hadn't faltered. He'd assessed the situation and taken immediate action. Mike was obviously a man used to taking charge in an emergency.

Of course, as a paramedic, he'd have had experience with such situations. It was a shame she hadn't learned more about him before he'd left. But he said he'd stop by on Monday, and she found herself eagerly anticipating seeing him again.

Hannah slowed the buggy as she saw the small phone shed that marked the drive leading to her home. She'd barely made the turn before Skip came running up, barking a boisterous greeting. Her *daed* followed the dog out of the barn and when he spotted her, moved to the buggy shed.

After they exchanged greetings, her *daed* waved her away. "Go see to your *dochder*. I'll take care of Clover and your buggy."

Dochder. She liked the sound of that. She was only Grace's foster mother right now, but she was looking forward to the day when her adoption of Grace would be finalized.

"*Danke, Daed.*"

She felt a pinprick of guilt for letting him take on her chore, but she didn't bother trying to hide her smile. Coming home to Grace in the afternoons was the highlight of Hannah's day. The Department of Job and Family Services had placed Grace in Hannah's care last year two weeks after she was left in their barn. For a few days, she'd worried that they wouldn't approve her as a proper foster mother. But Vivian Littman, Grace's caseworker from the department, had worked hard to make it happen, and in the end Grace had been placed in Hannah's care.

Since that time, Grace had become nearly her whole world.

When Hannah walked into the house, she spotted Grace holding on to the back of a kitchen chair. "Hello, sunshine."

As soon as the toddler spotted Hannah, her face lit up in that smile that never failed to warm Hannah's heart. Grace let go of the chair and started walking toward Hannah. After a couple of shaky steps, she plopped down on the floor and crawled the rest of the way.

Laughing, Hannah stooped down and scooped her up. "Have you been a *gut* girl today?" She squeezed Grace into a tight hug and her heart swelled as it always did when she felt the pudgy little hands reach around her neck.

Grace gurgled a laugh then said "Maa," her form of *Mamm*.

Hannah carried her to the kitchen table, then sat and settled the girl on her lap. Grace had brought such joy and purpose to Hannah's life. She couldn't imagine how she would have gone on if the adoption hadn't been approved.

"Hello, Hannah. I hope you had a *gut* day."

Hannah looked up to see Leah Burkholder, the neighbor and family friend who watched over Grace when Hannah was at work. "*Danke*. I did." She straightened Grace's *kapp*. "How did she do today?"

"Very well. She's always such a *gut* girl. And she's walking on her own more and more these days." Then she grimaced. "But she gave me quite a start this morning."

That didn't sound good. "What happened?"

"I'd set her on the floor in the front room with her doll so she could play while I folded laundry. I had my back turned to her for a few minutes and when I looked around I found her sitting on the sofa, grinning like she'd done a great trick." Leah shook her head. "She's turning into a monkey."

"You mean she climbed up on her own?" Hannah stared down at her little girl and felt a pang of disappointment. It was yet another first for Grace that she'd missed. Too many of those had happened this past year.

She gave Grace another hug. It was time—past time really—that she was more present in Grace's life. But how did she do that without giving up her bakery business, her only source of income? Raising a child came with financial responsibilities. And without a husband, she'd have to lean on her *daed* for that unless she could find another way to earn a living.

Martha entered from the basement, interrupting Hannah's somber thoughts. Her *shveshtah* went straight to the stove, throwing a quick hello Hannah's way. She lifted a cook spoon to stir whatever was simmering in her stockpot. "I hear there was some excitement at Rosie's this morning," she said over her shoulder. "Do you know anything about it?"

Hannah set a squirming Grace back on the floor. "How did you hear about that so quickly?"

"Verna stopped by right after lunch. She'd been to town and heard all about it."

Hannah should have known. Not much happened in Hope's Haven that Verna Bixlir didn't ferret out. And the woman enjoyed spreading the news around. In fact, she seemed to consider it her civic duty.

"So it's true? Did you hear from any of the people who were there?"

Verna wasn't the only one who enjoyed a bit of gossip. "Actually, I was there when it happened," Hannah said.

Martha turned around at that. "*Ach*, so you saw it all."

Hannah nodded. "I was there to pick up a lunch order and stopped to say hello to Carl Amstutz on my way out. While we were talking, Carl suddenly started choking."

Leah joined the conversation, her brow wrinkled in concern. "I hope he's all right."

"He is now. Before anyone else had a chance to react, another customer sprang into action and took charge. He performed the Heimlich maneuver, but it took a few minutes for Carl's throat to clear. By the time the town's EMTs arrived, the newcomer had Carl breathing again."

"And who is this hero?" Martha tossed the question over her shoulder again as she added some salt and pepper to her pot. Her *shveshtah* never seemed to stop moving—always busy, always looking for another project to tackle.

"His name is Mike Colder and he's visiting on some business. He's also an *Englischer* and a paramedic."

Martha turned around long enough to give her an arch smile. "It seems you learned quite a bit about this hero. I can hear in your voice that you were impressed, ain't so?"

Hannah ignored her tone. "What he did was impressive, for sure and certain."

"So, why is he in town? Does he have *familye* here?"

"He didn't say. But I did speak to him about getting some first aid training, and he said he'd help me look into it. So I expect to see him again on Monday." There was no point in telling her oh-so-responsible *shveshtah* how much she was looking forward to seeing him.

As it turned out, Martha was focused on the other half of her statement. "And why do you want to get first aid training?"

What a silly question. "If someone in the bakery chokes on his food the way Carl did, or worse yet someone here at home did so, I want to be prepared to help. And besides, it's a good skill to have, ain't so?"

Martha made a noncommittal sound indicating she wasn't convinced.

But Leah seemed more understanding. "Just so."

Hannah's *daed* walked into the house, pausing to stamp his boots on the mat. "I have Topper hitched to your buggy, and it's ready to go," he said to Leah. "We can head out to take care of your livestock whenever you're ready."

Normally Leah kept Grace at her own home, but two days ago Hannah had arrived there to find that a tree had crashed onto the roof during the night, seriously damaging the area over the kitchen. Once she determined Leah was shaken but fine, she'd insisted the woman move in with them temporarily, convincing her by saying how much she needed her help with Grace.

Her *daed* had gotten in the habit of helping Leah check in at her place when Hannah arrived home each day.

Leah stood and brushed at her skirt. "*Danke*, Isaac. If Hannah can spare me, I'm ready now."

The lightness in Leah's voice brought a smile to Hannah's lips. Her friend obviously missed her home and looked forward to these daily trips, even if it was just to take care of her goats and chickens.

After the door closed behind the pair, Martha paused, a thoughtful frown on her face. "Have you noticed how attentive *Daed* has been to Leah since she moved in?"

Hannah shrugged, more concerned with the game of patty cake she was playing with Grace. "They've been friends all their lives. Leah once told me the two of them and *Mamm* were scholars together when they were *kinner*. And Leah is a guest in our home."

"I suppose you're right."

But Martha didn't seem entirely convinced.

What was she worried about? Even though Leah's husband had abandoned her many years ago, in the eyes of the church and *Gotte*, she was still married. So the two older adults knew there could never be anything more than friendship between them.

Mentally shrugging it off, Hannah turned her thoughts back to how she could squeeze more time for Grace into her days.

* * *

Mike wasn't sure why he'd decided to stay at the B&B instead of the inn back in town. It certainly wasn't nostalgia or the desire to immerse himself in the local culture.

He'd driven by the place more out of idle curiosity than out of any intention to book a stay. His father used to sell applesauce and apple juice from their orchard to the Grabers and would often let him tag along. He had fond memories of getting the best melt-in-your-mouth snick-erdoodles from Mrs. Graber whenever he accompanied his dad on those deliveries.

But just about the time he'd been ready to turn around and head back to town, Mike had spotted a man, whom he later learned was Homer Graber, standing out in his field obviously having problems with a team of horses. In fact, it looked like one of the horses had come up lame. Mike had stopped to help and after they had the team stabled and had tended to the injured animal, Homer had insisted he come inside for a cup of coffee and a piece of his wife's cherry pie.

It turned out Homer was the son of the Grabers he remembered from his childhood. His wife, Ellen, was a plump, talkative woman who, like her husband, appeared to be in her late forties. By the time she had the coffee and slice of pie in front of Mike he'd learned the names of all their children, where they all lived, and a headcount of their grandchildren—twenty-three.

After twenty minutes visiting with the couple, he found himself agreeing to rent a room from them. Ellen mentioned that they normally leased only to Amish guests because it was an authentic Amish home, without electricity, but if he didn't mind that, she'd give him a good rate.

Mike, who sensed the couple could use the income, decided he could handle it for a day or two—it would be sort of like camping indoors. And if it became too uncomfortable, he could always move to the inn.

The Graber Farms Bed and Breakfast was for those who wanted the true Amish experience. There was no electricity, no fancy amenities. The appliances were powered by propane. The one concession he could see was the modern plumbing, though there was just one bathroom on each floor to be shared by all guests.

His bedroom was simply appointed. The only furniture was a bed, a nightstand, a pair of wooden chairs with cushioned seats, a dresser, and a wardrobe. Lighting was provided by a couple of battery-operated lamps. As expected, there was no place to charge his phone. But the bed was covered with a cozy-looking quilt and he could see several plump pillows.

Once settled in, Mike took a few minutes to call Clyde

Stafford, the EMT who'd given him his business card earlier. Mike explained about the training Hannah had asked for, and Clyde, who'd apparently pulled a Sunday shift, had invited him to come by their station the next day to discuss the request. While they were talking, it occurred to Mike that the firehouse was likely a safe-haven location just like his home base. His sister Madison was somewhat familiar with his work, so it made sense that she'd at least consider using a firehouse as a place to leave her baby.

Satisfied that he finally had a starting point for his inquiries, Mike decided to kill a few hours by checking out his current surroundings.

He walked the nearby fields, enjoying the brisk air and the exercise after being cooped up in his truck for that long drive. It hadn't helped that he'd missed his morning run today.

It was nearly dusk when he finally returned to the house. The Grabers graciously invited him to share their supper since he was their only guest at the moment.

When he retired to his room, Mike glanced at his watch, surprised to learn it was not quite nine. He was usually a night owl—not only by disposition, but because shift work had accustomed him to late hours.

He pulled out his sister's diary, once again reading through the experiences and thoughts she'd documented during the last seven months of her pregnancy. Was it wrong that he was more troubled that his sister hadn't wanted to tell him about her baby than by the fact that she'd actually *had* a baby?

She'd lied to him for months, both directly and by omission. She'd gotten pregnant out of wedlock. She'd stayed at school, even during breaks, to avoid the scrutiny

from him and their mom. The fact that she'd chosen to
have this baby on her own and leave her son, whom she'd
dubbed Buddy, in the care of a stranger rather than reach
out to him, showed a lack of trust that cut deep.

Was it because of the circumstances of her pregnancy?
Surely she knew he'd never turn his back on family,
regardless of the situation.

And how had she gotten herself in that situation to
start with? Madison had been a bit scattered and eccen-
tric, true, but she was also self-confident and not afraid
to stand up for herself.

Who was the father? And more important, *where* was
the father?

His nephew would be about a year old now, which was
both good and bad news. Bad because he'd missed a year
of the boy's life. Good because he was more confident of
his ability to care for a toddler than an infant, though he
had no experience with either.

He absolutely wanted to take guardianship of the
child. He owed Madison that much, even if she hadn't
trusted him to accept her child.

Without conscious effort, his thoughts turned to
Hannah. She was a strange contradiction. There was such
an innocence about her on the one hand. And on the
other there was this open curiosity that reached out and
drew you in.

But it was best he not let himself get drawn in. There
was too much unfinished business in his life right now to
pursue a female, even one whose eyes were as intriguing
as hers.

Especially when that female was Amish.

Chapter 4

I'm looking for Clyde Stafford. He's expecting me."

Mike had approached the first person he saw when he arrived at the firehouse Sunday morning. The garage doors were wide open and a few of the men were out front washing the firetruck.

The young man held out his hand. "My name's Steve Matthews. You must be the hotshot visiting paramedic who took care of that choking victim yesterday."

Mike took his hand and gave it a firm shake. "That's me. Name's Mike Colder. Job title, Hotshot Paramedic."

Steve grinned in response. "Glad to meet you, Mike. Ford's upstairs in the kitchen. Follow me."

So the man went by Ford—good to know.

They found him at the stove cooking a big pot of something that smelled amazing.

"Hey, Ford, you have a visitor."

The EMT glanced over his shoulder, then set his

spoon down and wiped his hands on a dishrag that had been flung over his shoulder. "Mike, you're early."

"I hope that's not a problem."

"Not at all. As long as you don't mind talking while I work at the stove."

Mike grinned. "Sounds like a good way to wrangle myself an invite to lunch."

"You got it. It's just firehouse chili, though."

"I've had my fair share of that back home. It'll be interesting to see how yours stacks up."

That earned him a grin. "I'll take that as a personal challenge." Ford turned his attention back to the pot. "So the Amish baker lady is interested in some first aid training."

Mike nodded. "After seeing what happened in the restaurant yesterday, she wants to be as prepared as possible in case the same thing happens at her bakery."

"Makes sense. She a friend of yours?"

"Never met her until she stopped me yesterday to discuss this." He leaned a hip against the counter. "So what about it? Are you open to setting something like that up for her and other interested parties?"

"Of course. We do it all the time, both general training and tailored training." He nodded toward a folder on a nearby table. "I put together a packet of information she can look at. There's a public session already scheduled for Tuesday evening, or we can do something special if it's needed."

Ford reached for a jar of spices, shook a liberal portion into the pot and then set the lid on it. "Now this needs to simmer for a bit. How about I give you a quick tour of the place?"

"Sounds good."

The station was set up much the same as the one Mike worked out of. The kitchen opened into a rec room with a big-screen TV and a large, comfortable sofa. There was a foosball table in one corner, and a pool table took up much of the rest of the room.

They wended their way through the equipment storage, the community meeting room, the weight room and training facilities and vehicle bays, pausing often for introductions and the exchange of stories.

As they toured, Mike looked for a natural way to bring up the subject of abandoned babies. About twenty minutes into the tour he found his opening. Ford stopped in front of a large metal box set in the wall.

"This is our safe-haven baby box," he said, patting the contraption.

Mike studied the box. It was about the size and shape of a large trunk and deep enough to comfortably accommodate an infant. "I've heard of these, but we don't have any in our area."

"I'm not surprised. They're not in wide use yet, but an anonymous donor provided the funds for our installation."

"Has anyone used it yet?" He tried to keep his voice and expression casual, but every part of him strained to hear the answer.

"Only once, about a year ago."

Mike's pulse jumped. Could he possibly have a lead on Madison's baby already?

"I was on duty at the time," Ford continued, "so I'm the one who received the little tyke. He was the cutest baby you'd ever want to see. I doubt Family Services had any trouble placing him in a good home."

It was Buddy—it had to be, the timing and location

fit. At least Madison had been responsible enough to leave her baby at a safe-haven drop. "What happened to him?"

Ford shrugged. "I assume he was placed with a foster family."

It appeared Mike's next step would be to contact Family Services. Waiting until the county offices opened tomorrow seemed intolerable.

For now, he would distract himself by getting to know this crew better and sharing a meal with them. So he dropped the subject and instead asked Ford about where he could find a good jogging trail.

* * *

When Mike finally left the firehouse, the sky had turned overcast and there was the feeling of an impending storm in the air. Despite that, he decided to do a bit of exploring. He drove around the town proper first, taking note of what still remained, what had been added and what had disappeared altogether. Of course, he'd last seen Hope's Haven through the eyes of a seven-year-old boy, so there were things he obviously hadn't been familiar with.

The sleepy small town he remembered as little more than a few stores and businesses to support the mostly rural Amish population had grown and modernized quite a bit. The road he'd driven into town on was now a four-lane highway, and there appeared to be as many if not more English vehicles than buggies traveling on it. How did the Amish community feel about sharing space this way?

But the most obvious change was that the town actively catered to tourist fascination with the Amish.

Many of the English-owned businesses advertised Amish or Amish-like wares, and there were stylized silhouettes of buggies and Amish folk everywhere.

When he drove north and east of town into the more residential areas, he saw the same sort of suburban housing you'd find in any Midwestern setting. By the time he turned his truck around and drove west of town, it had begun to drizzle. Still, he could see he'd found the landscape of his childhood.

There were barns and silos, buggies and horse-drawn equipment, hand-lettered signs advertising preserves, wicker baskets, quilts and rag rugs. Mike couldn't remember specific directions to childhood haunts, and the increasing tempo of the rain made it hard to pick out landmarks. Then he topped a hill and pulled up in front of a familiar sight—the schoolhouse.

He turned the engine off and stared at the simple one-room building to the sound of drumming rain and swishing windshield wipers. He couldn't tell if it was the same building or not, but it appeared smaller than he remembered. The playground equipment, swings and seesaws, were similar to what had been there when he was a kid, but the baseball field was new. In his day they'd scratched one out in the field and used feed sacks stuffed with dirt or sawdust for bases.

Through the curtain of rain, he could barely distinguish the shadowy forms of two outhouses on the far side of the building, one for the boys and one for the girls. It seemed that much hadn't changed.

What would he see if he looked in the window? The same single room with polished wooden desks and a wood-burning stove?

This place held so many memories for him, happy

memories of a carefree childhood, playing with friends, feeling secure and safe and as if he belonged. The transition from that to the English school—with its maze of hallways and crowds of students and teachers, none of whom knew his native language—had been shockingly abrupt and difficult.

And lonely.

Mike abruptly switched the engine back on and turned his truck around. This nostalgia was unproductive and distracting. He'd come back to Hope's Haven for one purpose only.

Time to find a place to eat. He'd seen chicken and dumplings on Rosie's menu yesterday. That sounded like just the thing on such a wet day.

Too bad the bakery wasn't open on Sundays. Those whoopie pies Hannah had given him yesterday had been every bit as good as the ones his mother used to make, if not better. And seeing Hannah, with her bright eyes and sweet smile, wouldn't be so bad either.

He pulled himself up short when he realized where his thoughts had strayed. The only business he had with the Amish baker was to discuss the training schedule with her.

* * *

First thing Monday morning, Mike headed to Millersburg, the county seat. He wanted to be the first one there when the Department of Job and Family Services opened.

But it turned out he could have slept in. The official he needed to speak to wasn't in the office.

"I'm sorry, Mr. Colder, but almost everyone is attending a meeting at the state capital today." The woman, whose nameplate identified her as Lisa Markham, held up a finger as she reached for the ringing phone. "Department of Job and Family Services. How may I help you?" She paused a moment, then "I'm sorry, ma'am, but Mr. Jacobs is out of the office until tomorrow. Can I be of service?" Another pause. "Of course. Let me transfer you to his voicemail."

After pressing a few buttons on the phone, she hung up and turned back to Mike. "I'm sorry, where were we?"

"I have a question concerning a baby who was left in Hope's Haven about a year ago."

"Right. If you want to come back tomorrow and speak to the supervisor—" The phone rang again, and the obviously harried woman again held up a finger and reached for the receiver.

With a nod and wave, Mike headed for the door. He'd made very little progress, but that was often the case with a cold call. He probably should have curbed his impatience and phoned first. Hopefully tomorrow would prove more fruitful.

An hour later, he stood in the doorway to Sweet Kneads. There were a fair number of people going in and out of the shops, mostly English with some Amish shoppers sprinkled in. Was it always this busy?

Hannah looked up from the customer she was helping, and her gaze met his. He liked the way her face immediately lit up in a welcoming smile.

She turned back to her customer, accepting his payment and giving back his change. Then she called for someone named Maisie, who shifted from restocking the breads to take her place behind the counter with the ease of long practice.

Hannah approached him with a warm hello.

"I hope I'm not interrupting," he said, returning her smile.

"Not at all. I needed to take a little break anyway."

He waved a hand toward the marketplace lobby. "Why don't we step out to the common area and find a bench?"

"Of course." She led the way to one of the few benches not already occupied.

As she took a seat, he glanced at the crowds milling around. "The marketplace seems to be doing a brisk business."

"*Jah*, the tourist season is picking up now that the weather is warming up. To be honest, more and more tourists visit us year-round." She shrugged with a teasing smile. "For some reason you *Englisch* seem to have a fondness for our ways and our goods, but not to the extent you want to actually follow our lifestyle."

What would she say if she knew he'd been born Amish? "Still, this all seems much too commercial for people who call themselves the Plain Folk." He mentally winced at the sharpness in his tone—he hadn't intended to take his cynicism out on her.

But if she took offense, she didn't show it. "We all must make a living, ain't so? And look around at these shops. Many of the goods we offer are those you might have found at a roadside stand a half dozen years ago. And still might if you look in the right places."

Then she changed the subject. "Have you been enjoying your stay here so far?"

He nodded. "It's been productive. And those whoopie pies you gave me were delicious. I tried to pace myself, but I'm afraid they were all gone by the time I went to bed Saturday night. Remind me to pick up a few more before I leave."

* * *

Hannah's chest warmed at his praise. But showing pride would be unseemly so she simply thanked him. Then she added, "If you want some variety, I do a special flavor each month. For April, it's lemon cream cheese filling."

"That does sound good." He gave his stomach a pat. "But you just can't go wrong with chocolate."

He didn't seem to be in a hurry to get to the point of his visit, so she waved a hand, taking in the entire marketplace. "Did you have a chance to look around at the other shops?"

He shrugged. "Not yet."

"You really should look around. Our shopkeepers are true craftsmen. You can find gifts for anyone here— parents, siblings, *kinner*." She wasn't prying about his marital status, really she wasn't. She was just encouraging him to support the shopkeepers here.

But Mike shook his head. "I don't have any family to speak of, and there's not anything I'm looking to get for myself right now."

"No *familye*." The very thought of such a situation broke her heart. "Oh, Mike, I'm so sorry."

He waved a hand dismissively. "No need to apologize, you couldn't have known."

She thought he was going to leave it at that, but a moment later he added, "My half sister and stepmom were killed in a car accident back in February."

She placed a hand on his arm in a reflexive gesture of comfort, then drew it away. She didn't want him to think her forward. "*Ach*, Mike, I'm so sorry." She knew she was repeating herself, but what else could she say?

"Again, there's nothing for you to apologize for."

She'd meant she was sorry for his pain, not for anything she might have done, but there was no sense trying to explain that. "Don't you have any extended *familye* at least, like *aentis* or cousins?"

He shook his head, tugging on the cuff of his shirt. "No other siblings, I've never married, and my dad passed away eleven years ago. There's no other close family."

She almost said she was sorry yet again but caught herself. "That must be difficult." She hoped he had close friends to support him.

The smile he gave her looked a bit forced. "I miss them, but I've always been something of a loner anyway."

He didn't seem bothered by his status, but Hannah wondered if that was the source of the guardedness she sensed in him. She believed one needed supportive connections with others to feel truly whole.

She sat up straighter as an idea hit her. "Do you have any plans for this afternoon?"

Chapter 5

Mike wasn't sure what Hannah had in mind with that question—was she trying to rope him into helping with something else? "No plans. Why?"

She leaned forward, her eyes alight with whatever she had planned. "On Monday afternoons I take some of my baked goods to Whispering Oaks, a local senior citizens' home. I visit with the residents and hand out the pastries and other goodies." She gave him a hopeful smile. "I thought perhaps you might be interested in going with me today. I know the residents would enjoy having a new visitor."

That certainly wasn't what he'd expected. To give himself a moment to figure out how to respond, he took a conversational detour. "I didn't know the Amish made use of retirement homes."

"*Nee*, none of the residents there are Plain Folk. But we are all *Gotte*'s children, ain't so?"

She waved a hand. "My friend Anna Mae Fisher

works there, and last December she asked if I would do it as a Christmas treat for the residents. I enjoyed it so much I just kept going every week. According to Anna Mae, some of the people who reside there have no one to visit them."

"That's very generous of you."

She shifted as if his praise made her uncomfortable. "Not at all. It only takes a little bit of time and some extra treats from the bakery. It's *gut* to assist others who need a bit of help, ain't so?" She had a feeling he needed this reminder that he was not alone in his loneliness.

"What time do you plan to head out this afternoon?"

"So you'll come?"

He nodded. "I have some time on my hands, so this seems as good a way to spend it as any."

"*Wunderbaar!* I usually leave here around two o'clock. You can meet me at the back of the building by the horse shed if you like and we'll go from there."

Then she tilted her head and studied him a moment. "You said there was something you wanted to discuss with me?"

He'd almost forgotten why he'd come here. "I just wanted to let you know I've got the info for you about the first aid training. I spent some time visiting at the firehouse yesterday. Ford, one of the EMTs there, tells me they're offering a training class tomorrow evening, and there are seats left if that fits into your schedule. Otherwise he can set up something special for you after the end of the month." He reached inside his jacket. "I have a folder here with more information."

"I don't want him to go to any special effort, so I'll make tomorrow work. I just need to let my sitter know she'll need to keep an eye on my little girl, while I'm out."

Her words blindsided him. She had a child?

It made sense, of course, for a woman like her to be married. He was just taken aback because she worked at a job outside the home, a rare thing for Amish mothers of young children.

"Will your husband be joining you for the class?" Even to his own ears, his words sounded stiff.

She waved a hand dismissively. "I don't have a husband. I—"

"Hannah."

She turned and smiled at the Amish woman approaching them.

While Mike absorbed the news that she was apparently a widow, Hannah performed the introductions. "Mike, this is my *shveshtah* Greta Stoll. She and her friend run the quilt shop." She gestured to the shop next to her bakery, and he saw it had The Stitched Heart Quilt Shop on a sign above the door.

Then she turned to her sister. "Greta, this is Mike Colder, the man who's helping me get the first aid training I told you about."

"I was hoping that's who you were talking to," Greta said with a bright smile. "I wanted to let you know that Noah and I would like to join you for that training if it's okay."

"For sure and certain." Hannah turned back to him. "Noah is Greta's *mann*. He runs the woodworking shop, and he's the one who developed this entire marketplace."

"It sounds like this place is pretty much a family affair."

Hannah smiled at that. "Noah is quite an enterprising

businessman. And he gladly shares his expertise and resources with others in the community."

Greta picked up the conversational thread. "*Jah*," she said proudly. "Noah started by expanding this building that housed his woodworking business to include three other Amish-owned shops. It was so successful he was able to add two additional shops this year, and renamed it The Amish Marketplace. And if all goes well he has plans to expand again next year."

As Greta spoke of her husband's entrepreneurship, it suddenly hit Mike. Could this be the same Noah Stoll he'd played with as a boy, the one who'd sat next to him in school, the one he'd practiced skipping stones with on Miller's Pond? Noah had lost his own mother at a young age, and when Mike's mother had her accident, Noah had tried his best to be a comfort.

But Greta was still speaking, dragging his focus back to the present. "Noah had first aid training about four years ago, but he admitted he wouldn't mind going through it again."

Mike nodded. "It's always good to have a refresher, especially if you haven't had to use the training in a while."

Hannah jumped in. "Mike just mentioned there's a class at the firehouse tomorrow evening."

"At six o'clock," Mike added.

"I'll speak with Noah, but I think we should be able to do that."

"You can leave your *kinner* at our house. Grace will like spending time with her cousins. And *Daed* and Martha will enjoy having them there too."

So she lived with her father and someone named Martha—probably the sister she'd referred to earlier.

While the two sisters discussed the logistics of childcare and transportation, Mike kept going over his memories of Noah. He hadn't thought about his childhood friend in a very long time but now he wondered what sort of man he'd turned into.

Impulsively, he turned to Greta. "Do you think your husband would mind if I got a look at his workshop?"

Greta seemed taken aback, then looked to Hannah as if asking her opinion.

Regretting his unguarded request, Mike waved a hand. "I'm sorry, I didn't mean to put you on the spot. Forget I asked."

Greta's expression immediately softened. "No need to apologize. I'm just not sure how busy Noah is right now, so I don't know if he has the time for a visitor. Why don't I just go ask him if this is a *gut* time?"

"Truly, there's no need. I'll be here for at least a week, so don't feel as if you need to disturb him now." The more Mike talked, the more foolish he felt. He wasn't one to give in to feelings of nostalgia or sentimentality.

But she just smiled away his protest. "I was already heading there to tell him about the first aid class, so it won't be any problem at all."

And before Mike could protest again, she was off.

Hannah smiled, no doubt sensing his consternation. "It doesn't do any *gut* to argue with Greta. She has a mind of her own." Then she straightened. "I should get back to the bakery. I'll see you at two o'clock." And with a wave she turned and headed back to her shop.

Mike stuffed his hands in his pockets, watching her walk away, feeling unsettled. In the space of ten minutes he'd agreed to help Hannah make a visit to a retirement home and tried to wrangle a visit with an old childhood friend.

What was happening to his resolve not to get involved in the Hope's Haven Amish community again? The problem was, he had too much time on his hands. The sooner he was able to find and lay claim to his nephew so he could leave, the better.

A few minutes later, he saw a door marked Employees Only open, and Greta appeared, waving him over.

As soon as he drew near, she smiled. "*Kum.* Noah said he would be more than happy to show you around the workroom."

Well, too late to back out now.

As Mike shook Noah's hand a moment later, he searched the man before him for some sign of the boy he remembered. But Noah now sported a beard and his frame had filled out. There were calluses on his hands from years of manual labor and lines on his face borne of experience.

Then he saw the almost-faded scar on the top of Noah's left hand and smiled. This was his childhood friend all right.

Noah, on the other hand, didn't seem to recognize him—not that Mike had expected him to. He, too, had changed quite a bit in the past twenty-plus years. And on top of that, his father had changed their names when they moved away.

Noah released his hand. "Greta tells me you want to have a look around my workshop. Are you a woodworker as well?"

Mike held his hands up, palms facing outward. "I have no talent in that area. I was just interested in seeing a craftsman at work."

"Well then, let me introduce you to the men who work with me."

Mike was tempted to tell Noah who he was, to have the opportunity to reminisce a bit about the good times they'd had together before everything changed. To get his former friend's perspective on what had happened back then.

Then again, he wasn't ready to reveal himself to the community at large, might never be ready. And he couldn't burden Noah with keeping that secret. Besides which, a small part of him wondered if his friend would welcome him back or if he sided with those who'd turned their backs on him.

So he held his peace.

But a feeling of unease settled deep in the pit of his stomach. Withholding his identity was like lying, even if it was a lie of omission.

And such dishonesty did not sit well with him at all.

Chapter 6

Around one thirty that afternoon, Hannah handed her latest customer their change and looked toward the door to see Mike standing there. He was early, which for some reason made her happy.

He smiled when he saw he had her attention and stepped forward. "Just wanted to let you know I'm here so you won't need to wait on me. Don't rush on my account, but whenever you're ready to go I thought I'd help you carry out whatever baked goods you planned to take with you."

How thoughtful. "*Danke.* Give me a few minutes to finish here and then clean my baking pans in the kitchen and I'll be ready to go."

"No rush, we're on your schedule this afternoon."

His words only added to her good mood.

"In fact," he continued, "if you don't mind my making myself at home in your kitchen, I'll handle dishwasher duties while you take care of what you need to out here."

That offer was totally unexpected. "*Ach*, I couldn't ask you to—"

Mike interrupted her protest as he headed around the counter. "You didn't ask, I volunteered. And don't worry, I've pulled my share of kitchen duty at the station where I work, so your pans are in good hands." And before she had time to protest again, he'd disappeared into the kitchen.

Fifteen minutes later, Hannah stepped into the back to see Mike placing a dishcloth over the sheet pans in the dish drain.

He raised a brow. "Do I pass muster?"

She frowned in mock-severity. "It'll do." Then she smiled. "Honestly, *danke*, you did a wonderful *gut* job." She hung her uniform apron on a peg. "If you don't mind helping me load those boxes into my cart, we can be on our way." And with that she fetched a collapsible wheeled wagon from a corner of the kitchen and pulled it open.

Once the wagon was loaded, Mike took charge and indicated she should precede him. As they exited the bakery, she turned away from the marketplace's front entrance. "My horse and buggy are out back, so we can use the rear exit."

"Lead the way," Mike said with a sweep of his free hand. Then, as they moved forward, "This load of baked goods seems a bit more than just the 'extra bits' you referred to earlier."

She felt warmth crawl up her cheeks. "There's always goods left over at the end of the day."

He raised a brow. "Lucky for the Whispering Oaks residents, I suppose."

By this time, they'd reached the exit and Hannah was able to change the subject. She moved to her buggy and set her tote bag inside. "If you don't mind, you can unload the cart in the back of my buggy while I take care of my horse."

He paused a moment before doing as she asked. "Are you sure you wouldn't rather take my truck? It's weather-proof and it'll be faster."

It was a kind offer, but she stood firm. "*Nee.* My buggy's quite comfortable, the sky is clear and quick doesn't always mean better."

He nodded and went to work.

Hannah stepped inside the horse shed and went to Clover's stall. She knew Mike had been hesitant to come with her today, but she hoped he would be glad he had. She prayed that her plan to help Mike find a measure of joy by interacting with her friends at Whispering Oaks would bear fruit.

Despite his profession he seemed like a man who needed to find those kinds of connections in his life.

* * *

Mike had forgotten about the slow pace of the Amish. It wasn't that they were lazy, in fact just the opposite. He supposed a good way to describe it was that they were always busy yet unhurried.

Without further discussion about taking his truck, he quickly stowed the baked goods.

That done, he headed inside the shed, where he heard her murmuring to a chestnut-colored horse. He joined her at the stall, watching how affectionately she stroked the animal's nose. "I take it this one is yours."

She glanced his way. "*Jah.* Her name's Clover and I raised her from a foal."

"She seems like a fine animal."

Hannah held out a handful of grain and Clover lipped it from her palm. "For sure and for certain. Clover and I are *gut* friends." She gave the animal a final pat, then opened the stall gate.

As she led Clover out of her stall, she gave him an assessing look. "How much do you know about hitching a horse to a buggy?"

"Not much, but I take direction well."

That earned him a smile, one that crinkled the corners of her eyes and lit up her face. "An admission like that is the mark of a man who's confident in who he is." She clipped her animal's lead to a strap nailed to the wall and grabbed a brush. Then she began vigorously combing the horse's coat. "First you have to make sure there isn't any dirt, bedding, or other trash on her coat." She spoke without looking up. "It's not just so she'll look her best. It's important because if you don't, the harness can rub against foreign material and make sores on the animal. It just takes a few minutes but it's well worth it if you prize your horse."

He remembered being a youngster and hearing his father saying something similar.

Once finished, she set the brush back in its place and reached up on the stall peg to retrieve Clover's collar and traces. "Ready for your lesson?"

At his nod, Hannah gave him directions on the various fastenings, interspersing her instructions with demonstrations. She spoke with the easy confidence of one to whom this was second nature. Mike listened intently, enjoying the sound of her voice and the way she avoided talking down to him. He did as she said, accepting correction without rancor, finding a natural rhythm to the task.

He finally stepped away from Clover. "Are we done?"

"With this part. Now we have to hitch her to the buggy."

He followed as she led Clover outside, and watched as she snapped the lead to the hitching rail. Then she moved to the buggy and lifted the shafts. Mike hurried forward and grabbed one side from her and together they slipped it around the horse. Again she gave him instructions, attaching the left side to the proper straps while he followed suit on the right.

"*Danke.*" She patted the animal before stepping away. Then she moved around and studied the work he'd done. Finally she gave him a beaming smile. "*Gut* job! You *are* a quick study, for sure and certain."

He found himself warmed by her praise.

"Whispering Oaks is about three miles north of here. You can ride with me in the buggy if you like or follow me in your truck if you prefer its comfort." The smile she gave him held a note of challenge.

Not one to let a challenge go unanswered, he returned her smile. "I'll join you in the buggy."

Her expression let him know he'd given her the right answer.

"Just let me get my go bag from the truck and I'll be right with you."

"Go bag?"

"It's a duffel that holds some basic medical equipment—stethoscope, bandages, blood pressure cuff, that sort of thing. I like to have it with me even when I'm off duty."

As he returned with his bag, he saw her nibbling on her lip. What was she up to now?

"Would you like to take the reins?" she asked.

Mike was surprised she would trust him, an apparent *Englischer*, with her buggy. "I'm game. But I may need a bit of coaching." He'd learned to handle a pony cart on the country back road near his family's place just a few months before he'd moved away from here. And his dad had let him take the reins of the family buggy a time or two. But he hadn't ridden in a horse-drawn vehicle since he was seven years old, much less driven one on a busy city street.

"I'll be happy to provide a bit of instruction, but you appear to live up to your claim of being a quick study."

"Sounds good." Mike stepped up in the buggy from the right, the driver's side, while Hannah went around to the left. Hers was an open buggy so there was very little protection from the elements. Not a problem on a fine day like today.

Before they set out, she gave him some quick instructions on how to set the horse in motion and direct the animal to turn left or right. Her instructions were again clear, concise and straightforward.

Finally she leaned back. "Ready?"

He nodded. "I just need the directions."

"Turn left when you leave the parking lot and then right at the first traffic light. And don't worry, Clover is used to the *Englischer* vehicles, so the noise won't spook her."

He could feel Hannah watching him closely as they started out, no doubt ready to jump in and take over if he should run into problems. But by the time he made the turn at the traffic signal, she'd leaned back and seemed to relax. Apparently his driving skills had passed muster.

"I suppose I should tell you a little bit about what to expect when we get there," she said. "The residents are friendly for the most part and most will be wonderful happy to see us. But, as with any group of people, there are some who can be more challenging."

He had a feeling she was being more than a little diplomatic with that description.

She gave him an earnest look. "But I believe those are often the ones who need us the most, ain't so?"

He let her question pass, focusing instead on the first part of her statement. "In what way are they challenging?"

"Let's just say they won't greet our visit with as much enthusiasm as the others. Some suffer from aches and pains, which makes them seem grumpy. Others have turned bitter because they feel abandoned or forgotten. We just need to keep all this in mind and smile and love them as we are instructed to."

Then she grinned. "Of course, it isn't always quite that simple. Anna Mae and I occasionally have some very interesting and, I'm sorry to say, not always charitable conversations."

He grinned in response. Good to know she was human after all.

Then he changed the subject. "Tell me about yourself. What do you do when you're not baking or visiting seniors?"

"I live on a dairy farm along with my *daed*, *shveshtah* and little girl. There's always work to be done, of course, but I spend as much time with Grace as I can."

"How old is she?"

"She'll turn one in just a few weeks." Hannah's voice had that unmistakable proud-momma quality.

So Grace was close to his nephew's age. Hannah could be a good source of information for what he could expect. "Is she walking and talking?"

"She babbles, but hasn't really started forming words yet. As for walking, she can as long as she has something to hold on to. I expect her to walk on her own any day now."

"And are you looking forward to that day?"

Hannah nodded. "*Jah.* I just hope I'm present to see it." She cut him a sideways look. "So many of her firsts happen while I'm at the bakery."

"And that bothers you?"

"*Jah.* But I am grateful for the time I do get to spend with her."

He was trying to figure out a way to ask about Grace's father when she changed the subject. "I probably should tell you what to expect when we get there."

After that, Hannah chatted about the people they would be seeing today, sharing anecdotes from prior visits. It was obvious she felt a real affection for the folks they were going to visit even though none of them were Amish.

When they arrived at Whispering Oaks, Hannah directed him to a place where he could park the buggy. He unloaded the boxes of baked goods into her utility cart while she tethered Clover to a hitching post. Had they set it up just for her? Or did they have other Amish visitors here?

She stepped back from the horse. "Ready?"

"Lead the way." He once again took charge of the cart.

When they entered the lobby, Hannah went directly to the reception desk and signed in. "Hello, Melba." She placed a muffin on the counter with a flourish.

"Is that one of your strawberry cream cheese muffins?"

"*Jah.* I know how much you like them." She slid the sign-in book toward Mike, then reached back in the wagon for a box. "And these cookies are for the rest of the staff."

Melba patted the box. "You're an angel. Everyone looks forward to seeing what you'll bring on your Monday-afternoon visits." Then she eyed Mike, speculation lighting her gaze. "I see you also brought a helper with you today."

"Melba Johnson, this is Mike Colder. Mike's visiting Hope's Haven for a few days and generously agreed to accompany me today."

"Welcome, Mike. Thanks for coming. Our residents are always glad to have newcomers drop by for a visit."

Mike sketched a half bow. "It's my pleasure." He grinned. "Not to mention, Hannah didn't give me much choice."

"Good for her." Melba turned back to Hannah. "They're all eagerly waiting for you and your goodies."

But Hannah didn't immediately move away. Instead she pulled her notebook out of her tote bag. "Are there any new residents or changes in dietary restrictions I should know about?"

"We have one new resident since you were here last, a gentleman named Frank Morris. Frank's on a low-sugar diet, but no other restrictions or allergies to worry about."

As Melba talked, Hannah penciled in her notebook. Then she closed it and turned to Mike. "Let me see that box on top." She looked over the packages and lifted one that had a blank label. "These peanut butter cookies should work for Frank today. And I'll make note of his favorite flavors for next time." With that she wrote Frank Morris's name on the tag.

Melba waved a hand to her left. "Most of the residents

are in either the common room or the library. They'll be glad to see you."

When Mike followed her into the common room, he estimated there were about twenty people already there. But it was a large room and well laid out so it didn't seem particularly crowded. The walls were painted a soft blue and several paintings, mostly landscapes, were scattered about. Off in one corner was a piano topped with a vase of bright-colored flowers and a tall table with an overflowing fern.

All in all, it was much cheerier than some senior living facilities he'd had occasion to visit.

There were two staff members present, one dressed in scrubs and the other in Amish garb—obviously Hannah's friend Anna Mae. The residents were all engaged in various activities—playing bridge, playing dominoes, working a puzzle, conversing. Before he could register more, everyone stopped what they were doing and greeted Hannah.

She returned their hails with a genuine smile. "*Gutentag*, everyone." She waved a hand in his direction. "This is my friend Mike Colder. I told him good things about all of you, so I expect you to be on your best behavior today."

There were a lot of good-natured protests and groans about how she was asking too much of them. From their reactions, it was obvious Hannah was well liked here, and not just for the goodies she brought with her.

She moved about the room, taking her time. She had a word for everyone, and it was personal. She asked after grandchildren and hobbies, inquired about past ailments and listened sympathetically to reports of new ones, and even commented on changes in appearance like the lady with the new hairdo, or one with a different color nail polish, or the gentleman with a jaunty bow tie. Most residents lit up when she spoke to them. And her smile was just as sunny when she was speaking to the grumpier residents as the cheerier ones. He noticed, though, that even those who didn't seem happy to see her didn't refuse her delectable gifts.

Of course she managed to draw him effortlessly into the conversations. He shared non-personal information about himself and anecdotes as appropriate and dodged the flirtatious overtures from several of the ladies. And as the time passed, he found he was enjoying himself more than he'd expected.

Hannah had already spoken to most of the residents in the room when she approached a group of four men playing dominoes. "Gentlemen, this is Mike. He's visiting in the area for a few days."

She turned to Mike. "These four are some of the keenest domino players you'll find anywhere." Then she grinned. "At least that's what they tell me."

She grabbed a cellophane-wrapped packet from the basket and turned to the man closest to her. "This is Ernest. He ran Ready Plumbers for over thirty years and also sat on the Hope's Haven town council." She smiled at the lanky gray-haired man with a cane near his right elbow. "I brought you your favorite, a walnut brownie."

Ernest accepted the bundle and captured her hand, planting a kiss on it with a flourish. "Tell me you're not still holding out for an Amish man and that I have a shot with you."

Mike felt a little pang of envy at the easy way the man flirted with her.

She laughed as she withdrew her hand. "As you can see," she said to Mike, "Ernest is something of a flirt."

Mike winked at the man. "Seems to me he's just a man who knows what he wants and isn't afraid to go for it."

Ernest gave her an arch look. "I like this man."

Hannah rolled her eyes and turned to a balding bear of a man with florid features. "And this is Mac. He's a landscaper. Some of the prettiest gardens in the area owe their beauty and design to his skill."

Mike shook his hand. "Actually, my dad was in landscaping and I spent a lot of my summers working with him before I graduated." He grinned. "Of course most of my efforts fell in the manual labor rather than design category."

Mac puffed his chest out a bit. "Nothing wrong with that. We all have to start somewhere."

While they spoke, Hannah pulled another package from the box. "Last time I was here you asked me to surprise you, so I brought you my April special, a lemon cream cheese whoopie pie."

"Don't know how you do it, Hannah, but that sounds like you picked just the thing for me again."

"It's because you're so easy to please." She moved around the table. "George here drove an eighteen-wheeler for over twenty years. He's visited every state in the continental US and has quite a few stories to tell about the things he's seen."

"True, but I don't like to go on about it."

Mac guffawed. "Don't you believe it, Mike. George'll break out one of his stories at the drop of a hat."

George stiffened. "At least I don't try to hog the extra Hawaiian rolls at suppertime."

Mike could tell there was no real acrimony in their bickering—it was a lot like the digs that went on among the firefighters and EMTs at the station back home.

"I like your stories," Hannah said as she handed George a packet. "I have the peanut butter muffin you asked for."

Then, as if that settled the matter, she moved to the final member of the quartet. "And last but definitely not least is Leon. He worked in food services and served as a volunteer fireman for many years."

Mike gave the man a respectful nod. "I've worked with quite a few firemen. They're definitely a special breed."

"What sort of job do you have that involves working with firefighters?"

"I'm a paramedic."

Leon nodded. "Also a special breed."

Hannah held out another of her cellophane-wrapped bundles. "Here are your chocolate chocolate chip cookies."

"My favorite." George gave Mike a probing look. "So how do you two know each other?"

"I ran into Hannah my first day here." Mike gave her a raised-brow look. "Ten minutes after we met, she recruited me to help her with some first aid training."

"That's our Hannah, always on the lookout for a likely recruit."

"I like to think of it as being resourceful," Hannah said, her nose tilted up in mock-affront.

Did she know how cute she looked when she did that?

"We're just about to start a new round," Leon said, meeting Mike's gaze. "We could use another player. What do you say?"

"Thanks, but I'm here to help Hannah—"

"Nonsense," Hannah said before he could finish. "I'm fine. In fact, there are a few bed-bound residents I want to visit before we go. So you have time to play a round or two."

"Unless you're afraid of getting soundly trounced," Leon challenged.

Mike pulled up a chair. "Well, I certainly can't walk away now, can I?"

"I'd say I'm leaving you in *gut* hands but I'm not so sure." Hannah gave the men around the table a mock-stern look. "You four take it easy on our visitor. None of your shenanigans."

Ernest put a hand over his heart. "My dear, you wound me with such accusations."

Hannah rolled her eyes again then turned to Mike, her gaze inviting him to share her amusement. "Consider yourself warned." And with that she turned and walked away, a basket of cookies and pastries on her arm.

Apparently, in addition to her other intriguing qualities, the baker had a playful side.

Chapter 7

Hannah settled back in the buggy as Mike took the reins. "It was *gut* of you to visit here with me today." She especially appreciated the fact that he hadn't just tagged along, he'd engaged with the residents, listening attentively, sharing his own stories, even doing a bit of teasing here and there.

He cut her a sideways glance as he turned the horse. "You didn't seem to need much help."

"It's more about giving time and attention to the residents than about handing out treats. And you definitely did well in that department." *And I hope you received something in return.*

"That one lady who came in after you left me in the clutches of your domino-playing friends—she certainly didn't seem happy to see you."

Hannah sobered. She hadn't realized he'd seen that. "Fay lost her husband, daughter, son-in-law and two grandchildren to a boating accident six years ago. It turned her bitter and she's pushed away everyone who tries to befriend her. I'm willing to endure her grumpiness if I must to bring what light I can to her life."

"You seem to know a lot about the residents."

"I just listen to whatever they want to tell me. Many of them are starving for attention, for some acknowledgment that they still matter."

"And you visit them every week?"

"*Jah.* Every Monday."

"Do you visit other facilities around here as well?"

"Not exactly."

"Not exactly?"

He certainly seemed curious about her activities. Was he interested in performing more of this kind of service?

"There is a group of us, the bishop calls us the *Yingah Shveshtra*, the Little Sisters. We take turns checking in on shut-ins around the community and carrying them meals and groceries. Wednesdays are my days off from the bakery so that is my day to perform this service."

"On your own?"

"We work in pairs. My friend Agnes is my partner, but she has three young *kinner* to take care of, so she prepares jars of soup and I make the deliveries."

"So your day off is not really a day off."

She shrugged. "Let's say it's a change of pace. And who wouldn't enjoy visiting a group of people who are always so happy to see you?"

She shifted, settling more comfortably on the bench. "Of course we focus on those who don't have close *familye* or whose *familye* can't drop by on a daily basis, so there's not a large number of people to visit." She knew many *Englischers* didn't put a premium on maintaining physically close generational ties, at least to the extent the Plain Folk did.

But Mike was nodding as if he understood. Was it because he'd lost his own family that he realized the value of close ties?

He didn't comment, and she was disappointed that he didn't offer to accompany her.

But naturally he had business of his own to take care of.

Once they arrived back at the marketplace, Hannah was impressed with how easily Mike parked the buggy parallel to his truck. Setting the brake, he handed her the reins then climbed down and grabbed his go bag as she slid over to take his place. He didn't head to his truck immediately, though. Instead, he stood with a hand on the buggy, smiling up at her. "Thank you for taking me with you today—it was...interesting."

"I was glad for the company. And the residents at Whispering Oaks were happy to have someone new to listen to their stories and who shared something of himself in return."

"I didn't do anything special." Then, before she could argue, he straightened. "I'll see you at the training session tomorrow."

That surprised her. "Surely the training will be too basic for you."

He shrugged. "Ford invited me to help out—an additional helper is always welcome at these classes, especially when it comes to demonstrations and monitoring the students' technique. Besides, it's always good to see how another group does things."

With a wave he headed to his vehicle.

After Mike left, Hannah turned her buggy toward home. Mike had impressed her today.

Hopefully her plan to help him focus on others who needed a helping hand had at least made some inroads into his lone-wolf outlook. Perhaps she'd have another opportunity to reinforce that lesson.

She certainly hoped so.

In the meantime, she had Grace to return home to. Being a mother was everything she'd dreamed of and so much more. Because of Grace, the future no longer stretched barren and meaningless before her.

Having Grace in her life gave her purpose and a quiet, ever-present joy.

She thought about Grace's mother often and prayed for her nightly. Try as she might, she couldn't figure out who would have abandoned her baby and specifically entrusted that precious child's care to her.

One thing she did know was that *Gotte* had given her this amazing answer to her prayers.

Still, was it wrong of her to sometimes wish for more, for a *mann* to love and be loved by?

Chapter 8

Mike got up extra early the next morning and tried out the jogging trails in the local park Ford had told him about. Then he took the EMT up on his offer to use the facilities at the firehouse to grab a quick shower.

Even with all that, he made it to the county offices shortly after they opened for the day. To his relief, today's visit went much better than the previous one had. After minimal delay, he was directed to Ramona Harper, the caseworker who'd dealt with the abandoned baby Ford had mentioned.

Not surprisingly, she wouldn't give him any information about the current whereabouts of the child or whether he'd found a permanent home. She did let him know, however, that the baby's parents had never been identified. When Mike explained what he'd found in his now-deceased sister's diary, she finally agreed to have a DNA test run to see if this child was indeed related to him. She cautioned him, however, that it would take at least a week to get the results, longer if the lab was backed up. She also wasn't ready to discuss next steps with him until those results were in hand. He felt confident, though, that he'd have a strong claim on the little boy when the relationship was proven.

Which he was certain it would be.

After all, how many infant boys could have been abandoned in Hope's Haven in that specific time frame? It was a relief to have found his nephew so quickly. He'd like to think Madison had subconsciously sprinkled these bread crumbs for him. Or perhaps for herself if she ever changed her mind.

He found himself at loose ends, full of nervous energy that needed some kind of release. It would have been nice to have someone to talk to, but this was not the kind of news to share with casual acquaintances. Fleeting thoughts of Hannah crossed his mind. Yesterday's outing to Whispering Oaks had provided an interesting insight into her personality and character. Much as he was reluctant to admit it, he had to concede that perhaps not all Amish deserved to be painted with the same broad brush he'd used all these years.

Not that he was ready to absolve the whole community of hypocrisy. As for how to spend time in Hope's Haven without getting too involved in the Amish community, perhaps the key was to be selective when it came to who in the community he interacted with.

* * *

Hannah looked up from the register and smiled when she saw Mike standing in line. She'd been thinking about him this morning, wondering how he was feeling after yesterday's trip to Whispering Oaks.

There were two customers ahead of him and she found herself acutely aware of him even as she served the others.

When it was finally his turn, she met his gaze with a smile. "*Wilkom* back. What can I get for you?"

"I've had a hankering for another of your whoopie pies. But don't get it just yet. I know it's only eleven, but I was hoping I could convince you to join me for lunch. There's something I want to discuss with you, and I thought maybe we could talk over a meal at Rosie's."

What did he want to talk about? It was tempting to accept his invitation, but she'd brought her lunch today. "I don't—"

"*Ach*, go on," Ada interrupted, making a shooing motion. "Maisie and I can handle this, and you have a delivery to make to Rosie's anyway, ain't so? You can get your friend to help you."

Norman, the owner of Rosie's, usually sent someone over to pick up the standing order for the diner, but he was running late today for some reason.

Mike made a quick half bow. "At your service."

Impulsively deciding she could save her sandwich for tomorrow, Hannah nodded. Sending Ada a grateful smile, she relinquished her spot at the register and motioned for Mike to join her in the kitchen.

"So what are we delivering?"

Hannah removed her bakery apron and grabbed the bags already packed awaiting pickup. "Caramel apple cheesecake bars."

"It sounds delicious," he said, taking the bags from her.

She smiled as she grabbed her tote. "Norman's customers seem to like it. I make him three dozen generous-sized bars a day, and he tells me he sells out most days. We have an agreement that I won't make it for anyone else or sell it here at the bakery."

"And I thought Rosie's was all about the pies."

"Oh, they do a good business in pies, but Norman likes to have some variety."

They chatted about inconsequential things on the walk to the diner, including how gray clouds were gathering overhead, but Hannah could tell he had something more than weather on his mind.

Once inside, she led the way to the counter. "Hello, Rosalind," she said to the cashier. "Norman didn't pick up his order this morning, so we brought it over." She studied Rosalind's harried demeanor. "I hope everything is okay."

As she spoke, Mike placed the bags on the counter.

Rosalind gave Hannah a grateful smile. "Bless you. It's been a crazy morning. One of the pipes burst during the night, and we came in at daybreak to a flooded kitchen. Getting it fixed and cleaned up put us nearly an hour late opening."

"*Ach*, I'm so sorry. Is there anything I can do to help?"

Rosalind picked up the bags and smiled. "Thanks, but you've already helped by bringing these over. Now, you don't need to hear any more about my troubles. Find a table and I'll send Patience over to take your order."

Mike let her pick the table, and almost as soon as they sat down Patience was there to take their orders. That done, Hannah couldn't contain her curiosity. "You had something you wanted to discuss with me?"

He leaned forward, placing his elbows on the table. "You mentioned you make deliveries to the shut-ins on Wednesdays."

That was an unexpected topic. "*Jah.*"

"And you go alone?"

She nodded. Where was he going with this?

He leaned back. "I was wondering if you'd like some company."

"That would be *wunderbaar*! But surely you have other things to do with your time here."

He shrugged. "I'm in wait mode right now, so I have some free time on my hands."

She wondered again what had brought him to Hope's Haven.

"In fact," he continued, "if your friend would like a break, I could take care of cooking something for the food baskets."

He'd surprised her yet again. "You cook?"

He stiffened in mock-affront. "Hey, don't sound so startled." Then he offered a crooked smile. "Not that I can cook a fancy meal or anything, but we all take turns handling the meals down at the fire station and I make a pretty mean chicken stew if I do say so myself."

Even though he'd made the offer seem offhand, she considered it quite generous. "Then *danke*, I'm sure Agnes would appreciate having a day off. I'll stop by and tell her on my way home this afternoon."

She lifted her water glass. "It will be *gut* to have company. Having someone with me will allow me to bring my little girl along. If you don't mind."

He spread his hands. "I don't mind at all."

She saw the truth of that in his eyes. "*Danke.* Wednesday is also the day my sitter has off so it would have fallen to my *shveshtah* to watch Grace. Not that Martha would mind. I actually think she likes having Grace to herself occasionally." She paused and gave him an apologetic smile. "I'm rambling, sorry."

His expression was almost indulgent. "No need to apologize—it's obvious how much you love your little girl. I imagine she brings a bit of sunshine to the shut-ins you visit."

Hannah nodded, pleased that he shared her view on the subject. "Nothing cheers the heart like the sweet innocence of a child's smile, ain't so?"

* * *

Mike smiled at her obvious love for her daughter, then changed the subject. "How many will I be cooking for?"

She pursed her lips, obviously ticking off numbers in her head. "We'll be visiting five households. Two of them have two people, two have one and one has six." She met his gaze. "If I figured right, that makes twelve."

Mike nodded. "Got it. Very doable."

Before he could say anything more, Patience returned with their orders. He picked up his fork, then paused as Hannah bowed her head for a silent prayer. That practice had once been second nature to him as well. He suddenly felt embarrassed that he'd let it drop.

When she opened her eyes, she smiled and dug into her meal with enthusiasm.

Mike took a bite of his pot roast and then saluted her with his fork. "This is delicious."

"Norman is a very *gut* cook." She took a sip of her

water, then stirred the ice with her straw. "Do you have friends you're visiting here?"

How should he answer that? He decided that honesty with a touch of evasiveness would be the best approach. "There's no one here I'm close to. This is more of a business trip."

He could tell she wanted to ask more about his reason for visiting Hope's Haven, but she was too polite to do so. And to make sure she didn't have another opportunity, he turned the conversation to something else.

"You mentioned your sitter—I assume it's someone other than your sister?"

Hannah nodded. "Leah is actually much more than a sitter for Grace. She was my *mamm*'s best friend and after *Mamm* passed, she became almost a surrogate mother to me."

"How old were you when your mother passed?"

"Eleven."

For once she didn't elaborate.

"That must have been a difficult time for you." He should know.

Hannah nodded, some of her usual happy glow dimmed. "Her death was sudden and it hit everyone in our *familye* hard, but in different ways." She pushed her food around on her plate with her fork, obviously lost in her memories. "*Daed* was devastated but he put on a *gut* face for us and threw himself into his work. Martha, who was sixteen at the time, immediately ended her *rumspringa* and did all she could to take over as lady of the house. Greta was thirteen and became determined to carry on what she called *Mamm*'s legacy of beautiful quilt work."

She gestured dispiritedly. "Everyone was so strong. Everyone but me. I tried not to let my weakness show, but there were times when I just couldn't put on a serene front. So I'd slip away to my special place."

She met his gaze for the first time since she'd started talking. "There's an old crooked oak tree with sweeping branches that grows in such a way that it forms an alcove of sorts. Several wild raspberry bushes grow nearby and I'd use gathering berries that summer as my excuse. I'd huddle under that tree, crying my eyes out until I couldn't cry anymore. And when I'd exhausted myself, I'd collect some berries and go home." She grimaced. "Pitiful, I know."

He reached across the table and touched her hand briefly. "Not at all. You were only a child, and you were grieving."

She seemed flustered for a moment, then shifted in her seat. "Anyway, that's the long way of telling you how I connected with Leah. She found me there one day. To do her credit, she could have quietly backed away because I didn't notice her at first. But she cleared her throat, and when I looked up she lowered herself to sit beside me."

Hannah paused, biting her lower lip before continuing. "I was mortified and tried to apologize. But Leah told me there was no need, that she understood my sadness and how losing someone you were close to was a difficult thing."

"She was right."

"But I couldn't accept the absolution. I explained it had been a little over a month since *Mamm* passed and except for those first few days, no one in our house cried. *Aenti* Hilda told us *Mamm* was in heaven with *Gotte* now, and it was selfish of us to wish she was still here."

Mike wanted to protest such harsh sentiment, but decided it was better not to interrupt.

Hannah tucked a wayward tendril back under her *kapp*. "Fortunately Leah explained to me that *Aenti* Hilda was only partially right. The way she put it went something like, *Your* mamm *is in heaven, for sure and certain. And I'm sure you rejoice for her that it's so. But to mourn the loss of a loved one is not selfish. It's a healing thing. The Bible teaches that there is a time for everything, including a time to weep and a time to laugh, a time to mourn and a time to dance. And even Jesus Himself, when He heard of the death of His friend Lazarus, wept. So if you need to cry, then cry you should. And you're also welcome to come visit and we can chat whenever you like.*"

"Sounds like a wise person."

"She is. Then she helped me to pick some of the raspberries and talked to me about all the different ways she used them besides making preserves. I think it was her way of giving me time to compose myself. But it was the start of my fascination with berries and their various preparations. As well as my deep friendship with Leah."

She straightened and gave him an over-bright smile. "I'm not sure why I just told you all of that—it was so much more than what you asked for."

"I didn't mind." In fact he was glad she'd shared so much with him. It gave him a much clearer picture of who she was.

She picked up her fork again and speared a chunk of carrot. "Now that I've gone on about myself, why don't you tell me a little something about you?"

That could be a tricky proposition. "What did you want to know?"

"Anything you feel comfortable sharing. How about why you chose to become a paramedic?"

He relaxed. That seemed a safe enough topic. "I never pictured myself sitting in an office all day. And I suppose I just liked the idea of helping people."

"But why a paramedic specifically?"

That was easy—he remembered the exact day. "When I was thirteen, I was involved in a school bus accident. Several kids, including me, were trapped and unable to get out. I wasn't hurt other than some scrapes and bruises, but two of the others were. The emergency responders who worked to free us—firemen, policemen and EMTs—appeared to me to be real heroes. Right then and there I knew I wanted to do what those men did. I wanted to make a difference, to help people in their darkest hour."

She smiled approvingly. "It sounds like a noble calling."

"No more so than many other callings."

"I know you're a blessing and a comfort to those you help."

Not sure how to respond to that, Mike changed the subject. After that they moved on to more inconsequential topics, keeping things light.

Later, as Mike walked to his truck, he pondered his actions. Why had he volunteered to help make those deliveries to the shut-ins? He knew it was partly because he was trying to fill his time with something productive. Still, he'd been determined when he arrived to hold himself apart from the Amish community, to take care of business and get out of Hope's Haven as quickly as possible. Yet here he was, less than a week since he'd come to town, committed to drive all over the area in a horse and buggy to visit Amish in their homes.

All because there was something about the Amish baker that tugged at him, that intrigued him in a way he couldn't get out of his mind.

There was no way this was going to end well.

Chapter 9

Mike spotted Hannah as soon as she walked into the fire station's training facility along with her sister and Noah. The trio paused just inside the room, and Hannah scanned the occupants, apparently looking for someone. As soon as her gaze connected with his, her face blossomed in a warm smile.

He couldn't help but respond in kind, and he quickly headed her way. "Glad to see the rain didn't scare you off." The weather had turned drizzly after lunch but had cleared up about an hour and a half ago.

"Of course." Hannah brushed at her cheek. "I'm looking forward to this."

Ford came up and greeted them with a smile. "Hello. You all must be Mike's friends. Welcome to our April first aid training session. I hope it lives up to your expectations."

"I'm sure it will," Noah responded, answering for the group.

Ford waved to some tables in the back of the room. "Help yourself to the coffee and cookies. And when you're ready, just find a seat and settle in. We'll get started in a few minutes."

With a nod, Noah escorted the ladies to a set of empty chairs near the middle of the room.

There were seventeen attendees in the class, including two other Amish individuals—no doubt the two from the marketplace Hannah had mentioned earlier.

The class lasted about an hour, giving time for the attendees to practice the techniques. Ford proved to be a great instructor, engaging the audience while driving home the pertinent points.

Mike surreptitiously kept an eye on Hannah, noting how she leaned forward slightly, occasionally looking down to make notes on the handout they'd been given.

Later, when it was time to practice what they'd been taught, Mike, along with three members of the local crew, roamed the room, making sure everyone performed the techniques correctly and answering questions or repeating demonstrations as necessary.

Once the class broke up and folks started drifting away, Mike approached Hannah and her companions. "Did the training give you what you were looking for?"

"*Jah.*" Hannah's eyes were bright with appreciation. "I feel better prepared now. I pray I never have to use any of this, but if I do, I hope I can approach it with the same presence of mind I saw you use with Carl the other day."

"I have a feeling, if the time ever comes, you will."

She ducked her head as if embarrassed and then quickly turned to her sister. "Greta has already faced such an emergency and was very competent and brave."

Greta waved away her sister's praise. "*Nee*. I was scared silly the whole time."

Mike lifted a brow. "Sounds like there's an interesting story here."

Noah spoke up. "I had an accident in my shop a couple of years ago—a heavy shelving unit fell on me after hours. Greta, who was watching my *kinner*, found me barely conscious and showed great presence of mind in getting the help I needed while keeping Anna and David calm."

Mike looked at Hannah's sister with new respect. "Impressive."

It was Greta's turn to appear flustered. "I merely phoned for help and tried to keep his little ones calm. The emergency responders were the real heroes."

One of the other Amish men who'd attended the training came up just then and captured Noah and Greta's attention.

Hannah, however, kept her focus on Mike. "Are you still sure you want to come with me tomorrow? It's not too late to change your mind."

"You can't get rid of me that easily," he teased. "In fact I've already cooked the stew, and Mrs. Graber offered to portion it for me while I'm here."

When he'd parted ways with Hannah after lunch, he'd gone to the grocery store and picked up everything he needed to make the chicken stew. He'd even purchased large plastic containers to put the finished product in. When he'd explained to Mrs. Graber why he needed to do some cooking, she'd gladly allowed him the use of her stove and pots and had even pitched in to help him with the prep work.

"I forgot to ask earlier, what time would you like me to meet you tomorrow?"

"Why don't I pick you up? The Grabers' place is on my way."

"In that case, what time should I be ready?"

"I have a few things to take care of first thing—how about nine o'clock?"

"I'll be ready." And strangely enough, he found himself looking forward to it.

* * *

"*Gut matin.*" Hannah's cheery greeting came from the seat of her buggy. Mike had been watching for her so she wouldn't have to get out and knock on the door, especially since she was bringing her daughter with her.

Today she was in an enclosed buggy rather than the open one she'd used Monday—probably the family vehicle. She'd no doubt switched up in deference to the little girl who sat beside her.

"Good morning, ladies. Just let me load up these boxes and I'll be ready to go."

Earlier he'd put the containers of chicken stew into two sturdy milk crates Ellen Graber had loaned him.

As he stored the crates, Mike noticed there wasn't as much room as he'd expected. "What's all this?" he asked. "There seems to be a lot more here than the simple baskets you mentioned Monday."

"Sometimes the folks on our list who can't travel to town ask us to pick up supplies for them."

"And of course you take care of it." So she did grocery runs too. Did all the so-called Little Sisters take that on or just Hannah?

He quickly loaded the other crate while Hannah placed

Grace in her lap and slid over to the passenger side. Apparently he was driving.

After he'd settled into his seat, he smiled down at the child, who had her thumb in her mouth. "And who is this pretty little ladybug?"

"This is Grace."

"I'm very glad to meet you, Grace." He smiled as the toddler ducked her face in Hannah's side. Then he turned to her mother. "Which way are we heading?"

"When you get to the end of the lane, turn right. Our first stop is Mary and Simon Fretz's place. Simon was blinded in an accident nearly four years ago, but he's trained himself to get around their small farm with the help of his service dog and he's able to do some of the chores like feeding their animals and milking their cow. Unfortunately his wife, Mary, sprained her wrist last week and hasn't been able to do much cooking."

"And they don't have family in the area?"

"Only one of their five children still lives in Hope's Haven. James Michael works at a butcher shop in town. His wife would have managed, but she cares for two preschoolers and a newborn in addition to caring for her own home. So we offered to visit Mary and Simon two days a week for a while to give her a little help."

"I'm sure she appreciated that."

When they pulled up to the Fretz home, Hannah filled a large basket with wrapped packages of bread and a half pie, adding a container of Mike's chicken stew. Then she pointed to one of the paper bags. "Would you grab that bag there, the one with the Fretz name on it?"

Mike retrieved the bag, then took the basket from her. With a *danke*, she lifted Grace out of the buggy and led the way up the front porch steps.

It turned out the Fretzes were an elderly couple, probably in their mid-eighties. Simon, who answered the door, was gray-bearded and had the unfocused gaze of someone who couldn't see. There was a large dog by his side, a mostly German shepherd mix.

Hannah, who had Grace on her hip, spoke up immediately.

"*Gut matin*, Simon. It's Hannah Eicher. And I brought Grace with me as well as a special guest."

"*Ach, wilkom, wilkom.*" He stepped to one side, gesturing to the dog to do the same. "Come inside. Grace will certainly brighten my Mary's day."

Mike followed in behind Hannah.

As Simon led the way into the house, he called out in a booming voice, "Mary, we have visitors. Hannah Eicher, and she brought little Grace with her."

A short, plump woman with a brace on her right wrist appeared from the back of the house. "*Ach*, Simon, I'm not deaf." Then she turned to the visitors. "Let me see that little *lamm*." She patted Grace's leg. "*Ach*, I wish I could hold you."

Hannah smiled and performed the introductions. "Simon, Mary, this is Mike Colder. Mike's a visitor to Hope's Haven and he volunteered to help me today. In fact you have Mike to thank for making the chicken stew you'll find in your box."

"*Ach*, a man who's not afraid to cook." Mary gave Mike a nod. "A rare treasure indeed."

Simon gave a loud huff.

Mary patted her husband's arm. "Don't worry, I include you as one of those treasures." She turned to Hannah and Mike as they all moved to the next room. "Simon's been helping with the cooking these past few days—I'm the eyes and he's the hands and between us we get it done."

Once in the kitchen Hannah set Grace on the floor and indicated Mike should set the basket and bag on the table. She lifted the bag first. "Here's the coffee and sugar you asked me to pick up for you."

"*Ach*, did you hear that, Simon? I don't have to ration your coffee anymore."

Simon took a seat. "Bless you, Hannah. Mary's been portioning it out as if we had the last bag of coffee left in the world. Can you believe she'd take advantage of a poor old blind man like that?"

Hannah laughed. "You might be blind, Simon, but you're neither poor nor old." Then she lifted the container of stew. "Would you like me to start this warming on the stove so it'll be ready when you want to eat lunch?"

For the next several minutes, Mike watched Hannah bustle around the kitchen with a breezy efficiency, chatting easily with the older couple, unobtrusively cleaning dirty dishes and taking care of anything else she saw needed attending to. At the same time, Simon pressed for details of where Mike came from and why he was in Hope's Haven. He managed to answer without revealing his past and present ties to the community.

Once they'd finally made their exit and climbed back into the buggy, Hannah bounced Grace in her lap and gave him a sunny smile. "They appear to be getting on well, ain't so?"

Mike nodded, picking up the reins. He had a feeling the shut-ins appreciated Hannah's presence and unsolicited help as much as, if not more than, the food deliveries themselves.

"Our next stop is Barnabas Moser's place. He's a

widower who—" She stopped, cutting him a worried look. "Is something wrong?"

Mike had been taken off guard at the mention of that name and apparently hadn't been quick enough in covering his reaction. "Sorry, I'm fine. What were you saying about Barnabas?"

She still looked worried, but to his relief she didn't pursue the topic.

Mike was, in fact, not fine. Barnabas Moser was his mother's brother, a man who trained horses and had an impressive way with animals. Mike had looked up to him as a little boy.

Barnabas was also one of the men who'd turned his back on Mike's father after his mother's passing. "What's wrong with him?" he managed to ask.

"Nothing. But *Daed* asked me to return a set of bridles he'd borrowed since I was passing near here."

She'd called him a widower earlier, which meant Aunt Sarabeth had passed. He remembered her as a tiny woman with a big smile who always seemed to be in motion, sort of like a hummingbird.

Even though he'd never planned to see any of his Amish relatives again, it saddened him to know that sweet, energetic woman was no longer in the world.

Quicker than he'd hoped, they arrived at his uncle's house.

Mike held back while Hannah knocked on the door, standing a couple of feet behind her. When the door opened, he immediately recognized the man standing there, even without the earlier heads-up.

While Barnabas and Hannah exchanged greetings, Mike took stock of the man. Barnabas had aged, of course. There were more than a few gray hairs in his beard and more lines on his face than the last time Mike saw him. But his voice still had a booming quality, and there was no mistaking the deep-set brown eyes and the nose with a bump on it from where it had been broken in his youth.

When Hannah turned to include him in the conversation, Mike pulled his thoughts back to the present.

"Mike, this is Barnabas. Barnabas, Mike's visiting our community and graciously agreed to help me today."

Barnabas held out his hand. "*Wilkom*, Mike. I hope you're enjoying your time here."

Mike grasped the hand and gave it a quick shake. There was no hint of recognition in his uncle's gaze, only a polite welcome. Which was probably just as well—recognition might have led to an awkward reunion. Still, Mike wondered how his uncle would react if he confronted him with his identity and asked for an explanation of how he'd acted twenty-two years ago.

Had their implacable shunning been aimed at his father only? Or had the vitriol included him as well?

He was so focused on his history with his uncles that he barely took in the conversation between Barnabas and Hannah.

Perhaps he'd confront his uncle, or rather uncles, before he left town, but now, with Hannah and her daughter standing there, was not the time.

It wasn't until they were back in the buggy that Mike could focus on the present again.

This was his fault. He should have realized he wouldn't be able to spend any length of time in Hope's Haven without running into one or more of his relatives. He should have prepared himself better.

But he was prepared now.

Because undoubtedly there *would* be a next time.

Obviously unaware of his inner turmoil, Hannah handed Grace a sippy cup.

"Our next stop is down the road a piece at Temperance Riehl's home. Temperance is a widow and unfortunately her daughter Laura Beth developed aspirations to be a nurse and left the Amish community to pursue additional education."

She said that as if the woman had committed a serious crime. "Is that so terrible? I mean if she felt led to pursue a nursing career—some people consider that a noble calling."

"I'm sorry if I offended you. It's just that Laura Beth has now married an *Englischer* and works at a big hospital in Georgia. She rarely returns to visit, and Temperance hardly knows her two grandchildren."

"So Temperance lives alone?"

"*Jah*. She lived with her *daed* until he passed away two years ago. She's getting on in age and suffers from arthritis in her hands, so we try to check in on her a few times a week. According to Nancy, who visited with her yesterday, Temperance was running a light fever. So if you don't mind waiting here in the buggy with Grace, just to be safe, I'd appreciate it."

"I don't mind a bit."

Hannah stepped down. "If everything is okay, I shouldn't be long."

"Take whatever time you need. Grace and I will get better acquainted while we wait."

He smiled down at the little girl. "That's a pretty doll you have there."

Grace held out the doll so he could see it better, but when he went to take it she quickly drew it back.

"Ah, I see," he said solemnly. "I can look but no touching."

Remembering the way Hannah had kept her entertained during the ride, he figured he could try singing, patty cake or peek-a-boo. Scratch the first item on the list—singing was definitely not his strong suit. He put his hands over his eyes and then jerked them away with a cry of *peek-a-boo*. Grace gave a delighted gurgling laugh, so he did it again with the same results. Really, was there any other sound quite so apt to make the listener smile as that of a child's laugh?

As Mike played with Grace, it hit him that Madison's son would be close to the same age as Hannah's daughter. Was he truly ready to take on the care of a toddler?

Hearing the little girl laugh again, though, convinced him it would be worth whatever it took.

His thoughts wandered to what Hannah had said about Temperance's daughter. What would she think if she knew he and his dad had left the Amish community? Would she feel the same as she did about Laura Beth? Or even worse, the way those members who wanted to shun him and his father had all those years ago?

* * *

Hannah climbed back in the buggy, unable to hide the smile on her face. The sight of the broad-shouldered, square-jawed paramedic playing peek-a-boo with her little girl had caught her unawares. The term *heartwarming* was overused these days but there it was—she'd felt as if she were melting on the inside.

"Where to now?" Mike asked when she had Grace once more on her lap.

"The Lantz place. It's the next farm south of here."

"What's the story there?"

"Asher Lantz owns the place. It was his father's before him, and his mother still lives there with him. His older brother Shem and Shem's wife passed away a few months ago. They left behind a preschool daughter and one-year-old triplets."

Shem Lantz was a name he remembered from his childhood. He had vague memories of a skinny boy with long legs and a wide grin.

"Asher and Dorcas, his mother, took the children in, and Asher's cousin Joan moved in to help them. But Joan has to be away for a few days this week and asked us to check in on them since Dorcas has trouble getting around."

She gave him a side-eyed look. "Just as a warning, I'm planning to put you in charge of the children while I persuade Dorcas to let me help with the housework."

"What about the language difference?"

Most Amish children didn't learn much English until they went to school. "I find most *kinner* do a *gut* job interpreting gestures and tone."

"I suppose I don't have a choice."

Hannah smiled at the slightly alarmed look on his face. Based on what she'd seen earlier, she had no doubt he'd do fine with the little ones. "Not at all."

He rolled his eyes but didn't argue further.

The stop at the Lantz place lasted a little over an hour. Hannah sent him down to the basement with the four Lantz children and Grace along with some toys and books. Then she began to tackle some of the housework while she insisted Dorcas sit and rest.

"*Ach*, bless you, Hannah. I just don't get around as well as I used to."

Hannah smiled. "Having to keep up with four little ones is enough to tire anyone out, for sure and for certain."

The older woman cast a worried glance toward the basement stairs. "Are you sure your friend is all right down there?"

Hannah nodded. "Mike is very *gut* with children. And if he runs into problems, the two of us are just a yell away."

Later, when Hannah was ready to leave, she headed down the basement steps. She found Mike on the concrete floor with the children and they were all industriously drawing on the floor with colored chalk.

Apparently communication hadn't been an issue. "*Ach du lieva*, what have we here?"

Mike, who'd been drawing as well, leaned back on his heels. "Don't you recognize a group of artists at work?"

By this time Grace had realized Hannah was in the room and lifted her arms to be picked up. Hannah complied while she studied the chalk drawings. Charlotte, the older girl, had drawn flowers and trees. The triplets and Grace had mostly scribbled. It was Mike's drawing that surprised her, though. It was the sketch of a horse and buggy. It was a simple chalk drawing, but somehow he'd managed to infuse it with life and movement. What could he do with pencil or brush?

"You are all wonderful *gut* artists," she said. "These are beautiful."

She bit her tongue as one of the triplets, with a mischievous grin, started scribbling on Mike's drawing.

But Mike didn't seem concerned. Instead he nodded approvingly at the culprit. "You're right, it needed a bit more color."

He stood. "It's time for me, Hannah and Grace to go, so let's clean this up." And with that he grabbed a shop broom from a corner of the room and went to work. Charlotte collected the chalk and put it away while the triplets did as much playing as cleaning.

Ten minutes later they were walking toward the buggy. "I didn't know you were such a fine artist."

He shrugged dismissively. "It's just doodles." Then he changed the subject. "Where to next?"

"The Geiser place. And don't worry, you won't have any young ones to watch over like you did here."

He took Grace from her so she could climb into the buggy. "Actually, it wasn't so bad," he said, giving Grace a squeeze.

Hannah smiled. Yes, someday he'd make a wonderful *gut daed*.

One thing was for certain sure, he had a heart for service. It came through in the pieces of his past he'd revealed to her so far. It showed in his career choice. And it shone brightly in his cheerful willingness to minister to the shut-ins with her.

It seemed unfair that he was so alone in the world, when he had a willingness to give this much of himself.

Why hadn't such a *gut* man married and settled down already?

If only things were different...

* * *

"*Gut* job! That's my sweet girl."

Hannah had some pumpkin spice sugar cookie dough on a floured sheet of waxed paper on the table. Grace stood on a chair in front of her, hands on the rolling pin, "helping" to roll it out.

Martha entered the kitchen and paused to smile at the two of them. "And what have we here? A junior baker?"

Grace held her hands out, happily showing their sticky surfaces from her earlier attempts to pat the dough with her hands.

Martha shook her head. "I see you're teaching her to follow in your footsteps."

Hannah smiled indulgently at her helper. "If eagerness is any indication, I won't have a choice in the matter."

"She wants to imitate you, that's a *gut* sign." Then Martha raised a brow. "I hope you'll also teach her how to clean up when she's done." And with another smile for Grace, Martha continued through the kitchen and headed down the basement stairs.

"Don't mind your *aenti* Martha," Hannah said to Grace. "She wasn't fussing. She just likes to have a tidy house."

She took a damp rag and cleaned Grace's hands, then set her on the floor with some spare cookie cutters. "Now, you play with those while I cut out the cookies." She'd had a last-minute order from one of her very good customers and decided to start on them this evening rather than wait until she was back at the bakery tomorrow.

As she worked, she thought about the morning's activities. Mike had been at ease during their visits, even with the Lantz children. The one time she'd sensed a stiffness in him was when they'd headed for Barnabas Moser's place. His hand had jerked slightly on the reins and his jaw had tightened. It had all happened in the blink of an eye and disappeared just as abruptly. But she was sure of what she'd seen, even as he'd brushed away her concerns. What did it mean? It was all quite puzzling.

What wasn't puzzling was the fact that, despite her intentions to the contrary, the feelings she had for Mike were growing warmer, deeper. Then again, what woman wouldn't find herself attracted to such a generous, confident man who was intelligent but also willing to learn from others?

And it didn't hurt that he had a winning smile and a set of brown eyes that could look right into you.

Chapter 10

Thursday morning Mike called Ramona to check on the DNA test, and as expected, there wasn't any news yet. She assured him once again that she'd call as soon as she knew something but that he shouldn't expect to hear anything before next week.

He decided to stop in at the local library to do some online research on foster parent and adoption laws and processes in the state of Ohio. He wanted to be ready to act when the results of the DNA test came back.

It appeared his being from out of state would add an extra layer of complexity. But perhaps the fact that his sister had crossed state lines to leave the baby here would allow the jurisdiction in the matter to return to Missouri where it belonged.

For good measure he also did some research on what he might need to purchase if—make that *when*—he brought the toddler home with him. The list was eye opening.

Before leaving, Mike also did a little online browsing through newsfeeds to catch up on what was going on in the world at large, something he'd been insulated from the past few days. It felt good to be back in touch with the world outside of Hope's Haven. Though to be honest, he hadn't felt the same sense of urgency to get online that he would have in the past. Must have had something to do with the slower pace of life around here.

By midafternoon Mike was headed back to Hope's Haven. It was a beautiful, clear day, so perhaps he could finish up that bit of exploration he'd started on Sunday.

As he drove on the winding back roads, he tried to picture what he'd find over the next hill or around the bend. There were lots of roadside signs inviting tourists to turn into this drive or that to find preserves or baskets or cheese or any number of other handmade goods. There were barns and silos and buggies near houses with large front porches furnished with rockers and benches. What he didn't see were utility lines, automobiles or satellite dishes.

He kept his eye out for his childhood home, but when he found himself back at the schoolhouse, he decided he'd missed the proper turn on one of the winding back roads. He'd have to try again another day.

Or maybe it was just as well he let it remain a pleasant memory.

As he drove back into town, he thought about Hannah. She was amazing—generous, hardworking and with a touch of mischievousness.

The Grabers were good people as well.

Had he been wrong to lump all the Amish together?

Perhaps it had just been his mother's family who'd turned their backs on the two of them.

He wasn't sorry his father had moved them away. He'd experienced so many things he never would have otherwise—an advanced education, music of all sorts with bands and orchestras, technology. The list was long. But maybe he shouldn't have allowed the bitterness into his life. He was starting to realize the opportunities he'd missed by turning his back on Hope's Haven entirely.

Should he confront those relatives who were still here? Reintroduce himself to old friends like Noah Stoll?

Maybe he would ask Hannah to help him reintegrate himself into the community, at least to a limited extent.

But not today.

He wasn't ready to explain his history to her or anyone else just yet. There was a kind of emotional safety in anonymity, in not having to come face-to-face with the depth of that bitterness just yet.

He turned his truck onto the main highway, leaving the Amish landscape in his rearview mirror.

* * *

Friday morning Ada nudged Hannah away from the register. "Why don't you take a short break. Someone is looking for some attention."

Hannah glanced down at the blanket she'd placed on the floor behind the counter. So far Grace had kept to the admonition not to stray from that boundary, but Ada was right—the toddler was getting restless.

"Good morning, Hannah."

Hannah glanced back up at the sound of that deep voice that had become so familiar to her. "*Gut matin.*"

Mike gave her an assessing look. "Forgive me for saying so but you look a bit harried."

She pushed a stray hair back under her *kapp*. "Just a little distracted." She gestured for him to step around to her side of the counter. "I have Grace with me today."

"Sitter problems?"

She nodded as she handed a customer the cinnamon roll he'd ordered. "Leah wasn't feeling well. Normally my *shveshtah* would take over, but she already had plans to work on a special project." Martha had decided she wanted to try her hand at cheese making.

Mike pulled her thoughts back to the present. "And you didn't feel you could just take the day off."

"*Nee.*" She waved a hand to the long line. "Not during the early-morning rush anyway."

"That's what happens when you have the best baked goods in town."

She glanced down at the little girl who was talking nonsense words to her doll. "And I do love getting to spend more time with Grace. But she requires a lot of attention." Another pause while she took an order.

"It's just for another hour, though," she said over her shoulder, "and we'll be fine for that long."

"What happens in an hour?" He handed her the proper-sized paper cup for the customer's drink order.

"That's when Greta comes in with her *kinner.*"

"And?"

"And she has a sitter who comes in to watch them. They've set up a nursery here and I've asked Naomi, the sitter, to watch Grace for me a couple of times before when I've been in this situation."

"Nice."

"*Jah*, it is."

"I tell you what. I'm free for the next few hours. I can keep an eye on Grace until Naomi arrives."

That was a tempting offer. And he had been really good with Grace and the Lantz *kinner* on Wednesday. "Are you sure?"

He grinned and spread his hands. "If it gets to be too much, I can always hand her back over to you. And as you said, it's only for an hour."

She returned his grin. "All right. Let's find you a table." She placed the toys she'd brought for Grace in a tote bag and led the way to a corner with a free table. She indicated Mike should take a seat and then handed Grace over. Remembering the chalk drawing session, she pulled a coloring book from the bag. "Grace, would you like to show Mike your book? He might even want to color a picture with you."

The little girl took tighter hold of her doll as she looked up at Mike hopefully.

He smiled down at her. "I love to color. And this looks like a very good book."

Hannah placed the tote bag containing Grace's things on an adjacent chair, then gave Mike a grateful smile. "Give me a minute and I'll bring you your order."

"No rush."

Hannah bustled off, the image of Mike smiling down affectionately at Grace lightening her steps.

* * *

Mike gave Grace a smile. "So, let's have a look at this book." He opened it to a random page and found a butterfly and flower on one side and a fish and some seaweed on the other.

"I think you should work on the butterfly while I tackle this fish, what do you say?"

She babbled a response and he smiled. "I'll take that as a yes."

He reached in the tote for the box of crayons and found they were the jumbo variety. He plucked the blue and red from the box and held them out to her. "Which one do you want?"

Grace carefully set her doll on the table and took the red color from him.

"Good choice." He figured she didn't understand his actual words, but apparently she got the general idea. She scooted forward to get closer to the book and began to happily scribble all over the page. Then she paused and looked up at him with a frown.

"Yes, of course." Mike grabbed a green crayon and went to work on the seaweed.

With a satisfied smile, Grace happily returned to her coloring. At one point she tired of her butterfly and began to scribble on his page as well, glancing up at him occasionally with a mischievous smile.

With a laugh he gave her a little squeeze. "Minx!" Then he nodded. "But you're right. This picture obviously needed some splashes of red."

The whole time he spent with Grace, he thought about his nephew. Very soon he could be doing similar activities with Buddy. The idea no longer scared him as it had before. While he had no illusions that it would be an easy transition, he now looked at the adoption as much more than a duty.

An hour later, Hannah returned and set a small pastry box on the table. "Guess what?" she asked as she lifted Grace. "It's time for you to go play with Anna, David and Peter."

The little girl clapped her hands and then placed them around Hannah's neck.

Mike gathered up Grace's playthings and stood. "Mind if I tag along?"

"Not at all. In fact, you can carry Grace's things and that box of cookies since I have my hands full with this *lamm*."

As they exited the bakery together, Hannah gave Mike a soft smile. "Thank you again for watching Grace. She's really taken a shine to you."

"It was my pleasure. She's a sweet little girl."

That earned him another smile. Mike cut her a sideways glance. "Isn't it unusual for someone to have a private nursery at their place of work?"

"It was actually Greta's idea for Noah's children before they were even engaged. His younger *shveshtah* Maisie, you know, the girl who works at the bakery, had watched them for him after his first *fraa* died. When she couldn't watch them any longer, he started looking for other solutions. Greta suggested he take some unused space up in the loft and convert it to a nursery so he could check in on them whenever he wanted to."

"That makes sense, especially since he owns this place. So why aren't we headed to the loft?"

"Because Noah decided having them going up and down the narrow staircase was a safety hazard, so he carved out a space downstairs to move the nursery to."

"So what's up there now?"

"Noah's office is at the top of the stairs. The room that used to be the nursery is next to it. It's become an informal meeting room for all of us shopkeepers."

They'd reached what he assumed was the nursery and Hannah gave the split door a soft knock. A tall, slim girl he'd guess to be about seventeen or so opened the top half of the door.

"Hello, Hannah." She smiled at Grace. "And hello to you, too. It's so *gut* to see you again. Are you going to join us today?"

Hannah nodded. "Leah isn't feeling well, so I hoped you wouldn't mind looking after Grace for me today."

"Of course." Naomi opened the bottom half of the door. "Come on in." Then she cast a questioning look his way.

Hannah quickly took the hint. "Naomi, this is my friend Mike. Mike, this is Naomi."

The two exchanged greetings as Hannah set Grace down near the other children. She took the tote bag with Grace's things from Mike and placed it in one of the cubbyholes in a nearby wall unit.

Then she held out the bag with the cookies. "And I brought these for you and the *kinner*."

Naomi's smile broadened. "You didn't have to do that, but I'm for sure and certain glad you did." She took the bag and placed it on a shelf.

"I'll pick Grace up as soon as I leave the bakery this afternoon."

Naomi waved her hand. "No need to hurry, we'll be fine."

"*Danke.* And stop by the bakery before you leave and pick out a pie to bring home with you."

As they moved away from the nursery, Hannah brushed at her sleeve. "I saw Grace fussing a bit earlier. She can be quite stubborn at times. So again, *danke.*"

He raised a brow. "Her temperament is not unlike her mother perhaps?"

She gave him a stern look. "Are you saying I'm stubborn?"

He lifted his hands, palms outward. "Let's say strong-willed."

She laughed outright at that. "So you're a diplomat." Then she changed the subject. "I hope helping me didn't take up too much of your time."

He shrugged. "The only thing on my schedule today is to spend time at the firehouse. Ford mentioned they're doing some spring cleaning around the place to get it spruced up for Mother's Day. Apparently all the businesses decorate."

She nodded. "It's a lovely tradition, for sure and for certain. Many townsfolk drive around to see the decorations that weekend, similar to the way some look at Christmas lights in December."

"So how long has this tradition been around?" He certainly didn't remember it from his childhood.

"About a dozen years or so. A local *Englisch familye* found out their *mamm* had terminal cancer and asked the community to help them make her last Mother's Day special. The idea took hold as a way to honor all mothers." She waved a hand. "The marketplace participates, too—we'll decorate in here next week."

They'd reached the bakery and paused at the entrance. He couldn't come up with a reason to detain her, so he stepped back. "I'll let you get back to work now. I need to head home—I mean, to the Grabers'—before I go to the firehouse."

As he headed back to his truck he wondered just when Hope's Haven had started feeling like home again.

* * *

Saturday evening Hannah pulled out a large mixing bowl, then gathered the ingredients for her special butter cookies. Mrs. Reynolds, an *Englischer*, had ordered three dozen of them decorated with a baseball theme for her son's birthday. The bakery had been too busy today for her to prepare these during regular working hours.

Part of the reason was because today had been the day they decorated Sweet Kneads for Mother's Day. Yesterday Noah and some of the shopkeepers and workers had stayed late to bedeck the marketplace itself. This morning there had been ribbons, spring wreaths and flowers everywhere. By noon each shop was beautifully arrayed in pastel-colored trimmings—it was such a cheery sight to see.

The fact that this year she felt like a mother herself only made it all the more special.

Grace crawled into the room just then, and Hannah paused to set out some plastic bowls and wooden spoons for her to play with. Grace gleefully began noisily playing with the makeshift toys. It was a bit distracting, but Hannah didn't mind. She liked having Grace nearby.

Hannah had the cookie recipe handy, but it was so familiar that she didn't need to so much as glance at it. She added the ingredients one at a time, mixing them by hand, enjoying the feel of the dough between her fingers, pausing from time to time to smile at Grace.

Once the dough was ready, she divided it and wrapped each section in plastic wrap and set it in the refrigerator to chill.

While she waited, she knelt beside Grace and joined in her play.

After a few minutes, Leah appeared in the doorway.

"It's Grace's bedtime," she said. "Do you want me to take her?"

"*Nee.* I'll do it." She always enjoyed putting Grace to bed. Their nightly routine was a special time she cherished too much to hand it off to somebody else, no matter how busy she was.

After getting Grace cleaned and changed into her nightclothes, Hannah brushed her hair while telling her stories—sometimes a fairy tale or nursery rhymes, other times, like tonight, it was one she made up herself. Then she rocked her while singing a lullaby, the same song her own mother had sung to her as a child.

When the song was over, Hannah tucked Grace into her bed and just before raising the side of the crib, gave her a hug and a kiss, which Grace returned. Feeling those pudgy arms go around her neck and the soft butterfly kiss on her cheek always made Hannah's insides go all soft and gooey, like warm caramel.

By the time she returned to the kitchen the dough was chilled properly. She went to work with practiced ease and within a few minutes had the first batch in the oven.

As she went to work preparing the second batch for the oven, her mind wandered to other things.

Or rather another someone.

How had Mike spent the day today? He'd stopped by this morning for his usual coffee and whoopie pie. But while he'd taken time to exchange pleasantries, he hadn't tarried. Was he taking care of whatever business had brought him to Hope's Haven?

He wasn't being secretive about why he was here, exactly. It was more that he hadn't been open and forthcoming about it. She knew her curiosity—some might say nosiness—was unseemly. But perhaps she could be forgiven as long as she kept it under control and didn't pry or invade his privacy.

She sprinkled more flour on the counter.

It was strange how much she'd missed his company, even though she'd only known him a week. And since tomorrow was Sunday, she wouldn't see him for at least another day.

What would it be like to be courted by a man like Mike? He was so strong, decisive, kind. And he'd been good with Grace. Watching him keep her daughter entertained and safe while she worked yesterday had touched her heart as nothing else could have.

Hannah stiffened abruptly, as if someone had thrown cold water on her. How could she have let her thoughts go there?

Not only was Mike *Englisch*, but she was still unable to bear children. And while the *Englisch* might not value large families as her people did, he would still undoubtedly want children of his own.

She realized she'd rolled this batch of dough much too thin and with a sigh started over.

It was going to be a long night.

Chapter 11

Despite his already wavering resolve not to revisit his past, Mike found himself wondering what had become of his childhood home. Hindsight might have soured his view of the Amish, but in his happy ignorance of the undercurrents he'd had some very good times there.

Perhaps, seeing his home again through adult eyes would help him come to terms once and for all with his past.

Since last Sunday had been what the Amish called a between Sunday when no services were held, this would be a church Sunday. Which meant every able Amish man, woman and child would be in services—it was an ideal time to check things out.

He'd gotten directions last night when he filled up his truck at the service station, asking about the apple orchard he remembered from when he was a boy, without feeling obliged to give his source any context for that memory.

Mike drove up the familiar lane and pulled his truck to a stop some distance from the house on the off chance that someone was at home. The lane was still mostly in shade because of the trees on the eastern side and wildflowers were everywhere.

Memories slammed into him from every direction. The oak tree with three trunks that he'd climbed often and fell out of once. The hill he'd labored to ride his bicycle up but gleefully flew down when going in the other direction. The now-taller trees that lined the fencerow between this property and the neighboring field. The half-buried boulder that his father had always had to plow around.

Did one of his relatives live here now? If he remembered correctly, his mother had had three sisters and four brothers. And they likely each had large families. Strange to think he had so many relatives, most of whom he'd never met. But then again, his aunts and uncles had been at the forefront of those who'd turned their backs on his father after his mother died.

When he got his first clear look at the house, he stopped in his tracks. A bright-blue tarp covered a large portion of the roof over the kitchen area. A downed tree on the ground nearby told the story of what had happened. As he drew closer, he noticed two windows on that side of the house were boarded up and the porch off the kitchen was a jumble of splintered lumber. As far as he could tell, the front portion of the house was unaffected.

He was tempted to go inside to see how much damage had been done and how much remained of the home he'd once known so intimately. But he balked at taking his trespassing quite that far.

He did go into the barn. There were no animals in

the stalls, though there were signs livestock had been there fairly recently. From the tack and milking pails, it appeared they'd bedded both cows and horses there.

He moved to the well-used but solid worktable that sat next to the door. Brushing away some of the debris with his hands, he felt the smoothness of the time-worn lumber. His finger traced the name his dad had carved into the wood on the day he finished it.

Straightening, Mike left the barn and continued his exploration of the grounds. To his surprise, there was still livestock here after all. A paddock behind the barn held four goats, and there were chickens in the coop.

So someone lived here but had likely vacated, at least temporarily, when the tree fell. But from the look of things, someone still came around regularly to tend to the animals. And the house and grounds, with the obvious exception of the damage done by the tree, looked well cared for.

He pulled out his cell phone and snapped several pictures of his surroundings. One of the things he'd regretted was that he'd had no photos from his childhood, nothing he could carry back to Missouri with him. He especially wished he could have one of his mother. It bothered him that the image of her he carried in his memory had faded over time, blurred to the extent that it was more impression than sharp image.

Then he remembered something, something he and his mother had done together all those years ago. He walked to the garden. It was just as he remembered it. Some of the fence posts had been replaced, but the same large, solid corner posts were there, guarding the boundaries. As a child he'd been digging around in the ground, planning to plant the seeds from an orange he'd eaten. He was certain it would grow into an orange tree and be a grand surprise for his mother come spring.

But while digging he'd uncovered a strange-looking rock that seemed to have something like a clamshell embedded in it. His planting project forgotten, he'd rushed to show his mother the treasure he'd found. She'd oohed and ahhed over it, congratulating him on his wonderful *gut* find. And after a while they decided to rebury it, an appropriate way to treat a treasure. They dug a hole near one of the corner posts, and after they buried it Mike found a handful of small, smooth stones to mark the spot. It was one of his last good memories of this place.

Two days later his whole world had changed—his mother had her accident and went into the hospital, the place where she would eventually draw her last breath.

Was the "treasure" still there? He had to find out.

He found the small pile of rocks, then looked around for a sturdy stick and started digging. It didn't take long for him to unearth the rock, fossil actually. He sat cross-legged on the ground and brushed the dirt from it. Closing his eyes, for just a moment he was a child again, listening to his mother's soft voice as she explained what a fossil was and her promise to find a book on fossils they could read together when the bookmobile passed through.

That had never happened.

Opening his eyes, Mike stood and carefully wrapped the fossil in a handkerchief and placed it in his jacket pocket. He wasn't sure who owned this place now, but he didn't want this to fall into a stranger's hands. He refilled the hole and placed the stones back on top, arranging them as close to how they were before as he could remember. He didn't think whoever had this garden would notice this corner anyway. And perhaps someday he could show it to his nephew and tell him the story of how he'd found it, reburied it and found it once more.

He looked around. This was probably the last time he'd stand here. He'd be gone from Hope's Haven as soon as he found Madison's baby and that would be that. There would be no reason for him to ever return.

But an image of Hannah's smiling face made him wonder if he wouldn't be leaving behind at least one thing worth returning for.

Chapter 12

On Monday Mike invited himself to accompany Hannah to Whispering Oaks again.

As they walked out of the bakery Mike asked about Grace.

"*Ach*, she's a regular little monkey. She walks all over the place now, as long as she can hold on to something. And she's learned to climb. If you turn your back for even a second, you're likely to find her on a chair or the sofa or even the kitchen table."

"Sounds daunting."

"Terrifying is what it is." She gave a mock-shudder.

"Sounds like there's something more there."

She lifted a hand, then dropped it. "It's just that I'm missing out on so many of her firsts. The first time she rolled over. The first time she crawled. The first time she pulled herself upright. And now the first time she climbed." She smiled. "Though to be honest, no one actually saw that. Leah found her on a chair after the fact."

"It's a dilemma every working parent faces."

Her gaze locked on something up ahead and there was a subtle shift in her demeanor, a stiffening and dimming of her smile. A split second later she looked down and brushed at something on her skirt, as if taking time to compose herself.

He tried to follow her previous line of sight, to see what had affected her that way. He saw an English woman pushing a stroller, a young Amish couple and an English woman with an arm full of purchases and a sullen adolescent girl in tow.

Had any of these pairings upset her? If so, why?

But Hannah had already returned to normal. "You're right, of course. It *is* something every parent must come to terms with. But these childhood years are so precious. I wish I could spend more time with her."

She was trying to carry on their prior conversation as if nothing had happened. But there was a brittleness under the surface now, a tension that hadn't been there before.

He watched her as the woman with the packages passed them going in the opposite direction, and Hannah had absolutely no reaction.

A moment later they passed the young Amish couple who had stopped to look in the window of the candle shop.

The woman glanced up and saw Hannah and gave her a bright smile.

"Hannah! Hello."

Whether she wanted to or not, Hannah had no choice but to stop. "Hello, Bethany, Timothy. I hadn't realized you were back in Hope's Haven."

Bethany nodded. "We're here to celebrate my *shveshtah* Rose's birthday."

As if just remembering his presence, Hannah turned to him. "Mike, these are two of my friends, Timothy and Bethany. And this is Mike, a visitor to Hope's Haven and a new friend."

As they exchanged greetings, Mike noticed a subtle stiffness from Timothy, a wary guardedness that seemed more personal than the usual polite reserve one experienced when dealing with the Amish. And it was directed toward Hannah.

As they chatted for a few moments, with Bethany carrying most of the conversation, Mike tried to size up the young man. He didn't see anything particularly memorable about him, but Mike still couldn't shake the feeling that there was some sort of tension between him and Hannah.

"It was nice seeing you," Hannah finally said, "but we have an errand to run this afternoon, so we should be on our way."

Mike hid a smile. With typical Amish humility she had said "errand" rather than mention her charitable activities.

Hannah didn't say anything as they exited, going directly to the horse shed and leaving him to load the baked goods in the buggy.

Once they were on their way, Hannah steered the conversation toward inconsequential observations, such as the Mother's Day decorations.

But, remembering how often she'd pressed him for personal details, Mike decided to do a little probing of his own. "Is there some issue between you and your friend Timothy?"

Her gaze shot to his as if he'd accused her of some crime. "What do you mean?"

"You can tell me to mind my own business if you like, but there's a tension between you."

Hannah folded her hands in her lap, her gaze focused on the road ahead. "Bethany, Timothy and I are friends. We were scholars together and even went through our *rumspringa* more or less together. Bethany's a sweet, generous person, and Timothy is a skilled leather worker."

"That's a very nice list of all the good things about them. It doesn't address the tension I felt."

She didn't say anything for a long while but at least she didn't deny it.

He finally decided he'd overstepped after all and tried to give her an out. "I apologize if I pressed too hard about your friends. If it upset you—"

"*Nee*, there's no need to apologize. I've done a bit of prying into your life and you've been very patient with me. To be honest, this is the first time I've seen Timothy and Bethany since they got married in November and moved to Shipshewana. I wasn't prepared to see them out of the blue like that and I guess it showed."

"And?"

She brushed at her skirt again. "The reason it felt awkward is that a year ago Timothy and I were courting. At the time I thought it would be the two of us getting married." She turned away from him to look at the passing scenery. "We broke it off rather abruptly."

The small stab of jealousy caught Mike off guard. Was she still pining for the man? Was that what had soured her mood?

"Mind you, I don't love him in that way any longer," she said as if reading his thoughts. "But seeing him reminds me of a particularly difficult time in my life."

It sounded like this Timothy fellow had broken off

with her rather than vice versa. But asking for details was taking his prying one step too far.

She turned back to face him, her smile overly bright. "You have nothing to apologize for. And we're here so let's have no more somber talk. We want to bring cheer to the residents and that means being cheerful ourselves, ain't so?"

He pulled the buggy to a stop, and before he could come around to hand her down, she had exited the buggy and was striding forward toward the hitching post.

Apparently the topic was well and truly closed.

But he still wondered just what had happened between the two to cause such a rift.

* * *

Tuesday morning Mike set himself a punishing pace on his morning run. He couldn't get what Hannah had said about her prior relationship with Timothy out of his mind. No, it was more than what she'd said, it was the way she'd looked—so bruised and vulnerable—when she saw her former boyfriend. She'd said she didn't love the man any longer, but was she lying to him, or to herself? Because he couldn't think of anything else that would elicit that kind of reaction.

What he really couldn't figure out, though, was why any Amish man who'd taken that first step of courting Hannah would back out on her. Especially when, given the timeline, she would have been a widow with an infant at the time they were dating.

He could see where something like that could leave Hannah feeling wounded.

It left him angry. How could someone do that to

her? Just when he thought he'd misjudged this community. Apparently there were self-righteous jerks in every
setting.

Thirty minutes later, Mike had showered and had
climbed into his truck. He checked his cell phone, which
he'd left in his truck while he ran, and discovered he had
a missed call from Ramona Harper.

He immediately came to attention. This was it, the
call he'd been waiting for. His whole life was about
to change. He just hoped that whoever had been caring
for Madison's child would be understanding about his
claim.

Taking a deep breath, he touched the redial icon. In a
matter of minutes he had the caseworker on the phone.

"Mr. Colder, thank you for returning my call."

He was too impatient for pleasantries. "Have you
gotten the results on the DNA testing?"

"I have. And I'm sorry to say that the baby in question
isn't related to you."

Mike plopped back against his seat. "Are you sure?"
He'd been so certain the child left at the fire station was
Madison's that the news hit him like a blow to the chest.
He'd never seriously considered that he would need to
look elsewhere.

"I'm very sure. The results are conclusive."

He rubbed the side of his jaw, trying to get his mind
working again. "What do I do now?"

"I'm not sure there is anything to do. Without additional information—"

He didn't let her finish that statement. "Can we find
out if any other babies were left in this area during the
same time frame?"

"I realize how important this is to you, and that you're

eager to find your nephew. But I'll need to speak to my supervisor to find out just how much time we can dedicate to this right now. You need to understand we're seriously understaffed at the moment with individuals out sick and on vacation."

"I understand. But as you say, this is very important to me. If it'll help, I'll speak to your supervisor myself."

"Let me see what I can do. I promise to get back to you, one way or the other, by tomorrow afternoon."

He didn't like the sound of that. "One way or the other" gave her an out that he found unacceptable. But he supposed there wasn't much he could do right now besides wait for her call.

Pocketing his phone, he started his engine and headed for The Amish Marketplace. He definitely needed his morning indulgence right now.

When he arrived at Sweet Kneads, before he could even say good morning, Hannah's brows drew down in concern. "Is something wrong?"

Was he so transparent? He shrugged, trying to ease her concerns. "I'm fine. I just got a little bad news is all."

"I'm sorry." Her sympathy seemed sincere, not merely perfunctory. "Is this related to the business you came to Hope's Haven for?"

"Yes." Suddenly he wanted to tell her about his missing nephew. "Would you mind having lunch with me today?"

She gave him a searching look. "Of course. Is eleven o'clock okay?"

He nodded, feeling better just knowing he had a sounding board. "I'll be back to get you then."

* * *

Hannah watched him go, cup of coffee in one hand and whoopie pie in the other. There'd been none of the normal chitchat this morning. He seemed truly troubled. She almost called him back and offered to go with him now.

But she couldn't abandon Ada at their busiest time of morning. Besides, it was too late—he'd already disappeared from view.

Hannah watched the clock all morning, waiting for the time when Mike would show back up. Had his lunch invitation had anything to do with the bad news he'd mentioned? Or did he just not want to eat alone?

When he finally returned, he seemed to be in a thoughtful mood.

"Much as I like Rosie's," he said as they exited the bakery, "I'm in the mood for something different today. Have any suggestions?"

"If you like burgers, Eberly's makes some of the best in town."

"That sounds good. And I've passed by the place, so I know right where it is." He cut her an uncertain look. "Do you mind if we take my truck? I'll be able to get you back quicker."

She hesitated a long moment, then nodded. "Since time is an issue, I suppose it'd be okay."

And he was right. They were there in just a matter of minutes.

Mike carried the tray with their orders while Hannah led the way to an open booth.

Hannah decided to let him lead the conversation. If he wanted to discuss what was bothering him, she'd be glad to hear him out. If not, she wouldn't push.

He took a bite of his burger and gave a satisfied *Mmmm*. "You were right, these are good."

"You should've tried one of the milkshakes instead of the soda. Those are even better."

"I never was much of a milkshake fan. That was more Madison's thing."

"Madison?"

His expression sobered. "Madison was my sister, actually my half sister."

"And you two were close?"

"She was nine years younger than me, but yes, in a big-brother, little-sister kind of way, we were close. Or at least I thought we were."

There was such sadness and regret in his voice.

"Madison is why I'm here." He stared at the straw in his drink. "The day before I showed up, I was sorting through the final bits of her and my stepmom's belongings when I came across one of Madison's diaries."

"And something she wrote caused you distress."

He nodded. "It covered October through April of last year." He dragged a french fry through a puddle of ketchup. "It opened with the statement that she thought she was pregnant."

Hannah set her cup down, getting a glimpse of his pain. "And you knew nothing of this before you read the entry."

* * *

There was no sign of judgment in her demeanor. Instead the gentle tone somehow conveyed sympathy and support. It gave him the impetus to proceed with his story.

"Nothing. I immediately read the diary from cover to cover, all the entries where she talked about her fears, her disappointment when the father disavowed responsibility or interest, her drive to see the pregnancy through on her own, her determination to keep the baby a secret, and her plans to give the baby up once he was born."

"He?"

"Apparently Madison had very few medical checkups during her pregnancy, and then only at free clinics. At least she did learn she was having a boy, or I wouldn't even have that much to go on."

"So what happened to the *boppli*?"

"I don't know." He felt the tension coil inside him again. "Madison was only nineteen, away at college, trying to hold on to an academic scholarship, and abandoned by the baby's father. She was scared, and she was going through this alone because she didn't want anyone to find out she was pregnant." His jaw tightened. "Especially me because she was afraid of disappointing me." How had she managed to carry it off? And how had he failed her so badly that she didn't feel she could come to him, no matter what?

Hannah touched his wrist briefly, bringing him back to the present. "You must not blame yourself."

How could he not? He straightened and returned to her original question. "The last few entries in Madison's diary indicated she planned to anonymously leave her baby—she referred to him as Buddy—here in Hope's Haven. That's why I came." It felt good to finally share his quest.

Her forehead wrinkled. "Why here?"

Mike chose his words carefully. He wasn't ready to go into his history here. "She'd gotten it into her head that leaving her baby among the Amish would guarantee he'd find a good family."

Hannah leaned back. "So you're here to find your nephew."

Relieved she wasn't digging deeper into why Hope's Haven, Mike nodded. "He's family. How could I not? He'd be nearly a year old now. I think it's high time I met him."

"*Familye* is important, for sure and for certain. But is meeting him all you want?"

Perceptive as well as quick. "I want to adopt him. But a lot will depend on his current situation."

"That's reasonable." She toyed with her straw. "I hope, though, that you'll proceed prayerfully. Your nephew may have been fostered or even adopted by someone who has grown to love him very much and would be heartbroken to lose him." Hannah took a sip, then set the milkshake back on the table. "Like I'd be if someone came along to claim Grace."

He sat up straighter. "You're not Grace's birth mother?"

"*Nee.*" She stiffened. "I've never been married. Have you thought all this time that I acted so shamefully?"

"I thought you were a widow." His mind was trying to shift to this new reality. "So Grace is adopted?"

"Not yet but it'll be final in a few weeks." A shadow dimmed the light in her eyes for a moment. "I can't imagine what my life would be like if Grace wasn't in it."

How did a young, single Amish woman end up adopting a child? "Is she the daughter of a relative or friend?"

"*Nee.* At least not that I know of. I think of her as a gift from *Gotte.*"

"Aren't all children gifts from God?"

"For sure and certain. But this was a very special kind of miracle."

"How so?"

She tucked a wisp of hair back into her *kapp* and he noticed some red splotches blooming in her cheeks. What was going on? "You don't have to share any information that makes you uncomfortable."

She took another swallow of her milkshake. "I don't like to talk about it, but it's not a secret. Last year I learned I'd probably never be able to bear children."

Mike's heart went out to her. This would be a blow to any woman who wanted children, but the Amish placed such a high value on large families that it would be devastating. Then he realized something else. "That's why Timothy broke it off with you."

She nodded. "I wasn't surprised, but I had hoped..." She lifted a hand, then let it drop back in her lap. "I should've known."

Mike had trouble believing any man would treat her that way. "I'm sorry."

"I couldn't really blame him." Was she aware of the slight tremble in her hands? "But it was only a few weeks later, just before Mother's Day, that Grace came into my life."

"Your springtime miracle."

She smiled. Then she picked up her burger. "But I didn't mean to sidetrack us from your story about searching for your nephew. Was there more to it?"

Her tone implied she was finished talking about herself. With a nod he accepted the change of subject. "I actually thought I'd found him. Ford told me about an infant boy who was abandoned at the firehouse last May and I thought for sure it must be Buddy. I tracked down the caseworker and convinced her to test our DNA to verify he was the one."

"That sounds promising."

"I heard today it wasn't a match."

"*Ach*, Mike, I'm sorry. I take it that was the bad news you mentioned earlier."

He nodded.

"So what's your next step?"

"I've asked the caseworker to follow up with other abandoned babies in the system who fit the situation. If that doesn't work, I'm not sure there's anything else I *can* do."

"And there was nothing in your *shveshtah*'s diary that gave you any idea of where specifically she left her baby?"

He shook his head. "The entries stopped before the baby was born. Honestly, I'm not sure she followed through on her plan to bring him here or even that the baby survived." He pushed his burger away. "And I worry I may never know for certain."

"What will you do now?"

"I'm heading back to Missouri tomorrow."

* * *

The next beat of Hannah's heart slammed against her chest in protest. "You're leaving?" She tried to moderate her tone. "Does that mean you're giving up?"

When he shook his head, her heart resumed its normal rhythm.

"Not until I've exhausted every possible avenue."

"Do you plan to continue your search from Missouri?"

"No, I still feel my best chance to find Buddy is to keep looking around here. But a while back I agreed to take a few shifts at work this week for a pal who's getting married and I need to live up to that commitment. I'll be back Sunday. Hopefully by then I'll have come up with a plan of some sort." He grimaced apologetically. "That means I won't be able to go with you to visit the shut-ins tomorrow."

"That's all right." She straightened. "In the meantime, I can speak with Vivian, the caseworker assigned to Grace, and see if there's any help she can provide."

"I appreciate that." Then he grabbed his burger. "We'd better finish these before they get cold."

With a nod, Hannah picked up her own burger. Her heart-stuttering reaction to Mike announcing he was leaving had surprised her. Had she developed feelings for him, feelings that could never be acted on?

That was unacceptable, for a whole wagonload of reasons.

While he was gone, she'd have to work on raising her guard.

Chapter 13

I have a favor to ask." It was Friday afternoon, and Hannah had made a decision. Now if she could only convince Leah.

Leah, who had just returned from checking on her animals, nodded. "Of course." She took her boots off by the door. "Does it involve Grace?"

"Not exactly. It has to do with my work. Our special-order business has been growing. People are wanting more and more custom-made items for parties and events."

"*Ach*, that's because the work you do is so *gut*. But what has that to do with me? If you want me to help at your bakery, I have to warn you that my baking doesn't live up to your standards."

Hannah waved a hand. "That's not true, I've tasted your black raspberry pie, remember? But no, that's not it. There are times when I have to take this work home with me. But when I do, I'm often in Martha's way and our oven at home isn't big enough to handle the larger batches."

"But what does this have to do with me? My oven isn't any bigger than yours."

"I've heard *Daed* say that when your home is repaired, you'll need to purchase new appliances since yours were ruined. I want to buy your oven for you."

"*Ach! Nee*, I couldn't let you do that."

"But don't you see, you'd be doing me a favor. I know it would mean you'd have to let me invade your home whenever I have a big baking project to do. And I'd have to store pans and staples there as well." She spread her hands. "So I understand if you don't want to deal with that."

Leah waved a hand dismissively, but still looked confused. "You know I wouldn't mind. But how is doing your baking at my house better than doing it at your bakery?"

"For one thing you're much closer to our house. For another, I can have Grace with me if I work at your place as opposed to the bakery."

She could see her words were making an impression, so she pressed on. "I meant it when I said you'd be doing me a favor. I'd install new ovens here, but our kitchen's not really set up well for that. And besides, this is Martha's domain and I'm not sure she'd appreciate my invading it."

"Your *shveshtah* would enjoy your company, I'm sure. But all right, I suppose if it'll make your life easier, then I don't mind."

Hannah took her friend's hands and gave them a squeeze. "*Danke*, Leah, this is going to not only help me out with my business, but also give me more time with Grace—which is even more important."

So part one of her plan was set.

* * *

Mike arrived back in Hope's Haven Sunday evening. He drove by The Amish Marketplace and it was, of course, closed. He was disappointed, though, that he couldn't speak to Hannah for another fourteen hours. It really was too bad the Amish didn't believe in personal phones.

Fortunately he'd made arrangements with the Grabers before he left so they were expecting him. Ellen welcomed him with her customary chatty cheerfulness. Before he'd so much as said hello, she started mothering him.

"*Ach*, you look tired out. Now you just let Homer take your bag upstairs and you follow me to the kitchen. We already finished our supper, but I have a slice of cherry pie and a cold glass of milk put aside for you."

He was tired, too tired for conversation, but fortunately none was required. The whole time he ate the thick slab of pie, his hostess kept up a constant chatter, telling him about the houseful of family she'd had for Mother's Day, what food they'd had and the antics of her numerous grandchildren.

Since she didn't seem to expect much of a response from him he let her chatter on, listening with only half an ear.

His mind kept wandering to thoughts of what Hannah's Mother's Day might have been like. Had her extended family all gathered together? Had she baked some of her specialty items? Had Grace enjoyed her day as well?

As for his time, it had been busy. He'd worked the evening shifts all three days.

The multiple call-outs for everything from vehicle accidents to accidental poisonings, from fires to falls from ladders and everything in between, had kept them hopping to keep up all the time he'd been on duty.

He'd been grateful for the chance to stay busy and focus on doing his job. Because there was really nothing waiting for him back at home.

* * *

On Monday morning, Mike made quick work of his run and then headed over to The Amish Marketplace.

He'd sure missed his morning whoopie pie while he was away.

Mike stepped inside the bakery and as he always did, he paused and waited for Hannah to notice him. And there it was, that warm, welcoming smile that said she was glad to see him.

"*Wilkom* back," she said. "It's *gut* to see you again. Do you want your usual order or are you ready to try something different?"

There was a note of challenge in her expression, but he decided to pretend he didn't notice. "Why mess with a winner?"

"Because during the month of May I offer chocolate whoopie pies with a special mixed-berry filling. Don't you think it's worth trying at least?"

He rubbed his jaw. "That does sound intriguing."

"I tell you what, why don't we ease you in and I'll give you one of each?"

"How can I turn down an offer like that?"

"*Gut.*" She quickly bagged his order and handed it over, along with a paper cup and lid for his coffee. "I hope you had a nice time back at home."

"It was busy." Given what had occupied his time he

wasn't interested in going into detail. He glanced over his shoulder at the growing line of customers. "But you have customers and I have an errand to run this morning. How about I join you for your trip to Whispering Oaks this afternoon?"

"*Jah*, I'd like that."

"Great." And with a quick wave, Mike headed for the door.

When Mike left the marketplace, he headed for Millersburg to visit the county offices of Family Services. He figured a meeting with Ramona Harper was in order. He needed answers and he needed to do this in person, face-to-face.

Fortunately she was in the office when he arrived. After they exchanged greetings she spoke first. "Mr. Colder, I'm afraid I only have a few minutes. I'm scheduled to do an in-home evaluation this morning and I don't want to be late."

"Then I'll get right to it. Have you checked into whether another baby boy was abandoned in the right time frame?"

She nodded. "I've personally checked through our records and there's no child in our system who fits the criteria you're looking for." She leaned forward. "Are you absolutely certain your sister left her baby in the Hope's Haven area? That she didn't perhaps decide at the last minute to leave him somewhere closer to home?"

If Madison had changed her mind, his search area would increase exponentially. "All I know is what she wrote in her diary. Unfortunately the entries end before the baby was actually born."

"I know it's not pleasant to think in these terms, but

you also have to allow for the possibility that she might have lost the baby."

He absolutely could not accept that. Too many family members had died on him already. "I suppose anything is possible. But I'm far from being ready to give up."

"Of course not. I'm just not sure what else I can do." She drummed her nails on her desk for a moment, then met his gaze. "If you like, I could look through the diary myself and see if anything jumps out at me. A fresh set of eyes might catch something you missed. But I know it's personal, so only agree if you want to allow me full access."

He hesitated. She was right about there being some very personal things in that diary, some things that didn't show his sister in the best light. But then again, if it brought him closer to her baby it was worth a shot. "All right. It's in my truck, let me get it for you."

He returned a few minutes later with the slim volume. "You do understand that this is very personal and private."

"Of course. And you can count on my discretion as well as the care I'll treat it with."

Mike handed it over and she gave him a serious look. "I'll let you know if I find anything. But you realize this is a long shot, right? I don't want to get your hopes up." The caseworker leaned back. "It's more likely that she simply changed her mind and left her baby somewhere closer to home."

When Mike walked out of the office, he wasn't confident that he was any closer to finding Buddy than he'd been when he walked in.

He arrived back in Hope's Haven about an hour before he was due to meet Hannah for the trip to Whispering Oaks, so he decided to swing by the fire station and see if Ford was available to talk. The man had been around a long time and might have some insight to offer. On his way, he stopped by a barbecue place he'd heard his friend mention and picked up a couple of sandwiches.

Once at the firehouse, he headed straight for Ford's office, where he found the door open and Ford at his desk. Mike knocked on the jamb and when Ford looked up, he held out the bag. "I come bearing gifts."

Ford inhaled deeply. "Benny's Barbecue, I'd recognize that aroma anywhere." He waved Mike over and cleared a spot on his desk.

Mike set the bag in front of his friend. "I figured a barbecue brisket sandwich, super-sized, might be just the thing to ensure my welcome."

Ford grinned. "Well, it certainly doesn't hurt your chances."

Mike handed the first sandwich and bag of chips to Ford and pulled the others out for himself, then slid the visitor chair closer to the desk.

"How was your weekend?" Mike asked as they settled into their meal.

"It was good. The kids came in for Mother's Day and we grilled and played with the new grandbaby." Ford lifted his cup in Mike's direction. "How about you? I assume you went back to Missouri to visit your mom."

Mike shrugged. "My mom's gone. My boss just needed me to pick up some shifts."

"So you don't live near your family?"

"Actually, most of my family is gone."

"Sorry, that's tough."

Mike decided he'd take advantage of the opening. "In fact, that's part of the reason I'm here in Hope's Haven."

"Oh?" Ford's tone indicated he was prepared to listen but didn't intend to pry.

"Somewhere out here I have a nephew I've never met."

Ford's brow went up. "I wasn't aware you had family in the area."

Mike gave him an abbreviated version of how it came about and what actions he'd taken.

Ford held his peace until Mike finished. "So you thought the baby that turned up here last year was your nephew."

Mike nodded. "Everything about the circumstances fit." He shrugged. "But it proved to be a dead end. And I'm not sure how to proceed from here."

"The approach you're taking, working with the folks over at the Department of Job and Family Services, is your best bet. I know they don't always move as fast as you'd like, but they are good at what they do."

"I just feel like I should be doing something more."

Ford grimaced sympathetically. "Frustrating, I know. And I'll keep my ear to the ground for you of course."

"Thanks."

"How long are you planning to stick around? Not that I want to get rid of you, but I was wondering how open-ended this search is?"

"I have enough vacation time that I can stick around until the end of the month. If I haven't found him by then, I'll just have to monitor the situation long-distance." Then Mike realized what he was saying. "Not that I'm doing much by being here. But I feel better having face-to-face meetings with the county folks rather than doing it over the phone." And if he was being strictly honest with himself, spending time with Hannah was another draw for him to be here in person.

Ford leaned back in his chair. "All kidding aside, Missouri, I appreciate you giving us so much of your free time these past few weeks."

"Glad to do it. It gives me something to occupy my time."

"If you ever consider moving up this way, I'd sure like to talk to you about joining up with us."

That caught Mike completely by surprise. "You don't know anything about me."

"I know what I need to."

"I appreciate the offer, but I'm not really looking to move."

Ford nodded. "I figured. But the offer still stands if you ever change your mind."

If Ford had any idea what this town represented for Mike, he would never have bothered to make the offer.

Chapter 14

Once they settled into the buggy that afternoon, Hannah took the conversational lead. "How was your trip home?"

"Busy." He gave the reins a little flick. "But let's not talk about my work. How was your Mother's Day?"

"It was nice. It was a between Sunday, so Greta and her *familye* spent the day with us. Grace had cousins to play with and the rest of us played board games all afternoon." Too late she remembered he didn't have any *familye*. Did it bother him to hear about such gatherings?

Something Hannah had realized during his absence was that her grand plan to tamp down any feelings but those of friendship toward him wasn't working very well. Not if the way her heartbeat quickened and warmth flooded her body at the sight of him was any indication.

Then again, emotions weren't something you could control. The best you could do was to control how you dealt with those emotions.

She decided to change the subject. "Did you come up with a plan to find your nephew?"

"Of course I'll continue to work with the Family Services people. Wherever Madison left her baby, they had to have been involved in some way. But rather than just waiting on them, I also plan to get the word out myself. I spoke to Ford, and he's going to put feelers out. And I'm going to visit the firehouses and other baby drop locations in neighboring towns just to be sure I'm covering all the bases."

She touched his arm briefly. "I'm glad you're not giving up."

"I won't. Even if I ultimately decide he's better off where he is than with me, I need to know he's okay."

Hannah prayed he would find his nephew soon and that it worked out for him to be a part of the boy's life.

When they arrived at Whispering Oaks, Melba greeted them with an eager smile. "I have an idea I want to run by you."

"Oh?"

"How would you feel about doing a cookie or cup-cake decorating class here at the center? We could work around your schedule, and I've already gotten approval to reimburse you for all your materials. We might even be able to kick in a little stipend for your time as well."

"Oh, that sounds like fun." Hannah pulled out her notebook. "I'll have to look at my schedule." She chewed on her pencil for a moment. "Since next Monday is my regular day to come here anyway, if I can get Maisie to work a full day, I could take the whole afternoon and do it then. Would that work?"

"That would be perfect."

"Let me talk to Maisie and I'll get back to you."

As they walked to the common room, Mike shook his head. "Cookie decorating classes for all the residents. You believe in keeping busy, don't you?"

"How could I say no? And I'm sure it will be wonderful fun."

"Well then, if it'll be such fun, would you like some help? Assuming I'm still here."

"For sure and certain. In fact, having you there might encourage more of the men to participate."

"Well I'm not sure my participation will change anyone's ideas, but I'll be glad to give it a try."

The smile she sent his way made him very happy he'd agreed.

* * *

The next day, when Mike returned to the county office, he discovered Ramona was out but she'd left a large sealed envelope for him. When he opened it, he found his sister's diary along with a handwritten note.

Mike,

Reading your sister's diary did give me an idea of one more place to look for her baby. It's a long shot and will take me a few days to check out. Be patient and I'll contact you when I know more.

Ramona

Mike tucked the note back in the envelope with the diary and slowly made his way back to his truck. What had the caseworker seen that he'd missed? And why was she being so annoyingly cryptic?

But he felt much more optimistic today than he had yesterday.

He stopped in at the fire stations in the towns on the way back to Hope's Haven and made some good connections.

It was midafternoon when he made it to Hope's Haven. He stopped in at the firehouse and was just in time to join the crew for a game of basketball. When they finished, he offered to order pizzas for the men on duty.

That earned him a raised brow from Ford. "Is this your idea of cooking lunch for us?"

Mike laughed. "When I do cook, you're going to find it was worth the wait."

He mentally grimaced—he certainly hoped he could live up to that bit of boasting.

One thing for certain, if he brought some of Hannah's pastries along for dessert, the meal would end on a high note.

Too bad he couldn't bring Hannah herself along.

* * *

Hannah had asked if he would meet her at her place Wednesday morning rather than vice versa as they'd done it before. "The first home we're going to visit today is in the opposite direction of Graber Farms and it'll save time," she'd explained.

When Mike arrived, Hannah already had her buggy loaded and ready to go.

"I hope I didn't keep you waiting," he said when he climbed in beside her.

"*Nee*. I was ready early. And Grace likes to be outside

when she gets the chance, especially if she can play with Skip."

"Skip?"

"Our dog." She pointed to the white-and-black English shepherd near the barn.

"Ah, I see. Well I hope Grace likes cats as well."

"She does. Why?"

He reached into his jacket. "I picked up a little something for her." He pulled out a fluffy yellow-and-white stuffed kitten and held it out to the toddler sitting on Hannah's lap.

Grace's eyes lit up and she reached for the toy with a happy gurgle.

Hannah's gaze softened. "*Ach*, what a nice gesture. *Danke*."

He waved her words away. "It's just a little thing."

She gave him a knowing look. "You were thinking of your nephew, weren't you?"

She continued to surprise him with her perceptiveness. "I was. I'll have a child's room to furnish when I bring him home with me."

"Since you live alone, will you have someone to help care for him?"

"I've started researching day care centers and nanny services." He set the buggy in motion. "I imagine the first six months will be a period of adjustment for both Buddy and me."

He kept trying to picture what that life would be like, but it was still pretty hazy. Out of nowhere the thought popped up that if he stayed around here, Buddy and Grace could grow up together.

"Turn left at the end of the lane." Hannah's words pulled him back to the present.

Then, like before, she told him about the people they would be visiting.

The visits went pretty much as they had when he accompanied her before. Except there was one fewer today—Mary and Simon Fretz's daughter was visiting from Sugarcreek and so there was no need for Hannah to provide meals.

* * *

Once they'd visited the last shut-in, Mike turned the buggy toward the Eicher farm. He'd enjoyed the morning, especially since it involved spending time with the woman seated next to him. He'd never met anyone quite like her before.

Hannah gave him a sideways look. "If you have a little time when we get back to my place, I'd like to introduce you to my *shveshtah* Martha and my *daed*. I'm sure Martha will have some kind of snack available."

"That sounds good." Should he read anything into this invitation?

When they arrived back at her family's place, Mike pulled the buggy to a stop near the horse barn. He set the brake then came around the other side to take Grace while Hannah climbed out. He was touched by how trustingly the little girl went to him.

By the time Hannah had her feet on the ground, an older man had approached them from the barn.

"Mike, this is my *daed*, Isaac." Hannah took Grace back from him. "*Daed*, this is Mike Colder, who's been visiting in Hope's Haven. I invited him to come inside for a snack."

"*Wilkom* to our home."

"Thank you for your hospitality, sir."

Her *daed* waved her away. "Why don't you go ahead and let Martha know we have company. Mike and I can take care of your horse."

Hannah looked at him as if to ask if he'd be okay.

He smiled her way then turned to Isaac. "It looks like you have a nice spread here."

Isaac went to work on the harness. "*Danke*. I understand from Hannah that you've been staying at the Grabers'."

Mike worked the straps on Clover's other side. "I have. They've been treating me well."

"Not many *Englischers* stay there. They seem to prefer the Blueberry Inn where they have access to more of the conveniences they are used to."

"The Grabers are good people, and I have no complaints about my accommodations."

Isaac nodded. Then, as the horse was freed from the buggy, he waved Mike away. "Go on to the house, my *dochder* will be waiting for you. I'll take care of Clover and be there shortly."

Mike nodded and turned his steps toward the house. Had Isaac been assessing him? If so, had he passed muster?

Mike knocked on the door he'd seen Hannah disappear through earlier, and a moment later she opened the door and stepped aside for him to enter.

Once inside he found himself in a typical Amish kitchen, not very different from the one at the Grabers'. Or the one in his childhood home for that matter.

Hannah gestured toward a woman standing at the stove. "This is my *shveshtah* Martha. Martha, this is my friend Mike Colder."

"*Wilkom* to our home, Mike. Can I get you a cup of coffee?"

"Thank you." Mike rubbed his hands together. "That would be very welcome. I hope my presence hasn't cost you any extra work."

"Not at all. Company is always welcome."

Hannah waved to the other side of the room where Grace sat on the floor next to a set of blocks. She was currently placing her new stuffed cat on top of a pile of the wooden cubes. "As you can see, Grace is introducing her kitty to the rest of her toys."

"Oh, I see you made it back." Someone entered the room from the basement stairs. "How was Barnabas?"

"He was fine. Full of stories from his trip."

Mike looked around to see who'd entered the room and for a moment the entire world stopped. There was no sound, no movement, no one else in the room.

It couldn't be.

His eyes had to be playing tricks on him. It was like his first time at Rosie's—just a trick of the setting and clothing and name.

But this time it didn't shift back into a more acceptable image. Suddenly he couldn't breathe, had to get some air.

"Excuse me. I need to step outside for a moment." And without further explanation he turned and left. It was all he could do not to outright flee, to keep his steps steady and even.

Once outside he started walking, not picking a direction or even checking his surroundings.

That woman standing in Hannah's kitchen was the woman his father had told him died twenty-two years ago.

His mother.

Chapter 15

Hannah wasn't sure what had happened to affect Mike so strangely, but she was worried. Mike's face had drained of all color when Leah walked in and his voice had taken on a strangled quality. The abrupt-to-the-point-of-rudeness way he'd left was unlike him as well.

Ignoring the startled looks from Martha and Leah, she hurried after him. She could see him striding at a ground-eating pace, heading across the field toward the wood that separated their property from Leah's.

She set off after him, rushing past her surprised *daed*, returning his greeting without pausing. She had to almost run to catch up, and still the distance between them barely closed. She called out his name, but she had to do so four times before he finally stopped. Even then he didn't turn.

When she finally reached him, he was breathing heavily and his eyes were unfocused, haunted looking. She was out of breath herself and had to take a moment before she could speak.

"I'm sorry." His voice was ragged, as if he was under some powerful emotion. "It was rude of me to leave so abruptly."

"What's wrong?" she asked, trying to keep the worry out of her voice.

He stuffed his hands in his pockets, but not before she noticed they were trembling slightly. He started walking again, but this time he set a more reasonable pace. "I can't talk right now. I need to keep moving."

"All right. But I'll be here when you're ready." And she walked beside him, matching his pace, holding her peace, waiting.

It was several minutes before he said anything. When he did, he didn't look her way, seemed to be almost speaking to himself. "One of the things that bothered me when I found Madison's diary was that she kept her situation secret from me."

Although he hadn't answered her question, Hannah let him talk, sensing he was trying to make sense of whatever was bothering him.

"It felt like she'd been lying to me," he continued, "even though technically she hadn't. It was more a lie of omission."

Hannah nodded.

"But I just realized that I've done the same thing to you, actually to everyone I've encountered here in Hope's Haven, but mostly to you."

She still had no idea what he was talking about. Whatever it was, it obviously had him agitated.

"What I failed to tell you was that I was born in Hope's Haven, and in fact was raised here until I was seven years old."

Surprising but not earth shattering. "There's no need

for you to feel bad about not telling me. It was none of my business." Then she connected a few of the dots that had been puzzling her. "So this is why Madison brought her *boppli* here."

"In a way." He waved a hand. "I suppose you could say we have Amish in our blood."

That put a hitch in her step. "You mean you're not *Englisch*?"

He grimaced. "When I was seven, my mother was in a serious accident. She had to be hospitalized and was in a coma for several weeks. When she eventually died, my father couldn't stay here and took me and moved away."

"I'm so sorry. That must have been difficult." She'd been eleven when her mother had passed with a whole community of *familye* and friends to support her, and she'd still been devastated. Had Mike not had that same kind of support?

He nodded his acknowledgment of her sympathy. "According to my father, my mother's family blamed him for what happened and were so angry over it that they convinced the bishop and community to shun him after he left."

That didn't sound right. A shunning was a very serious matter, only undertaken for a deliberate offense against the tenets set down in the *Ordnung*. There had to be more to it—

But he was still talking. "I haven't been back since that day. Until now. In fact, the real reason Madison chose to leave her baby here is because she knew this was the one place I'd never come to."

"You dislike Hope's Haven so much?" It was difficult to leave the hurt out of her voice.

The look he gave her softened the impact of his previous statement. "I used to."

"But I still don't understand. What does this have to do with why you walked out a while ago?"

He raked his fingers through his hair. "One of the things my father did to cut ties with the community after he was treated so terribly was to change our names. The name I was born with wasn't Mike Colder." He paused and she saw his jaw tighten and a small tic at the corner of his mouth jump. "It was Micah Burkholder."

Hannah stopped in her tracks as the meaning behind those words slammed into her. "Leah's son."

"Yes." His hands fisted at his sides. "Except according to my father, my mother died in the hospital without ever coming out of her coma." He turned to her, his expression bleak, broken. "But if this was all some horrible miscommunication, if she actually survived despite what my father believed, why didn't she look for us?"

"Because she was told you had died," Hannah said as gently as she could. "And afterward your *daed* divorced her."

She saw him struggle with the implications of that news. "Then it wasn't a miscommunication. He knew all this time that she was alive." His fists clenched at his side. "He *knew.*"

Hannah didn't say anything. It hadn't been a question.

"Why would he keep this from me, outright lie about something so important?"

"I didn't know your *daed*, but he must have had his reasons. Instead of looking back, you should look forward. You've found your *mamm* now and that's a wonderful *gut* thing. She'll be so full of joy to have you back in her life."

He rubbed his jaw. "What do I say to her? She's a stranger to me now. And if what you say is true, she thinks I died over twenty years ago. We no longer have anything in common."

"She's your *mamm*. That will be enough, ain't so? Besides, she may have believed she lost you all those years ago, but she never stopped loving you. Never."

She touched his arm, intending to emphasize her words and perhaps offer comfort. But when he stared down at her hand on his arm something shifted in his gaze, something that tugged at her, warmed her from the inside out.

With effort she pulled her hand away, tucking some stray wisps of hair under her *kapp*. Looking ahead instead of at him, she found the distraction she needed.

"Do you remember when I told you how I first became *gut* friends with Leah?"

He appeared confused by the change of subject, but he nodded. "Yes, she found you crying in some secluded spot."

Hannah pointed. "Do you see that large, split-trunk oak tree up ahead? If you go around to the other side, you'll find that natural alcove I mentioned. That's where she found me." She looked away a moment. "I still go there sometimes when I need to be alone."

"We all need a safe place to retreat to at times."

She met his gaze, composed once more. "But this isn't one of those times. You've been given a very special gift, a second chance to spend time with your mother. And now you must share this wonderful *gut* news with her at once."

Mike nodded and turned. The walk back to the house progressed at a slower, more deliberate pace and neither of them spoke.

When they neared the horse barn, Hannah saw her *daed* hitching Topper to Leah's buggy and impulsively placed a hand on Mike's arm, pausing their walk. "I have an idea. Every afternoon, *Daed* escorts Leah home to help her check on her place and tend to her remaining livestock. I think it might be a *gut* idea if you take his place today."

Mike hesitated, and she thought for a moment he'd balk. Then he nodded. "You're right. The sooner I do this, the better." He met her gaze and she saw the mix of longing and anguish there. "What if she doesn't believe me?"

"She will." Leah would see the truth in him, Hannah was sure of it. "Now *kum*, I'll let *Daed* know you're going to drive Leah."

She changed direction and hurried forward. Mike followed at a slower pace.

"*Daed*, I hope you don't mind but Mike would like to take Leah to her place today."

Her *daed* gave her a questioning look, but after a moment studying her face, he merely nodded. "Of course. I'm almost finished hitching Topper to the buggy. You can go let Leah know it'll be ready whenever she is."

Mike stepped forward to help her *daed* finish up, and Hannah left them there.

She found Leah at the kitchen table with Grace in her lap. She looked up, a worried crease furrowing her brow. "I hope your friend is okay."

"He will be. He just got a bit of a shock." She took Grace from Leah and gave her friend an encouraging look. "I hope you don't mind but he's going to drive you to your place today instead of *Daed*."

That earned her a startled look. "Whyever would he want to do that? Didn't he come here to visit with you?"

"This is more important." She hoped her expression was encouraging. "Don't worry, this is a *gut* thing."

When Leah still appeared hesitant, Hannah touched her friend's hand. "Trust me."

Finally Leah nodded.

Hannah watched her friend, knowing her whole world was about to change. How would she react? She would rejoice to have regained a son. But this was not the little boy she remembered—he was a grown man, one who had lived among the *Englisch* most of his life. One who had, for all intents and purposes, become *Englisch*.

Her *daed* walked in just as Leah was making her exit.

Martha gave Hannah a questioning look. "What was that all about?"

Hannah shook her head. "It's Leah's and Mike's story to tell, not mine."

Martha and *Daed* exchanged curious looks, but thankfully neither pushed her for an answer.

Hannah carried Grace into the living room. And she said a prayer that Leah and Mike would find their way to a happy reunion.

* * *

Mike headed the buggy down the Eicher's drive in silence. He wasn't really sure where to begin. His mother was not only alive but sitting right beside him. It was almost more than his mind could process.

When they reached the end of the drive his companion—he couldn't yet think of her as his mother—broke the silence. "You'll need to turn left here."

He turned the horse onto the road. "I know."

"Did Hannah or Isaac give you directions?"

"No." He took a breath. "I've been there before."

"And when might that have been? I don't remember seeing you there."

"Sunday before last."

"I would have been at Sunday service."

He nodded.

She didn't say anything else for a long moment, but he could feel her scrutiny, her curiosity. Then she spoke. "Young man, is there something you want to speak to me about?"

"Yes, ma'am. But if you don't mind, I'd like to wait until I'm not driving this buggy."

She leaned back, folding her hands in her lap. "Hannah told me to trust her and I do. So I can wait a few more minutes."

The closer they drew to their destination, the tighter the tension coiled in his gut. He wanted simultaneously to get this over with and to draw it out. How would he break the news to her? How would she react?

His dad had divorced her, something unthinkable for an Amish woman. Had she forgiven him? Or was this why his father had been shunned?

By the time he stopped the buggy near the front porch and helped his mother down, he'd convinced himself she wouldn't be as happy to see him as he was to see her. "Would you like to find a place to sit?"

She nodded. "We can go inside. The living room is fine. It's just the kitchen that's a disaster."

"When did this happen?"

"About three weeks ago."

"I'm surprised a frolic hasn't been organized to make the repairs."

She again gave him that curious, assessing look. "Not many *Englischers* know what a frolic is." Then she led the way to the front porch. "As a matter of fact, a frolic has been scheduled for Friday."

He made a mental note of that—he definitely wanted to take part. Assuming nothing changed when he revealed who he was.

"In the meantime," she continued, "the Eichers have taken very *gut* care of me."

"The Eichers seem like good people."

They climbed the front steps together, and Mike opened the door and let his mother precede him into the house.

She moved to the rocker, a piece of furniture he remembered from his youth, and settled down. Then she looked at him expectantly.

He rubbed the back of his neck, not quite sure where to start.

As if reading his mind, she gave him a gentle, understanding smile. "I have found that when you have difficult news to deliver, the best approach is to just come out with it, ain't so?"

He grimaced. "*Difficult* is a good word for it." He straightened and braced himself for her reaction. "Mike Colder is not the name I was born with. My father had it changed when I was just a boy."

She went very still, and her gaze sharpened as she studied his face carefully. "And what is the name you were born with?" Her voice was not quite as steady as it had been earlier.

"Micah Burkholder."

She stood slowly, pushing herself up with effort, but her gaze never left his face.

Did she believe him?

Once on her feet, she reached up and put a hand on each side of his face. "Micah, my Micah. It really is you. *Gotte* be praised, it's a miracle."

"Not a miracle." He reached up, placing his right hand over hers. "But the truth uncovered."

He led her to the couch, and they sat together. She clung tightly to his hand as if afraid he would disappear if she let go.

"My Micah, what a fine young man you've grown into. I want to learn all about you, about the life you've lived and what drew you back to me." Then she smiled. "But we have time for all of that. For now, it's enough that you're here."

Mike mentally winced. Did she think he was moving back here? How did he tell her he had a whole life and career in Missouri?

She must have seen something in his expression. "We do have time, don't we?"

Mike gave her hand a squeeze. "I'll be here at least until Memorial Day."

He saw the flash of disappointment in her eyes, and the effort she made to hide it. "Of course. You've made a life for yourself elsewhere."

"It's only been about an hour since I saw you and learned you're still alive—I haven't really had time to figure out my long-term plans yet." He smiled reassuringly. "But I do know that I want you to be a big part of my life going forward."

Her expression softened. "I'd like that, too, for certain sure."

"We've lost so much time, time we could have spent being part of each other's lives even if we lived apart."

Then she frowned. "You said you only learned I was alive when I walked in the room. So you thought I was dead?"

He nodded. "It's what Dad told me."

"Just as he told me you had passed." She looked down at her lap. "He came to visit me while I was still in the hospital. He told me you had died in a swimming accident and that he would be filing for a divorce."

Even if his father had wanted to sever ties, that seemed unnecessarily cruel. "I don't understand, why would he do such a thing?"

"Samuel had been feeling restless for some time before I had that accident. And to be fair, I was told later that the doctors didn't think I would ever regain consciousness. They told me I was in that coma for over three weeks. And even when I woke up, the doctors doubted I would ever walk again."

"All the more reason that we should have been there for you." How awful it must have been to go through that knowing her husband had abandoned her just when she needed him most? Could he ever forgive his father for what he'd done?

"I had other friends and *familye* to help me. It was nearly a year before I could walk on my own again and an even longer period before I could be fully independent, so I wouldn't have been a *gut* mother to you during that time." Her gaze turned earnest. "But your *daed* always loved you very much. I think you were the only thing keeping him anchored to the community for as long as he stayed. Perhaps he wanted to make certain when he filed for divorce that I wouldn't try to take you away from him." She looked down at her hand on his. "How is Samuel?"

It surprised him that she didn't know, but then he realized she'd have had no way to hear. "Dad died of a heart attack about ten years ago."

He was startled by the sorrow he saw in her expression. Did she still love him after all this time, after all he'd done?

"I'm sorry," she said softly. "You would have been about nineteen when that happened, ain't so? Were you left to face that loss on your own?"

Yet more uncomfortable news to deliver. "Dad remarried when I was nine, and the two of them had a daughter the next year. So I still had my stepmother and half sister."

"*Ach*, you were not raised without a *mamm* to love you, that's *gut*. And you have a *shveshtah*. It seems you had a full life after you left us."

"My stepmother was a good woman, but she wasn't you. And Madison, my half sister, was a sweet girl who I loved but she was ten years younger than me. Unfortunately, both were killed by a drunk driver last February."

"It pains me that you've had to face so much loss." Her expression shifted. "Is that why you came back here, to find the *familye* you have here? Because they'll be so happy to welcome you back."

"Yes, but not in the way you think." How much should he tell her? Then he straightened. There'd been too many secrets, too many out-and-out lies in their lives. No more. "I'm afraid it's a long story and a bit complicated as well."

She stood. "Then perhaps we should feed the chickens while we talk."

For the next hour Mike told her about finding his sister's diary and all the steps he'd taken since. She in turn told him some things about her recovery and life since she left the hospital, but only the good. He was left to read between the lines to figure out some of the hardships she'd faced. Again he wondered that his father could have abandoned her that way.

But he would make it up to her. Now that he'd found her, he would see that she had everything she needed.

* * *

When Mike and Leah returned to the Eicher farm a couple of hours later, they shared their good news with Martha and Isaac. Mike was surprised Hannah hadn't already filled them in, then took himself to task. Of course she would've respected their privacy, would have waited for them to explain, or not, on their own schedule.

Mike followed his mother's lead and glossed over the role his father had played, saying merely that a miscommunication had caused the belief that they were dead and thus caused the long separation.

Martha and Isaac were amazed and excited for the two of them and supper turned into a celebratory event. Leah made plans for how to reintroduce Mike to his Hope's Haven *familye* and friends.

"I've actually already run into one of my uncles," Mike admitted. "Barnabas."

"That's right," Hannah said, "he's one of the people on our shut-in list."

Later that evening, Hannah walked him out to his truck. "So, when do you plan to let everyone know who

you really are? I ask because I want to know how long I
need to watch what I say."

He rubbed the back of his neck. "It could be a bit
awkward. After all, I've already run into a few old friends
and didn't let on that I knew them."

He'd certainly been good at keeping his secret to
himself. "Another of the shut-ins we visited?"

"No, actually, it's Noah Stoll."

"You knew Noah from before?"

He nodded. "We're the same age and were school-
mates. We were good friends once upon a time."

"Then you should definitely tell him next time you
see him. Or better yet, make time to tell him tomorrow.
Noah's a *gut* man. He'll understand why you didn't say
anything right away."

He reached for the handle of his truck door. "I'll think
about it."

Did he need a bit of gentle prodding? "Surely you'd
rather he hear it from you than someone else. Because
whether you do the telling or not, word will get around."

He grimaced. "The joys and the curse of living in a
small town."

She laughed. "*Jah.* But better a small town than a
big city."

"You can't know that until you try living in a city."
And with that he climbed in his truck and turned on
the engine.

Hannah stepped back and turned toward the house.
His last words had caught her off guard. Sometimes it
was hard to remember he was an *Englischer*. Amish-born
as it turned out, but an *Englischer* nonetheless.

It would be best if she kept reminding her heart of that.

Chapter 16

As Mike ran on the jogging trail in the park the next morning, he contemplated what a difference a day could make. Yesterday he'd been without family, he was firmly and happily grounded in his English identity and he'd resented what he considered Amish hypocrisy.

Today he had a mother, he still held out hope for finding his nephew, and he was ready to try to mend his relationships with his Amish friends and family. It had been a long time since he'd felt this sense of satisfaction with his life.

Now if only there was some way for him and Hannah to work things out between them. Because no matter what his head told him, his heart had a mind of its own.

Granted the fact that she was baptized Amish and he had no intentions to go down that road was a tremendous gap to try to bridge. But it wasn't unheard of for members of the Amish community to decide to spread their wings in another direction. Would she ever look on him as someone worth taking that step for?

Later when Mike stepped in the bakery, he admitted, to himself at least, that he came here every morning as much to see Hannah's sweet smile as to eat her sweet pastries. And she didn't disappoint—this morning her smile had ramped up another notch. "I hope you know how happy you've made Leah. She just keeps saying over and over how wonderful *gut* you look and how happy she is that she's able to have you back in her life. It took her a while to settle down enough to go to bed last night."

"I've had similar feelings. I halfway expected to wake up this morning and learn it was all a dream."

"While she's staying with us, feel free to come over anytime you want to visit with her."

"Thanks. I'll definitely be taking you up on that." Then he changed the subject. "What time do you finish up here today?"

She handed him his order. "Around three. Why?"

"I have an errand to run this afternoon and wondered if you'd help me out."

"Mind if I ask what kind of errand?"

"I just learned the emergency responders in Hope's Haven do quarterly visits to the children's ward at the local hospital and they bring gifts to pass out. I thought I'd pick up a few things to donate." He accepted his change and put the coins in a tip jar. "I thought you might be willing to help me pick some things out."

"*Jah!* That sounds like fun." Then it was her turn to change the subject. "Have you spoken to Noah yet?"

"He's my next stop."

"*Gut.* Stop by afterward and let me know how it went." Then she reached back in the display case. "In fact, here's a butterscotch muffin you can bring him to break the ice. I happen to know he has a weakness for them."

"Good to know."

Then she remembered something. "By the way, Noah's not in the workshop. I saw him head to his office in the loft a few minutes ago."

With a nod, he took the treats and headed out the door.

When Mike reached the top of the stairs, he paused a moment to look down on the marketplace. Even at this early hour it was busy. And Noah had created all of this, given all the Amish shopkeepers down there the opportunity to be entrepreneurs. Would his friend understand why he hadn't identified himself? Or would he hold the deception against him?

Mike straightened. There was only one way to find out.

Turning to the open door, he knocked on the jamb.

Noah looked up and stood with a polite smile. "Mike, *kum* in."

Mike entered and held out the butterscotch muffin. "This is courtesy of Hannah."

Noah accepted it with a grin. "I'd never turn down one of her offerings." He waved Mike to the chair in front of his desk as he sat back down. "Are you just delivering this or is there something I can do for you?"

It was best to be direct. "I came to apologize."

"For what?"

"I wasn't totally honest with you when we met. Or I should say there were certain things I failed to mention."

Noah's expression sobered and the muffin sat on his desk, forgotten. "Is that so?"

"I recognized your name as soon as Hannah introduced us. It's one I was quite familiar with from my childhood."

This time Noah's forehead furrowed in confusion. "Should I know what you're referring to?"

Mike leaned forward in his seat. "You would likely have recognized mine, too, except my name was changed as a child."

"I don't recall having any *Englisch* friends as a child."

"The name I was born with was Micah Burkholder."

Noah leaned back, his gaze sharpening as he studied Mike's face.

"I see you recognize the name."

"Micah died."

Mike spread his arms. "As you can see, I'm very much alive."

"Does your *mamm* know?"

"She does now." He settled back. "Up until I walked into the Eicher home yesterday and came face-to-face with her, I thought she was dead."

"*Ach*, that must have been quite a reunion."

"For sure and certain." The Amish phrase slipped out without thought.

"Micah Burkholder. It's been a long time since you were last here." He raised a brow. "Do you still bite your lip when you try to hit a baseball?"

Rather than answering, Mike asked a question of his own. "Do you still chew on your pencil when you're working through math problems?"

Noah laughed and held up a pencil with visible teeth marks.

"Some things never change." And some things did, whether you wanted them to or not.

Then Noah sobered. "But how did this happen? Your *mamm* mourned your loss for a long time."

Mike explained the bare minimum, but even so it was an indictment of his father's deceptions.

He finally moved on to a different topic, a second subject he'd come here to discuss. "I understand a frolic to repair my mother's roof is scheduled for tomorrow."

"*Jah.*"

"I want to help. What can I do?"

"The men are gathering early, around six thirty. Extra hands are always welcome."

"I'll be there. I have some tools in my truck, but I'm not sure I have the right stuff."

"There are always extra tools available. In fact I'll bring some from the shop."

"What about shingles and other materials we're going to need?"

"Everything is being delivered this afternoon. Isaac took charge of figuring out what was needed and ordered it for her. Carl Amstutz, the man you saved from choking, runs the local hardware store. He provided the shingles and windows at cost."

"What about the lumber and nails?"

Noah shifted in his seat. "They're taken care of, too."

Mike sat up straighter. "You're providing them, aren't you?"

"It won't take very much."

"That's generous of you, but I'd like to reimburse you." He spread his hands. "It's my mother's home, after all."

Noah nodded. "I understand. I'll let you know how much it comes to."

Mike leaned back, satisfied he'd do just that. "There's another way I might be able to help. I drive a pickup truck. We can load the materials in the bed and I'll transport them out there." He held up a hand before Noah could protest. "I know you have special wagons for this, but it'll save your horses some work and it's something I can do to help."

Noah nodded. "All right. Give me thirty minutes to finish up here and then pull your truck around to the side entrance."

Mike's steps were much lighter going down the stairs than they had been going up. Having Noah's acceptance meant more to him than he'd realized it would.

* * *

"I suggest we go to Spellman's," Hannah said as Mike started the truck's engine. "They have a good selection and they're not too pricey."

"I defer to your suggestion. It's that big store on the north edge of town, isn't it?"

"*Jah*." She folded her hands in her lap. "Is there any news on your nephew?"

"Not yet. But the caseworker did say it would probably be the end of the week before she got back to me and it's only Thursday."

"I'll continue to pray for both you and your nephew." He seemed far less discouraged today than he had before. Was it because he now had his *mamm* back in his life—his own springtime miracle?

When they entered Spellman's a few minutes later, Hannah grabbed a shopping cart. "Are you looking for any particular kind of gift? Or for a particular age group maybe?"

Mike rubbed his jaw. "We've done this sort of thing back at my station house in Drifton, and it seems to me the eight-and-under group get the bulk of the gifts whereas the gifts for the older kids lag behind."

She nodded. "Then if you want to get some gifts for adolescents, I'd suggest things like board games, puzzles, books and art supplies."

"I like all of that. Let's see what we can find."

Hannah headed for the aisle with the books first.

"This age group is too old for coloring books."

She shook her head. "Actually there are some made specifically for older kids. You can pick up a few of these along with colored pencils or markers. There are also puzzle books, craft books and some great how-to books for kids."

"Hey, look at these." Mike pulled out a book on paper airplanes, one on origami and another on how to draw animals. "What do you think?"

"*Jah*, I think those would be fine gifts."

Nodding, Mike tossed the books in the cart, then paused in front of some reference books. With a smile he pulled a book on fossil hunting and dropped it in as well.

Hannah held out an armload of six books. "Here are some fiction and nonfiction books I think might be *gut*. Do you see any you like?"

He waved to the basket. "Toss them all in."

"It looks like you have a nice selection here. If you like we could pick up some wrapping paper and ribbons as well."

"We'll do that on the way out. Right now we have more shopping to do."

"You're being very generous."

He waved aside her words without comment. "Let's check out the board games next."

Hannah watched as Mike settled on classic games—

Clue, Scrabble, Uno, Chinese checkers. He also grabbed a few wooden and metal brain-teaser-type puzzles. Hannah finally held up a hand with a laugh. "If you try to add anything else, we'll have to go back for another basket."

Mike looked over the shopping cart with a sheepish grin. "I guess I did get a bit carried away." He took hold of the cart handle and turned it toward the checkout. "Thanks for your help."

"I enjoyed it. It was fun to picture the faces of the children who'll get these." And to see this additional proof of his generous nature. Did Mike even realize how special he was?

* * *

After dropping Hannah off near her buggy, Mike headed for the firehouse with his purchases. But his thoughts remained with Hannah. As they'd headed toward the checkout, she'd paused to pick up a couple of stuffed animals. "These make *gut* companions for children in such a place as a hospital," she'd said by way of explanation.

When he'd told her to go ahead and toss them in the basket, she shook her head. "These are my contribution," she'd insisted, and she refused to be dissuaded. The sweet, gentle baker certainly had a core of steel.

When he pulled his truck around behind the firehouse he spotted Ford, sipping on a soda and watching a basketball game in progress.

"Hey, I thought your shift would be over by now. Don't you ever go home?"

"Patsy's visiting her sister for a few days, so I figured I'd hang out here and cook supper for the evening crew."

"And this is how you cook?"

"The chowder is simmering on the stove as we speak." He lifted his can in salute. "You're welcome to join us if you like."

"Thanks, but I'll take a rain check. I stopped by because I have a few things for your hospital toy drive. They're in my truck—where do you want me to put them?"

"We have a bin in the community center. Come on, I'll lend you a hand."

"None of them are wrapped but there's gift wrap in the load as well."

"That's okay. We need to mark it for age appropriateness anyway. Some of the spouses like to help with that part of the project."

Mike opened the door of his truck and Ford whistled. "That's quite a haul—did you buy out the whole store?"

Mike grinned. "We did go down every aisle in Spellman's toy section. And faced with so many choices..." He shrugged.

"We?"

Mike reached into the backseat, effectively turning his face away. "I asked Hannah to help me. She actually purchased some of these items herself." He grabbed a couple of bags and backed out, then turned to see Ford had a knowing smirk on his face.

"Hannah, huh? Been seeing a lot of her, have you?"

"It's not like that."

"If you say so."

Mike refrained from further comment. Did Ford not understand what it meant that Hannah was Amish and he wasn't?

Romeo and Juliet had had an easier gap to bridge.

Chapter 17

Hannah, along with Martha and Grace, arrived at Leah's place at eight o'clock Friday morning. They'd brought cleaning supplies and an abundance of food hampers, ready to tackle whatever needed attention inside the house. The work on the outside was already in full swing and the sound of hammers and saws filled the air.

They found Leah, who'd gone on ahead with their *daed* earlier, trying to set things up inside. She welcomed them with a smile and an apology. "The workers stirred up quite a bit of debris when they took the tarp off the roof. I've been working on the cleanup all morning."

"That's what we're here for," Martha said. "You watch Grace until some of the girls get here and Hannah and I will get to work in here." She turned to Hannah. "If you'll get the cleaning supplies from the buggy, I'll start clearing debris."

Hannah hid a smile as she headed back to the buggy. Martha was definitely in her element in situations like this.

By the time she'd wrestled an armload of brooms, mops, rags and soap from the buggy, other groups were arriving. In short order, Martha had the women organized. One of the first things they did was move the large kitchen table into the living room and wipe it down. That gave them a place to set the food while they worked. Before long the house was filled with industrious women, chatting, laughing and working together.

The older children and elderly women looked after the younger children, making sure they didn't get underfoot with the workers. Some of the boys pounded nails into scraps of wood, imitating their dads and older brothers.

At one point when Hannah passed by Leah, the older woman stopped to speak to her. "I wanted to let you know Otto just delivered the ovens."

Hannah looked past her, trying to see. "How do they look?"

"They're larger than I'd expected."

Hannah met her gaze again. "I hope that's not a problem."

Leah lifted her hands palms out. "Not at all. Otto showed me where and how they'll be installed, and it will work out nicely." She patted Hannah's hand. "You'll be able to do quite a bit of baking at one time in those."

"That was the idea. I only hope you won't regret having me underfoot so much."

"*Ach*, it will be *gut* to have the company. Especially if Grace is with you."

"As much as possible. That's the reason I want to do this." Hannah looked around. "The cleanup is going well, ain't so?"

"For sure and certain." Leah gave a sigh. "I truly

appreciate all you and your *familye* have done for me, but I'm looking forward to sleeping under my own roof again. And having my son here with me." She squeezed Hannah's hand. "My son, Hannah. I can still hardly believe it. *Gotte* is so *gut*."

"Amen. Does that mean Mike decided to move in with you?"

"*Jah*, for the remainder of his stay. It'll make it easier for us to get reacquainted."

Hannah felt a little twinge of disappointment that the unexpected miracle of him and his *mamm* finding each other hadn't convinced him to stay permanently.

Later, when she went outside to bring water to the workers, she found herself searching the crowd for Mike. It didn't take much effort—he stood out among the men. And not just because he was dressed differently. Something about him drew her gaze like a raven attracted to a shiny bauble.

He was up on the roof along with a number of others. The damaged section had been removed and new timbers and decking laid down. Now they were installing the shingles.

Tearing her gaze away from the men on the roof, Hannah moved around the yard, passing out drinks poured into paper cups from the gallon jug. Paulette Eicher, the twelve-year-old daughter of one of her older cousins, sat on the front porch, reading a book to Grace and a couple of other toddlers. Three of the younger men were cutting the downed tree into firewood-sized pieces. Another group worked on reconstructing the kitchen porch. One broken window had been replaced, and Cyrus Slabaugh was already working on the second.

By the time she got to the men who were tossing

trash and debris onto the burn pile, Hannah had run out of water.

And all the while her heightened senses kept her keenly aware of Mike's presence there on the roof.

* * *

Mike had felt a spotlight on him since he'd arrived this morning. It was an uncomfortable feeling, but he'd borne it with stoicism for his mother's sake.

Of course everyone knew who he was—as Hannah had warned, word spread quickly in a small town. Especially juicy news like this, that a man everyone thought dead now walked among them.

There was an awkward moment when he came face-to-face with his uncle Barnabas, but the man smiled and clamped him on the back. "*Wilkum* home, Micah. I haven't seen such a bright light in your *mamm*'s eyes since before her accident."

Several cousins introduced themselves and more than one asked whether he planned to rejoin the community. He deflected the question with noncommittal responses and a change of subject.

Noah made sure he had the proper tools and suggested he work alongside him, at least at the outset. It was obvious most of these men had worked together many times before. There was a rhythm to their work, an unspoken understanding among them of what needed to be done and a willingness to tackle it with gusto. Very few orders were issued, yet the work got done.

From his vantage on the roof, Mike had a good view of everything around him—the work going on at ground level, the children playing in the yard, the same yard he'd played in twenty-two years earlier, the women providing refreshments and helping his mother get the inside of her house set to rights. The talk that was a mix of Pennsylvania Dutch and English spoken with the unique patterns of the Amish.

All around were the sounds and sights of his childhood.

The men ate their lunch in shifts. Since many of Leah's dishes had been destroyed, they were eating on paper plates and drinking from plastic cups. Which was fine by Mike—it had the added advantage of making cleanup easier. While he sat on the front porch steps eating his lunch, he kept his eye out for Hannah. She was like a bluebird flitting from job to job, pausing to throw some sticks on the burn pile, comfort a fallen child, or take the empty paper plate from one of the workers and dispose of it. At one point he captured her gaze from across the yard and she shared a smile that seemed somehow intimate even though they were in the midst of a crowd.

It was midafternoon when the work was done and the folks began dispersing. Finally it was just him, his mother and the Eicher family.

Hannah eyed his mother in concern. "You look exhausted, and it's been a long day. Why don't you go back to our house with Martha and *Daed*? I'll finish cleaning up and take your buggy home for you."

"I need to feed—"

"I'll take care of the goats and chickens," Mike said, interrupting her protest.

"*Jah*, that's a good idea," Isaac said.

Leah hesitated a moment, then nodded. "*Danke*. I think I'd like to lie down for a while."

"I'll take Grace with us," Martha added. "I'll have her all cleaned up and fed by the time you join us."

After they'd gone, Mike turned to Hannah. "Is there something I can do to help before I tend to the animals?"

"You can double-check that all the windows are closed. I heard *Daed* mention that there was a chance of rain tonight."

With a nod, Mike did as she requested. He paused a moment when he came to the room that had been his as a child.

None of his personal possessions were here, of course. His father had packed everything up when they left. But the same blue-and-green quilt covered the bed. As a child it had simply been a bed covering, something to keep him warm at night. But looking at it now, he saw the time, effort and love his mother had put into creating it.

When he moved back here tomorrow evening, he'd be much more appreciative of what was covering him.

When he came back downstairs, Hannah was gathering up the last of the cleaning supplies. She glanced up and met his gaze. "I just need to load these in the buggy and then I can help you feed the animals."

He took the cleaning paraphernalia from her. "Why don't I just throw these in the back of my truck since I'm headed to your place when I leave here."

They left the house in companionable silence. Interesting how neither of them felt the need to fill the void with empty chatter.

Once he'd tossed the supplies in his truck, they headed for the barn where the feed was kept. "So how does it feel?" she asked. "Being back at your childhood home I mean."

"A little bit familiar, a little bit strange."

She smiled. "I imagine the strange will fade soon."

"Perhaps. If I stay long enough."

He saw the disappointment that briefly shadowed her face. Did that mean she would miss him when he left?

Time to change the subject. "Mother showed me the new ovens. She also told me your plans to take care of some of your special orders from here."

Hannah nodded as she scratched the head of one of the goats. "She kindly let me talk her into this. I'm afraid I may have taken advantage of her."

"Nonsense. You know she likes having you and Grace around. And to be honest, it'll make me feel better when I'm back in Missouri knowing you'll be stopping by regularly." He met her gaze. "So are you doing this mainly to be able to spend more time with Grace, or is there some other reason behind it?"

She gave the goat one last pat then stepped out of the pen behind Mike and closed the gate. "It's all about Grace, for sure and certain." She slowly led the way to the chicken yard. "In fact, I'm thinking about changing my work schedule even more."

"How so?"

"I want to be a bigger part of Grace's everyday life. But I can't afford to give up the bakery altogether, exactly because I have Grace to think of now. And while I know I'll always have a home with *Daed* and that I have his and Martha's support, I need to make certain we can also stand on our own should the need ever arise."

"It sounds like you've given this a lot of thought."

Hannah nodded. "It's been weighing on me for a while."

"And have you reached a decision?"

"*Jah.* I want to hire Maisie to work full-time. I'd only go into the bakery one or two days a week, but I'd take care of any special orders from home—actually Leah's home. I could even make some of the specialty doughs and batters from home and deliver them to the bakery."

That was a big step. But it sounded like she'd made up her mind. "When would you start this new schedule?"

"There's a lot I still have to get figured out. And of course I need to speak to Maisie to see if she's even interested. But if I had my way, I'd start in early July."

Mike nodded. "That gives you time to ease into things."

"I hope so." Then she changed the subject. "Leah mentioned you'll be moving in here with her. She's wonderful happy to have you with her again."

"It'll give me time to get to know her again before I leave. And when I find Buddy, Mom will get a chance to get to know him as well." Against all odds he was becoming part of a family again.

"She'll enjoy having a *kins-kind* of her own." Her expression turned somber. "I hope you're planning to remain a part of her life."

"Of course. I can see me and Buddy making several trips here a year, and I hope I can convince her to come visit me as well."

She nodded but didn't comment. Instead she changed the subject. "I'll see if there are any eggs while you feed them." And with that she ducked into the henhouse.

* * *

After supper that evening Hannah helped Martha with the dishes. Leah and their *daed* were in the living room reading. *Daed* had received a new copy of *The Budget*, which he always read in great detail. Leah was about halfway through an issue of *The Connection*.

Hannah dried a bowl Martha had just washed and stored it away in a cabinet.

Martha paused before handing Hannah the next bowl. "Is that *daed*'s snoring I hear?"

Hannah nodded with a grin. "When I stuck my head in there a little while ago, both Leah and *Daed* seemed to be doing more dozing than reading."

Martha gave a short nod as she finished passing the dish. "They both worked very hard today so they can be forgiven their need for a little extra rest."

Before Hannah could respond, Grace, who was playing on the floor, started fussing.

"What is it, sunshine?" Hannah asked the toddler.

When the little girl kept fussing, Hannah moved closer. A quick inspection showed that the stuffed cat Mike had given her was caught between two spindles of a dining room chair.

Grasping the toy from the other side of the chair, she easily pulled it free.

"Here you go," she said, holding it out to Grace. "Mike would be wonderful pleased to hear how much you like his gift."

"What are you doing, Hannah?"

Hannah kept her gaze on Grace. "What do you mean?"

"You know what I mean. You're falling for him, aren't you?"

Hannah tried to ignore the warmth rising in her cheeks. "If you're speaking of Mike, we are just *gut* friends."

But Martha wasn't ready to let the subject drop. "You might be fooling yourself, but you're not fooling me. Or anyone else for that matter. People are beginning to talk about how much time you're spending with the *Englischer*."

Did Martha expect her to spend less time with Mike simply because the gossips were trying to stir things up? "People should find other things to talk about." She mentally winced at the sharpness in her tone.

"You didn't answer my question."

Hannah shrugged. "I said we were just friends. But if it ever developed into something more, would it be so terrible?"

"He's not one of us."

"How can you say that? Micah is Leah's son and he was born right here in Hope's Haven."

Martha dried her hands with more force than necessary. "He's never been baptized, and he's been part of the *Englisch* world for over twenty years." She frowned. "Do you honestly believe he's going to give up that world, a world that includes all those gadgets and luxuries the *Englisch* are so fond of, to live the Plain life?"

Hannah didn't have an answer for that. Up until this afternoon she'd wondered if, having found his *mamm*, he might be tempted to stay with her. But despite it all, he still seemed quite ready to return to his life in Missouri.

Martha's expression softened. "I know you believe you'll never find a *mann*, but I know *Gotte* has plans for you. You must just learn patience."

Hannah stared down at her skirt as she brushed at an imaginary bit of lint. Were those plans to have her live her life as a spinster? *Gotte* had found a way to provide her with a child, and that should be enough—it was greedy of her to expect more. "It doesn't matter. Mike doesn't share my feelings."

"And if he did share your feelings? If he asked you to
follow him back to the *Englischers'* world, what would
you do?"

"I would tell him no."

"Then there you have it." Martha's gaze softened. "I
just don't want to see you get hurt again."

"Pain is a part of life, ain't so? It's not something we
can escape."

"*Ach*, but you don't have to rush to embrace it."

Was Martha right? Was she rushing into something
that would only bring her pain in the end?

Still, she could hardly control her heart. The only thing
she could control was her reaction to those feelings.

And based on the fact that Martha hadn't had any
trouble seeing through her, she needed to do a better
job of it.

* * *

On Saturday, Hannah went in to the bakery, but she'd
previously made arrangements with Maisie to work a full
day so she could leave at noon. She wanted to free Leah
up so her friend could take the time she needed to settle
back in her home.

During a slower part of the morning, Hannah pulled
Maisie aside to speak to her about future plans.

"Would you be interested in working here full-time?"

"You mean permanently?"

"*Jah.* I want to stay at home more to spend time with
Grace. I'd still be involved, but I'd do a lot of my baking
from home."

"How would that work?"

"I'd take care of most of the special orders for parties

and such. And I'd prepare the doughs and batters for my specialty items and deliver them here for you to bake so they could be offered fresh."

"Would I eventually have the opportunity to develop specialty items of my own?"

The question caught Hannah by surprise. But then she nodded, pleased Maisie was showing that level of interest. "Yes, but I'd want you to be conservative, not introducing too many new things at one time." Then she smiled. "Does this mean you *are* interested?"

"For sure and certain." Maisie clasped her hands together. "Does Ada know?"

Hannah nodded. "I spoke to her before you came in this morning. She'd be happy to work with you." Then she straightened. "We can discuss it more later. Right now it looks like we have a big group of customers walking in."

She thought she saw a little bounce in Maisie's step as the girl moved back to the counter. Hannah knew that when Maisie's brother Calvin had gotten married a little over a year ago, he and his wife, Wanda, had settled into the family home. Which meant Wanda had taken on a lot of the responsibilities Maisie had previously held in the household. She had a feeling the girl was looking for something she could make her own. And hopefully she'd find it right here at Sweet Kneads.

Later that morning Vivian Littman, the caseworker assigned to Grace, left word that she needed to speak to her in person and would be coming by her home that very afternoon.

Hannah tried to tell herself it was merely another home visit to make sure things were in order before the adoption, but she had a nagging worry that something might have come up to delay or interfere with the entire process.

* * *

By the time Hannah arrived at home Mike was there, helping Leah get packed up to move back to her own house later that afternoon. She found him on the floor of her front room, helping Grace stack blocks.

"Hello there. Are you trying to take over your *mamm*'s job?"

He grinned as he stood in a lazy, fluid motion. "Just temporarily. Mom's in the basement, washing the sheets and pillowcases."

Hannah frowned. "There's no need for her to do that."

Mike shrugged. "She said she wants to leave her bedroom just as she found it when she arrived."

That sounded like Leah.

"You're home earlier than normal. Special occasion?"

"I wanted to let your *mamm* go home early if she wanted to take some extra time to settle back in."

Leah walked in just then. "That's wonderful thoughtful of you, Hannah, but there was no need."

"Actually, I did have another reason. Grace's caseworker is stopping by this afternoon."

Mike frowned. "Is there a problem?"

"Not that I know of. It's probably just routine."

His gaze never left her face, studying it as if he could sense her unease.

Before he could say anything, she changed the subject. "Have you moved your things over to your *mamm*'s house yet?"

"Everything I brought with me fits in a duffel, so it didn't take much."

"I imagine the Grabers were sad to see you go."

He shrugged. "Ellen Graber sent me off with a big country breakfast and a streusel coffee cake wrapped up to eat later."

Hannah grinned. "You obviously made a *gut* impression on her."

Skip's barking alerted Hannah that they had a visitor. She exchanged an unguarded look with Mike and then went to the door, reaching it just as someone knocked. As expected, when she opened the door she found Vivian standing there. "*Wilkum.*" She stepped aside. "Please come in."

"Thank you." As she entered, Vivian looked past Hannah. "Oh, I see you have other visitors."

"Vivian Littman, this is Mike Colder." As she made the introductions, she noticed a slight shift in Vivian's demeanor.

"How do you do, Mr. Colder? Ramona Harper has mentioned your case to me." She turned back to Hannah. "I'm sorry, but may we speak privately?"

"Of course."

Mike moved toward the door. "If you'll excuse me, I think I'll check with Isaac about moving Mom's cow back to her place." He nodded to the caseworker. "It was good to meet you, Vivian."

Leah picked Grace up. "And the two of us will go down to the basement and finish up the laundry I was working on."

Once the room cleared, Hannah gestured toward the sofa. "Please, have a seat." She noticed Vivian's demeanor wasn't as positive as it usually was. "Has something happened to delay the adoption?"

Vivian took a deep breath. "I didn't realize you knew Mr. Colder. Have you been acquainted long?"

Why had she changed the subject? "I met him when he came to town a few weeks ago. We've become friends." She folded her hands in her lap. "Why?"

Rather than answering, Vivian asked another question. "And do you know why he's here?"

"*Jah*. He's looking for his nephew."

"He's looking for his sister's child." Vivian tugged on her sleeve nervously. "As it turns out that child is a girl, not a boy."

"Are you certain? Mike seemed so sure." And why was Vivian telling her something that was clearly none of her business?

"Actually it was merely a hunch and Ramona wanted to be certain before she said anything. However, the hunch was confirmed this morning."

"Does Mike know yet? I'm sure he'll be just as happy to know he has a niece as he was when he thought it was a nephew." She smiled. "He is very *gut* with Grace, and she's taken to him as well."

Then she saw the uncomfortable, almost pitying look Vivian was giving her and realization hit with the force of an avalanche.

"It's Grace, isn't it?"

Chapter 18

Hannah stilled as everything slowed and became unfocused. For a moment her mind refused to process what Vivian's news meant.

But the caseworker was nodding and studying her sympathetically. "I'm afraid so."

"Are you sure?" Then she shook her head, trying to clear it. "Of course you're sure or you wouldn't be here."

"We did an expedited genetic materials test. There's no question—Grace and Mike are related."

How did this affect the adoption? Then she mentally grimaced—did the fact that that was her first concern make her a bad person?

Her thoughts scurried around, trying to find a way to convince her everything would be okay.

But Vivian was still watching her, waiting for a response. She struggled not to be selfish, not to focus on how this affected her, but she felt as if she were suffocating.

"Mike will be so happy to know his *shveshtah*'s child has been found." Even to her ears her voice sounded stiff.

"You need to understand that if Mr. Colder wants to take guardianship of Grace, he has the stronger claim." Vivian's tone was gentle, her expression searching.

The ground beneath Hannah's feet started to crumble. "He'll make a *gut* father for Grace."

"Hannah, I'm so sorry." Vivian reached out a hand, but Hannah stood.

If the woman touched her, she'd lose all vestige of self-control. "It's best this came to light now, before the adoption is finalized, ain't so?" She needed to be alone right now. "We shouldn't keep Mike waiting. He should know his *shveshtah*'s child has finally been found." Then her heart thumped painfully in her chest. "You don't have to take Grace away right now, do you?"

"No. Mr. Colder hasn't laid any claim on her yet. For all we know, he may not."

Hannah very much doubted that. After going to such lengths to find his *shveshtah*'s child, he wouldn't walk away now. Especially since he'd already formed a bond with Grace.

"Since the child in question is Grace, Ramona handed over Mr. Colder's file to me. I'd intended to get in touch with him on Monday. I just wanted to make you aware of the situation first since this will likely impact the adoption."

Hannah tried not to think about that. "But now there's no need to wait since he's actually here and you've already talked to me."

Vivian frowned. "I should discuss this with him at my office. There's access to the appropriate information and forms if he wanted to pursue legal action."

Next steps. Like assuming guardianship of Grace. "*Nee*, he shouldn't have to wait. Mike knows who you are. He'll take one look at my face and know something's changed. He'll want to know what that is, and I won't lie to him."

Vivian studied her a moment, then nodded. "Very well. Let's at least get the notification done."

Hannah nodded. "*Danke*. If you'll wait here, I'll let Mike know you want to speak to him." And before the caseworker could change her mind, Hannah left the room.

As soon as she stepped outside, she stopped and took a deep shuddering breath, vowing she would not cry. The fresh air was welcome, bracing.

She finally straightened and set off to find Mike. The sooner she sent him in to talk to Vivian, the sooner she could find some solitude.

She found him sweeping the bed of his truck. He looked up and smiled. He raised a hand to wave and a greeting formed on his lips, but he must have seen something in her expression because his smile faded. He immediately set the broom down and hopped out of the truck. "What's wrong? Did she bring bad news?"

She pasted on what she hoped was a convincing smile. "*Nee*. In fact it's *gut* news." For Mike at least. "And she wants to speak to you as well."

His brow furrowed. "Me? I don't understand. Did Ramona send a message with her?"

Hannah gestured toward the house. "Just talk to her— your questions will be answered."

And with that she turned and walked away.

* * *

Mike wasn't sure what was going on, but Hannah certainly didn't look like someone who'd just received good news. In fact, she looked as if she'd just been told her best friend died.

His instinct was to go after her, to find out what was wrong and help her work through it. The only thing that restrained him was the sense that whatever the caseworker had to say to him was an important piece of the puzzle. So he turned and all but sprinted to the house. If he was going to slay Hannah's dragon, he needed to know what that dragon looked like.

As soon as he entered the front room, Mike got straight to the point. "I understand you have something to tell me."

Vivian nodded. "I know you've been working with Ramona Harper, but she's unavailable today so you'll have to make do with me."

Mike, still seeing the crushed look on Hannah's face, wanted to yell at her to hurry up, but he managed to hold his tongue.

"We found your sister's child."

Mike stood up straighter. They'd found Buddy? He was finally going to be able to see and hold his nephew. "When can I see him?"

"Not him, her. The reason it took so long is that your sister's child isn't a boy, it's a girl."

Mike sat on the sofa, trying to adjust his image of what the future would be like. So life with a niece rather than nephew might hold more tea parties than football games but he could live with that. Especially if the girl was anything at all like Grace.

Then it hit him—why the caseworker had come to speak specifically to Hannah instead of him—after all, she'd had no way of knowing he was here. And why Hannah had had that bruised, bereft look on her face earlier. "It's Grace, isn't it?"

Vivian nodded. "It is. I know that this is... unexpected. You probably have questions and things you'd like to discuss."

Right now he had to find Hannah. "If you don't mind, I'd like to get back to you on Monday."

"I understand." She stood and handed him a business card. "You'll be working with me in the future instead of Ramona. Just call me whenever you're ready to discuss."

She paused a moment. "I don't know if your and Hannah's friendship makes working this out easier or more difficult. But if either or both of you need to talk through options, I'm available."

She took her leave and Mike immediately set out to find Hannah. What should he say when he found her? She was obviously worried that she'd lose Grace to him. And the truth was, he didn't have any idea yet what he was going to do. The thought of wresting the little girl, her miracle child, away from Hannah was unthinkable. But the idea of leaving Madison's baby behind when he returned to Missouri was equally so.

He set out in the same general direction Hannah had headed in, but she didn't seem to be anywhere in sight. He stood in the middle of the field, turning in a full circle, but still couldn't spot her.

Then he remembered her thinking spot. With long purposeful strides, he headed there. Sure enough, when he stepped around the tree, he saw her sitting on a limb that nearly touched the ground before shooting up again. To his relief, she wasn't weeping. But neither did she look at peace. The urge to put his arms around her and offer comfort and reassurances was strong, but he knew it wasn't the appropriate response right now. So instead he merely said, "Mind if I join you?"

She didn't look up, just shifted, making room for him to sit beside her, which he did.

When she still didn't speak, he opened with a neutral topic. "This is a great spot. I can see why you come here to think."

She merely nodded.

He was just about to make another inane comment when she finally broke her silence. "Congratulations on finding Madison's child," she said softly. "Your niece is a wonderful sweet little girl."

"Hannah, look at me." He waited for her to comply, and his heart broke at the anguish he saw reflected in her eyes. She seemed to be barely holding herself together.

"I'm not exactly sure what all this will mean"—he gently brushed a wisp of hair from her forehead—"but we'll work it out. You are the only mother Grace has ever known and I can't see taking that from her. Or from you."

Her gaze searched his face as if looking for what was in his heart. Then she nodded and her expression seemed a little less strained, a little more hopeful.

She braced her hands on the limb, one on either side of her. "It's nice that Grace already knows and likes you. It'll make things easier for both of you."

He rubbed the back of his neck. "The thing is, now that I know the truth I wonder how I didn't figure it out myself. Grace has Madison's eyes, her dimple and her pointy little chin."

"It's *gut* that Grace will be able to learn about her mother from you when she gets older."

Mike tried to lighten things a bit. "I have lots of stories to tell about Madison and albums full of pictures to share."

He could tell she was working very hard to be positive. He wasn't sure he'd be able to do the same if the roles were reversed.

She stood and brushed at her skirt. "I suppose I should get back to the house."

Mike stood as well and let her set the pace as they began the trek back. "So what happens now?" she asked.

He wished he knew. "We figure this out. Together."

Hannah kept her gaze focused straight ahead. "Whatever happens, Grace's well-being should be our primary goal."

"I absolutely agree."

She squared her shoulders. "The others will be curious about what Vivian had to say and why I disappeared. We should be prepared for questions."

"It might be better not to wait for the questions but just tell them outright what we've learned."

"In that case, I think you should be the one to speak."

Was the subject too difficult for her right now? "I can do that." He studied her closely, trying to gauge how ready she was to face questions. "I'd like for us to stand together in presenting this as a good thing. But only if that's what you want, too."

She nodded resolutely.

How could he take Grace away from her? Then again, how could he walk away from his own niece?

Chapter 19

As soon as they walked in the house, Grace, who'd been playing on the kitchen floor, started crawling toward Hannah calling for her maa. Hannah scooped her up and hugged her tight, wondering how many more opportunities she'd have to do that. Because, regardless of what Mike said about them working out a solution together, she didn't see how they could both have the kind of close relationship they each wanted with Grace. She had to fight against the bitterness that threatened to overwhelm her.

She glanced up to see Martha, *Daed* and Leah looking at her and Mike with some concern. Fortunately, Mike cleared his throat and claimed everyone's attention.

"I know you're wondering why Grace's caseworker stopped by today to speak to both Hannah and me. The news she brought is going to affect everyone here to one extent or another, so Hannah and I want to fill you in."

He glanced Hannah's way, and she nodded. "Why

don't we all go into the front room where we can be comfortable?"

They trooped into the living room and somehow Mike maneuvered it so that the two of them and Grace sat on the sofa facing the other three, who took seats in nearby chairs.

"Before we talk about Ms. Littman's visit today," Mike began, "I need to explain something to you, Isaac, and you, Martha—namely why I'm in Hope's Haven to begin with." He smiled at Leah. "My mom's already heard this."

And in a surprisingly succinct manner, Mike proceeded to explain about his sister, what he'd found in her diary and his search for her child.

Hannah kept her gaze on her *shveshtah* and *Daed* while Mike spoke. As usual, it was difficult to figure out what *Daed* was thinking, but Martha looked by turns shocked and sympathetic.

When Mike finished, Martha leaned forward. "*Ach du lieva*, did you ever find your nephew?"

Hannah gave a little nod as Mike cut a quick glance her way. Then he turned back to Martha. "Not until today."

"Is that the news Vivian brought you?" Leah asked. "Has the little one really been found?"

"Yes."

Hannah couldn't help it, she gave Grace another tight squeeze.

"*Wunderbaar!* When can you see him?" Leah's face practically glowed. And why not? Her friend had discovered her son was alive only a few short days ago and now she potentially had a new grandchild.

"One of the things Ms. Littman had to tell me was that my sister didn't have a little boy, she had a girl."

Martha smiled. "Girls are nice, ain't so? Just look at our Grace."

Hannah caught her *daed* staring at her and this time his expression was easy to read—he'd already guessed what was coming next. She sat up straighter. It was time she stopped being a coward, forcing Mike to take the lead. This was her story as well. "Interesting you should say that, Martha. As it happens, Mike's niece is our very own Grace."

For a moment no one said anything. The three seated in the chairs looked at one another, then back at her and Mike.

Martha was the first to break the silence. "But surely you'll still be adopting Grace?"

Hannah tried to hold her smile. That was the question, wasn't it? "Grace is Mike's blood kin. Naturally he'll want to play a big part in her life."

"No decision has been made yet." Mike interjected quickly. "Hannah and I both want what's best for Grace. And we've only just learned about this. We're going to take our time discussing this over the next several days to make sure we're looking at all sides of this before anything is settled."

Did he really intend to include her in that decision? "And we'll also be praying for the wisdom to know *Gotte*'s will in this," Hannah added.

"As for right now, nothing will change. Grace still lives and sleeps here, and Hannah still has primary responsibility for her. I'll spend time with her as well, of course, but since my mother will be caring for Grace when Hannah's at the bakery, I shouldn't have to get in anyone's way."

It seemed he'd already given the future some thought in just the little time since Vivian had left.

Martha stood. "I left a pot of chicken and dumplings on the stove. I should get back to it."

Was it her imagination or did Martha sound stiffer than usual? Hannah stood, still holding Grace. "Leah, I know you're anxious to settle back into your home. Now that I'm here, please feel free to go on whenever you're ready." Right now she felt the need to be selfish, to have Grace all to herself. She knew none of this was Mike's fault, was no one's fault, but the end result was going to be the same—her dream of adopting Grace had crumbled.

"*Danke.*" Leah stood "Micah, if you'll help me put the last of my things in the buggy we'll be on our way."

Her *daed* stood as well, but not before he shot Hannah a silent reprimand. "Martha is cooking enough for you both to eat with us. You'll have much to do as you settle in, there's no need to add cooking a meal to your plate."

"That's very kind of you, but I've imposed on your *familye* long enough. Besides, Micah did some grocery shopping for me earlier today, so we'll be fine."

She approached Hannah and took one of her hands. "We'll see you at the service tomorrow." She gave the hand a squeeze. "Trust in *Gotte*. All will be well."

Hannah nodded, feeling both embarrassed for her actions and glad that they were leaving.

* * *

The next day was a church service Sunday and, in deference to his mother's feelings, Mike decided to attend. When he told her so her face lit up. "That's *gut*." She studied his clothing. "Perhaps, before the next church Sunday, I can make you a set of proper Amish clothing."

Mike shook his head. "Don't go to all that trouble. I understand you can purchase them ready-made now." Besides, he wasn't sure how many more of these services he'd be attending.

As Mike hitched the horse to the buggy, he thought about how he had Hannah to thank for his ability to do so. And of course, Hannah hadn't been far from his mind lately. The bruised, hurting look he'd seen on her face when he found her in her thinking spot yesterday had haunted his dreams last night.

He didn't want to hurt her by stealing away what she'd seen as her only chance to have a child.

But Grace was his niece and, regardless of what his father and then his sister had done, one didn't abandon family.

The service that Sunday was held at the home of Debra Stoll, Noah's stepmother. Mike was sure he'd visited the place during his childhood, but he didn't really remember anything about it.

There were a lot of rituals and practices around how one acted during the Amish Sunday service that he'd long forgotten. Like the fact that the men and women did not sit together, did not even enter the room together. When it came time to file into the service he took his place among the single men, easily identifiable because of their clean-shaven faces.

He'd also forgotten how long the service lasted— around three hours, almost entirely in High German. He recalled enough of the language of his childhood to understand a little of the preaching and singing, but not enough to fully participate. There was something familiar and comforting about the service—the cadence of the speakers, the long, drawn-out syllables of the hymns sung a cappella from the Ausbund, the arrangement of the congregation by gender and marital status, which should have been divisive but curiously served more to show there was a place for everyone here. The sense of peace and reverence stirred something inside him, something long buried from the days of his childhood. It made him shift in his seat, unsure if he wanted to lean in or leave.

After the service he was able to shake that feeling off and look forward to the traditional congregational lunch, which was served in shifts. As one of the single men, he ate in the second shift. The meal, he discovered, was something else that hadn't changed much from his childhood. The homemade bread and peanut butter spread, ham, pickles, beets, cheese and boiled eggs were reminiscent of the meals he'd had every other Sunday of his childhood.

The biggest drawback of the morning for him was the fact that because there was a strong separation by gender in not only the service but in the pre and post activities, he was only able to catch brief glimpses of Hannah. She'd had Grace with her during the service. The little girl sat on the bench next to Hannah most of the time, sometimes napping against her side or cuddled in Hannah's lap. Like other mothers, Hannah had brought a small pouch containing a few toys and snacks, just enough to keep the child quiet and entertained during the long service. Later he caught a glimpse of her among the women setting out the food for the meal. He assumed Grace was with one of the many adolescent girls who were recruited to keep an eye on the younger children.

He supposed he'd have to wait until everyone had been fed and the meal cleared away before he had a chance to talk to her.

Had she had as sleepless a night as he had? Had she come up with any potential solution to their dilemma?

* * *

Hannah helped out in the kitchen, cleaning dishes and wiping down tables alongside other women of the congregation. She usually enjoyed this part of church Sundays— the interaction with friends across the community, the chatter and laughter and just general catching up on life. Some of these women she rarely saw anywhere other than these gatherings. These gatherings wove them together as a community.

But today she felt restless, unable to focus. She'd been surprised and pleased to see Mike at the service today. Was this a signal that he planned to rejoin the church? Or was he merely doing what he thought would make his *mamm* happy?

When most of the work was finally done, Hannah turned to Martha. "Looks like things are in hand here. I'm going to go check on Grace."

Martha nodded and made a shooing motion with her hand.

Hannah found Grace being rocked by one of Leah's nieces. It only took a glance to see Grace was sound asleep. For a moment Hannah thought about taking her anyway—sleep seemed a wasteful way to spend whatever time they had left as mother and daughter. But Grace needed her naptime to recharge and enjoy her afternoon.

Feeling at loose ends, Hannah headed outside. Maybe a walk would improve her mood.

* * *

Mike saw Hannah strike out by herself and headed after her. They needed to talk.

He caught up with her just past the barn. When she spotted him her steps faltered a moment, but then she moved forward again.

"Mind if I join you," he asked, matching her pace.

"*Nee.* I'm just getting some fresh air."

He grinned. "Perfect. I happen to like fresh air myself."

She smiled at his attempt to tease, but didn't say anything.

They walked in silence for a while, until Mike finally felt he had to say something. "Are you ready to teach the cookie decorating class at Whispering Oaks tomorrow?"

"*Jah.* In fact I already have the cookies baked and packed."

"When did you find the time to do all that?"

"I mixed the dough Friday evening and baked it last night." She shrugged. "I had trouble sleeping anyway."

He ignored the last part and focused instead on the first statement. "I thought you had those ovens installed at Mom's so you could bake there."

"I did and I will. But yesterday was Leah's first night back in her home after several weeks away, not to mention your first night there in twenty-two years." She raised a hand and rolled her wrist. "I decided I'd wait a day or two before invading her home."

Was that the only reason? Or had she been avoiding him? But of course he couldn't ask her that. "What time did you want to head to Whispering Oaks tomorrow?"

"I told Melba we'd arrive by one o'clock, so if you want to meet me at the bakery at twelve thirty, that should give us plenty of time."

"I have a better idea. Why don't I meet you around eleven? We can take time over lunch to discuss what happens with Grace."

Her gaze flew to his, obviously surprised. "Have you made any decisions? After all, I know your intention was to find Madison's child and bring the toddler back to Missouri with you."

"No. Like I said before, the two of us need to talk it through first. But whatever I do decide, it'll be with Grace's best interest in mind."

She nodded without meeting his gaze. But he noticed they'd changed directions and were now headed back toward the house.

He tried again. "I know this news about Grace being my niece has upset you, even though you're too gracious to cast blame. But I don't want it to insert any awkwardness between us." Which was a foolish thing to say because they both knew it already had.

After a moment she turned to face him. "Actually, I'm ashamed to admit I haven't been gracious. You don't deserve that. Finding your niece should have been a joyous occasion, but I spoiled that for you."

He touched her arm briefly. "Hannah, you love Grace like she was your daughter. There's no way this wouldn't hit you hard."

"*Danke.*" Then she rolled her eyes. "I suppose that proves you're the gracious one."

Mike smiled, some of his tension easing. At least she'd thawed enough for a bit of teasing.

But he knew, unless some miracle happened, this was going to drive a wedge between them that no one could remove.

* * *

Hannah settled into the back seat of the buggy with Grace. She savored the feel of the drowsy toddler nestled against her, playing lazily with her *kapp* strings. But she was also distracted by Mike's request that they meet tomorrow to discuss how to move forward with the issue of Grace's guardianship. Could she possibly convince him to let her adoption procedure go forward? Should she?

Martha spoke up from the front seat next to *Daed*. "It appears Mike is stepping back into his role as Leah's son with more ease than I'd expected."

"Leah is happy to have him back, for sure and certain." *Daed* tugged on the reins to coax the horse to turn left. "I haven't seen her so happy in a long time."

"Perhaps he'll change his mind about going back to his former life." Martha turned to look at Hannah. "Do you know yet what his plans are for Grace?"

Hannah shook her head. "We're going to discuss it over lunch tomorrow."

Martha's expression tightened in a worried frown. "Surely he won't take her with him when he returns to Missouri."

"He has the right to do so." Hannah was grateful her voice didn't quaver or break. "And when you look at this from his perspective, Grace is the daughter of his now-deceased *shveshtah* and he's the closest living relative she has."

"You're right, *dochder*, Grace is his *familye*, and he wants to be a part of her life. But I will miss that sweet little *Liebchen* if Mike does take her away."

There was no response she could give to that.

"And speaking of Grace," he continued after a moment, "I have a favor to ask of you, Hannah."

What could he want from her?

He gave the reins a flick. "While Leah stayed in our home these past few weeks, you and Grace could sleep a little later in the morning because you didn't have to go to Leah's house before you turned around and headed for the bakery, ain't so?"

"*Jah.*" What point was he trying to make?

"I'd like to take Grace to Leah's in the mornings for you. It would give me a little special time with her, and it'd save you from making that extra stop. What do you think?"

Hannah was torn. She didn't mind making an extra stop in the mornings, actually preferred time spent with Grace over a few extra minutes' sleep. And there probably wouldn't be many more of these opportunities.

But this seemed to be important to *Daed*.

"*Danke, Daed.* That would be right nice. We can start tomorrow."

Later that evening, while Hannah helped Martha clean up the kitchen, she noticed that her *shveshtah* seemed agitated. She was scrubbing the counter with more effort than required, her lips were tightly compressed as if to hold something in and her eyes were narrowed. Twice Hannah tried to start conversations with her only to get one-word responses and nothing more.

Finally, she'd had enough. "Martha."

"Hmm." Her *shveshtah* didn't bother to look up.

"Martha, look at me."

That got her attention. Martha stopped scrubbing the already clean counter and met her gaze. "What is it?"

"What's wrong? You've seemed distracted ever since we got home."

"Didn't you hear what *Daed* said on the ride home?"

Hannah shrugged. "*Daed* said several things."

Martha waved a hand impatiently. "I mean about bringing Grace to Leah's in the mornings."

"*Jah.*" Why would that have her so upset? "He just wants to spend more time with Grace before everything changes. I think it's sweet."

"Don't you see—it's not just about Grace."

Hannah finally got a glimmer of what was bothering Martha. "Do you still think there's something between *Daed* and Leah? We already discussed this and decided they were just *gut* friends."

"You decided that, I didn't. Besides, last time we discussed this we assumed Leah was still a married woman. Now we know she's a widow. There's nothing to keep them from courting."

Hannah paused. She hadn't considered that. "I still think they're just *gut* friends." Then she raised her chin. "But even if they do feel something more for each other, would that be such a bad thing?"

Martha turned away, ostensibly to hang up her cleaning rag. "You're probably right, I'm just imagining things."

Martha didn't sound like she truly believed that. Why was this bothering her so much? Hannah gave her *shveshtah* a sympathetic look. "You do know that if *Daed* ever remarried, it wouldn't mean he's forgotten *Mamm*?"

Martha waved that off. "Of course. I already said I was imagining it anyway."

As Hannah climbed the stairs, she mulled over what it would be like to have Leah as a *shteef-mamm*. She already had a sense of what it would be like to have her live under the same roof. And if it would make their *daed* happy, why shouldn't he marry again? Why did Martha seem so upset by it? Was it just the idea of change she objected to?

Before retiring to her own room, Hannah looked in on Grace. The battery-powered lamp she carried cast a soft glow into the room. She smiled at the sight of the little girl on her side, her doll and kitty safe within the curl of her body. Such a sweet picture of innocence.

Would Mike truly take her away?

Chapter 20

I plan to pursue the adoption of Grace."

Hannah paused with her hamburger halfway to her mouth. Leaning back against the booth in Eberly's, she set the burger back down on her tray and took a sip from her cup. "So you've made your decision." It was what she'd expected, yet the reality hit her anew like a punch in the chest.

"Only about the adoption."

"Only?" Wasn't that the main thing, the thing that decided who would have Grace in their lives and who would be left on the outside looking in?

He leaned forward. "She can't stay in limbo—someone needs to adopt her to keep her out of the foster care system. And I'm sorry if you still hoped that someone would be you, but she is my family."

Hannah tried to swallow a sip of milkshake through the lump in her throat. "Of course." So much for them deciding this together.

"But I was thinking," he continued, "perhaps we could come up with a schedule that allows us both to be an important part of Grace's life."

"And how would that work?"

"We'd decide who would have charge of Grace on what schedule—alternate weeks, alternate months, something else—whatever we think will work best for each of us and for Grace."

Hannah took a bite of her burger while she thought about what he'd said. "How would that work with you back in Missouri and me here in Hope's Haven?"

"Now that I've found I still have a mother, I plan to come back often to visit her. Whatever schedule we work out, I'm sure I can arrange to transport Grace back and forth between our homes on the appropriate dates."

"It sounds like you've given this a lot of thought."

"I've thought of little else since the truth came out. I don't want to split you and Grace up completely. You two need each other." He picked up his own burger. "I know this isn't ideal. I'm open to suggestions if you have a better idea."

She shook her head. "*Nee.* But it seems like it could get confusing for her." And what was best for Grace had to be the deciding factor.

He touched the top of her hand as it rested on the table, and she was surprised by the little tingle of awareness that shot through her, causing her hand to jerk reflexively.

Mike looked slightly off balance as he drew his hand away. Had he felt it too?

Whatever the case, he continued as if nothing had happened and she tried to do the same.

"Let's at least give this a try." He spread his hands. "And we really don't have to change anything for a few weeks. It'll take time for me to find out what's required for me to formally adopt Grace. And I'll have to get my apartment childproofed, convert the guest room into her room, make arrangements for a sitter to watch her when I'm at work, and find a pediatrician."

It sounded as if he'd done some research.

He shrugged. "I figure it'll be at least the end of the month before I can get all the wheels in motion."

Did he really think nothing would change immediately? Already she could sense the change in the dynamics between them. All the decision-making was now in his hands. It was almost as if Grace had become a visitor in her home rather than part of her household.

And her heart was breaking.

Hannah had to change the subject before she thought too much about the future. "Did you find out how the mistake was made about Madison's *boppli* being a boy?"

His wrinkled brow indicated he was surprised by her change of subject, but he went along. "I called the caseworker this morning to ask about that. When she read Madison's journal, she picked up on something I'm embarrassed to say I missed. The date on the diary entry where Madison noted she'd learned she was having a boy showed she couldn't have been more than thirteen or so weeks along. Unless she'd had specialized tests, no medical professional would tell her the gender of her child with relative certainty so early in her pregnancy. I'll never know what convinced her it was a boy, but it was obviously in error."

"You did say she was naïve."

He'd taken a bite of his burger so he merely nodded.

She changed the subject again—anything to keep the

talk away from Grace. "How have things been with you and Leah?"

"We're still getting to know each other again. But it becomes more comfortable every day." Mike gave her a crooked grin. "It helps being back in that house. I can't believe how much stayed the same in the past twenty-two years. The only difference is the addition of some basic indoor plumbing." He grinned. "For which I am very grateful."

"Leah told me yesterday that you're doing some work around the place." If there was one thing Mike definitely wasn't, it was lazy.

"Just a few maintenance odds and ends. After all, a son should make sure his mother is safe and cared for."

"And I know she appreciates it, for sure and certain."

As they ate, they settled into other topics. Hannah tried to tell herself that Mike adopting Grace was a good thing. Mike would have *familye* again, and Grace would grow up knowing who she was and where she came from.

Above all, she tried to remind herself that *Gotte* was in control of everything.

But the knowing and the meekly accepting were two very different things.

* * *

During the ride to Whispering Oaks, Mike could sense the change in Hannah. Her talk was still upbeat and she still wore a smile. But something in her expression had dimmed, and there was a slight slump to her shoulders that hadn't been there before.

Hopefully this was temporary, a period of adjustment to her new relationship with Grace. And it could be a good thing, not the mother-daughter relationship she'd wanted, but certainly one of favorite aunt. They *could* make this work—Hannah would see that as they moved forward.

When they arrived at Whispering Oaks, he loaded up her portable cart with the cookies and decorating supplies. And there was quite a bit to load. He looked at her from the corner of his eye. "You must have spent hours getting this much baked and prepped."

Hannah shrugged. "I find working with dough relaxing."

Placing the last box precariously on the overloaded wagon, he shook his head. "Then judging from the quantity you have here, I'd say you must be very relaxed indeed."

She rolled her eyes and grinned.

And with the mood somewhat lightened, they walked through the front entrance.

Melba looked up as soon as they stepped inside and came around the desk to greet them. "We're all ready for you. The tables are set up in the common room, plastic tablecloths have been laid down, paper plates and paper towels have been made available and the residents are eagerly waiting for you."

"*Danke.* I think we're going to have a wonderful *gut* class." She gave Melba a challenging smile. "There's room if you'd like to join us."

Melba shook her head. "I wish I could, but someone has to watch this desk."

"In that case I'll save you some of the cookies." And with a wave she headed for the common room.

Mike followed more slowly, keeping an eye on the overflowing cart he pulled behind him.

Hannah stepped into the makeshift classroom and

Mike could immediately feel the energy in the room go up, the mood lighten. Did she know what a positive impact she had on people around her?

"Hello, everyone. Give us a few minutes to set things up and then we'll get started."

Conscious of his role in pulling in the male residents, Mike called out to the domino-playing friends. "Mac, George, you guys mind giving me a hand here?"

The two men came over, and a moment later Ernest and Leon joined them. With a little direction from Hannah, he and his helpers had the cart emptied in a matter of minutes.

"All right, everyone, find a spot at the table."

After all the shuffling was done, Mike noticed the always biting, unsocial Fay stood to one side, aloof and alone. Should he try to draw her in? Would she even welcome the gesture?

He sought and met Hannah's gaze across the room, and something in her expression stopped him.

Then she spoke up. "I'm going to need someone to help me, someone confident enough to not mind being part of the demonstration." She scanned the room and met the loner's gaze. "Fay, there you are. As a former high school art teacher, you'd be perfect. I've saved you a place right here next to me."

As if Fay's compliance was a foregone conclusion, she turned to the rest of the group. "Here's an overview of what we're going to do today. Everyone should have a sheet in front of them with some basic designs outlined. I'm going to show you some simple tricks for how to trace them onto your cookie. Then we'll learn how to apply the frosting and candies to make your picture come alive on the cookie. The cookies are packaged up with two cookies per bag, one square and one circle. Now, before we get started, are there any questions?"

"Can we eat them when we're done?" Mac asked.

Hannah laughed. "You can do with them as you please."

"Can we use our own design?" a lady whose name he'd forgotten asked.

"Absolutely."

She glanced around. "It looks like there's no more questions, so let's get started."

Mike was impressed once again with her teaching style. As before, her instructions were comprehensive and yet easy to follow. And as she demonstrated, she had a subtle way of showing Fay in the best possible light. She had the former schoolteacher going around the room and helping those who were having problems with the instructions.

Just another demonstration of how good she was with people.

* * *

The next morning Mike parked his truck behind the fire station. His back seat was full of bags of groceries and he was feeling pretty pleased with himself. He'd called Ford last night and offered to make good on his promise to cook for the crew. He not only was looking forward to it, but felt he owed it to them as well. After all, he'd spent quite a bit of time here these past few weeks, made use of their showers, and eaten more than one meal with them. He was in his element here—they talked the same language, shared the same type of experiences. He was going to miss hanging out with these guys when he left Hope's Haven.

Recruiting the handful of men in the parking lot to help, he transported the groceries up to the station's kitchen. Ford was there, waiting on him. "So what do you have in store for us, Missouri?"

"Get ready for the best chicken and sausage jambalaya you've ever had the privilege of tasting."

"Those are mighty big words. I look forward to seeing if you can live up to your claims."

Mike grinned and then made himself at home, digging through their pots, utensils and spices to find what he needed. In addition to the jambalaya, he planned to make some cheesy garlic bread, using loaves he'd purchased at Sweet Kneads and his own blend of cheeses, butter, garlic and spices.

Several of the men were in and out, checking in to sneak tastes, offer advice and get their good-natured digs in.

While he worked, there were two call-outs, one involving a kitchen fire that was quickly put out and another involving a motorcycle accident that required transport to the local hospital. It seemed strange to be left behind while the others rushed out.

But by the time the food was done, everyone on the current shift was back in house. And as soon as he announced it was ready, the men lined up for lunch.

He was gratified to see that the men cleaned their plates, several coming back for seconds in quick order.

"Well," he said to Ford, "do I pass muster?"

Ford's brow furrowed. "I suppose it'll do." Then he stood. "Although I may need another taste to make sure."

"Well, save room." Mike pulled a large box out from under the counter. "When Hannah heard I was cooking for you guys, she insisted I bring this along." He lifted the lid to reveal a large sheet cake. "According to Hannah, it's a chocolate pecan brownie cake." Before he'd finished his description, men were grabbing paper plates and circling the counter.

Ford laughed as he moved to the stove for another serving of jambalaya. "Looks like it's a hit."

"I'll let Hannah know."

Then Ford's expression took on an authoritative look. "You do know that house rules state that whoever has kitchen duty does both the cooking and the cleaning."

"Funny, I don't seem to remember that being the case when I've eaten here before."

"Apparently your memory's faulty."

"I suppose your men would verify that such a rule exists if I asked."

Ford grinned. "Absolutely."

Mike laughed as he carried the sheet pan to the sink. He really didn't mind—not the good-natured fib or being tapped to do cleanup.

Later, while Mike worked on the dishes, Ford leaned back against the counter, arms folded. "Any word on your nephew?"

"Actually, quite a bit has happened the last few days. For one thing, it turns out I have a niece, not a nephew."

"Wow, no wonder the caseworkers had trouble finding the kid."

Mike nodded. "Once that mistake was uncovered, they came through in quick order. My niece was located on Saturday."

Ford studied him critically. "I'm not seeing the level of excitement I expected."

"There are complications. Grace was living with a foster mom who was in the process of adopting her."

"That would definitely complicate things. But still you

have a strong claim on the child, assuming they're certain she's your niece."

"My claim isn't the sticking point, everyone agrees Grace is my niece."

"Then?"

"It turns out her foster mother is none other than Hannah."

Ford straightened. "You mean your Amish baker lady?" He gave a long, low whistle. "That's tough."

Mike found himself scrubbing the pot with more ferocity than required.

"What are you going to do?"

"Adopt Grace myself. Try to work out some kind of arrangement where Grace can spend time with each of us." *Try to hold on to Hannah's friendship with every ounce of my being.*

* * *

When Hannah arrived at Leah's Tuesday afternoon, Mike was on the front porch, replacing one of the railing spindles. Since she was planning to be here for several hours, she proceeded on around to the back where she could park her buggy and unhitch Clover.

By the time she'd pulled the buggy to a halt, Mike had joined her.

He offered his hand to help her step down. "Mom tells me you plan to do some baking here this afternoon."

She nodded. "Lots of graduation and wedding-related activities happening in the next few weeks. I've got orders for hundreds of elaborately decorated cookies and cupcakes along with several cakes."

He went to work unhitching Clover. "Sounds ambitious."

"It's doable, but it'll take more than one afternoon to accomplish."

"I'm sure Mom won't mind." He waved her away as she moved to help with the horse. "I've got this. Why don't you go on in the house and get started?"

"*Danke.*" Hanna reached inside the buggy and pulled out a large hamper.

"What do you have there?"

"I mixed up some of the dough yesterday. It has to chill overnight so this is what I'll bake today."

"Looks heavy. Need some help?"

"*Danke*, but I can manage." By the time she reached the kitchen door, Hannah was regretting not taking him up on his offer. The rolls of dough in the hamper were weighing her arm down. But she couldn't very well turn and ask for help now.

Besides, Grace was inside, and Hannah couldn't wait to see her.

* * *

Mike watched Hannah cross the yard, carrying a basket that was obviously too heavy for her. And they said the Amish eschewed pride. For a woman who appeared soft and sweet on the outside, she could be surprisingly stubborn at times.

Shaking his head, he went back to work on the horse's straps. As he worked, he felt a few raindrops on his head. But by the time he turned Clover loose in the paddock, the drizzle had already stopped.

When he stepped inside the kitchen he halted on the threshold, transfixed by the sight of Hannah down on the floor playing patty cake with Grace. They were the perfect picture of a loving mother and daughter. How could he break them up?

"Okay, sunshine, *Mamm*—" Hannah cut a quick, abashed glance Mike's way then turned back to Grace, "I mean, *I* love you, but I need to start baking."

Mike saw the lost look that flashed across Hannah's expression when she made that slip. They hadn't discussed what Grace should call her, it hadn't even crossed his mind to ask. But he could see it mattered to her—mattered a lot. He personally had no problem with Grace continuing to refer to Hannah as *Mamm*. But it could be confusing to the girl as she grew older.

Leah, who'd been working at the stove, set down her cook spoon and turned. "The longer this simmers, the better it will be. The kitchen is all yours, Hannah. Just don't remove the lid from the pot while you work."

Hanna stood. "*Danke*, Leah. I don't have a reason to use your stove, so your soup is safe."

"Since you have so much work to do this afternoon, I'll take Grace into the front room with me."

"*Danke*."

Then Leah turned to Mike. "Why don't you see if you can make yourself useful."

When she and Grace made their exit, Mike turned to Hannah. "You heard her—what can I do?"

She waved a hand dismissively. "There's no need for you—"

He raised a brow. "Don't you think I can be of any use?"

She didn't say anything for a moment, and he wondered if this was going to be one of her stubborn moments. Then she nodded. "All right." She went to the freestanding supply cabinet she'd purchased at the same time she'd ordered the ovens, and retrieved a roll of parchment paper and a stack of sheet pans. She set the sheet pans on the counter and handed him the roll of parchment paper. "You can line each of these pans, edge-to-edge, while I prepare the work surface."

"Starting me off with the hard jobs I see."

That earned him a grin, but she still hadn't met his gaze since that slip earlier. Would they ever be able to regain the easy camaraderie they'd had before they learned Grace was his niece?

While he worked on lining the cookie sheets, she quickly wiped down and dried the table. Then she grabbed a canister of flour and dusted her work area.

A few minutes later he added paper to the last pan. "All done here."

"*Gut.* Me too."

"So what's next?"

She tilted her head and finally met his gaze. "You're sure you want to keep going?"

"I do."

She gave him a mock-warning look. "Don't say I didn't give you an out."

Good, she was relaxing.

"I put the cookie dough in the refrigerator when I arrived. If you'll get two of the disks for us to work with, I'll get the rolling pins."

Once that was done, Hannah went into instructor mode. "We need to take these disks of dough and roll them out to a thickness of about a quarter inch. Try to make the overall thickness as uniform as possible."

She demonstrated. "If the dough begins to stick to your rolling pin or your hands, you'll want to sprinkle on more flour."

He enjoyed watching her when she was in her element this way, confident and relaxed. And standing side by side as they worked was nice too. Was she even aware that she hummed softly when she worked?

"How's this?" he asked when he had it rolled out.

Her mouth scrunched to one side as she focused on his sheet of dough. "The center seems a little thicker than the edge. Otherwise I think it's ready."

Mike studied his dough critically, then rolled gently from the center out.

This time she nodded and gave him an approving smile. "You're doing so much better than I did on my first attempt."

"Why, thank you. I have a good teacher."

"Of course, I was six my first time."

That surprised a chuckle out of him, and he saw an answering grin on her face. Promising.

"So what's next?" he asked.

She checked her ever-present notebook. "This first set is for a graduation party. I'll do a dozen round cookies, decorated with graduation caps, a dozen rectangles decorated with diplomas and a dozen plaque shapes decorated with the year." She retrieved the appropriate cookie cutters and handed him one. "You can work on the rectangles."

Did she know she had a smudge of flour on her cheek? Even though he thought she looked absolutely adorable, he couldn't resist reaching up to brush it away.

As soon as his hand touched her face, sensations jolted through him with the force of a flashover—sudden, overwhelming, undeniable.

She felt it too. He could see it in the way her eyes widened and darkened, in the sound of her breath catching in her throat. For that moment in time everything shifted.

They weren't rivals for the guardianship of Grace.

They weren't Amish and English.

They weren't Ohioan and Missourian.

They were just a man and a woman.

And standing right here in his mother's kitchen, he wanted nothing more than to take her in his arms.

Chapter 21

Hannah's gaze was locked to Mike's, and she couldn't seem to look away. It felt as if a sparkler was going off in her stomach. His hand on her cheek felt both gentle and strong, protective and yielding. For a moment she could see a future where he was more than just a friend.

And abruptly, from one heartbeat to the next, she came to her senses. She stepped back and looked away from those draw-you-in eyes.

How long had they stood like that, gazes locked, his hand caressing her cheek? It felt like both a single heartbeat and something that could stretch into forever.

She picked up one of the cookie cutters. "Any questions before you start? We have a lot to accomplish tonight." She still wouldn't trust herself to meet his gaze.

"I think I've got it." His voice, huskier than normal, did nothing to ease the flutters in her stomach.

They worked in silence, cutting the dough into shapes and setting it on the prepared pans. When this first batch was ready for the oven, Hannah wiped her hands on the dishtowel she'd set on the back of a kitchen chair. Finally trusting herself to meet his gaze, she smiled. "All right, into the oven these go."

To her relief Mike seemed to have returned to his usual friendly self. With an easy smile and a nod, he helped her get the pans in the preheated ovens.

That done and the timer set, she turned back to him. "There are four more disks of dough in the refrigerator. Do you mind working on those by yourself for a while?"

"Are you going somewhere?"

"*Nee.* But I need to mix more dough and get it in the refrigerator so it'll be ready to bake tomorrow."

"In that case, I don't mind at all. Just let me know which cutters to use and how many of each to cut."

For the next hour and a half or so they worked together, Mike getting yesterday's doughs prepped and in the oven, her mixing fresh dough to chill overnight.

The mood had shifted again to something more companionable and less tense. Their work and movements seemed to develop a sort of complementary rhythm and they chatted mostly about the events these baked goods were for.

But beneath it all was an edgy awareness of the attraction they couldn't act on and the still-unresolved issues surrounding Grace's future.

* * *

Leah returned to the kitchen with Grace on her hip. "Have either of you noticed the weather?"

Mike immediately pushed away from the table and

went to the kitchen door. What he saw drew a low whistle out of him. "Where'd this come from? I looked out the window thirty minutes ago and there was only an occasional drop or two coming down." It was times like this that made him miss easy access to his cell phone and laptop. He should have checked the forecast at the first sign of rain.

"Well, there's a lot more coming down right now," Leah said, stating the obvious. Then she turned to Hannah. "I don't like the idea of you getting back on the road in this, especially with Grace. The two of you should spend the night here."

"I don't know—"

"Mom's right. This won't let up anytime soon." He rubbed his jaw. "I could take you in my truck, I guess, but unless it's been fixed since I moved away I seem to remember there's a low spot near the end of our lane that tends to flood in heavy rains."

"It still does," Leah confirmed.

Mike turned back to Hannah. "There's a phone shed at the end of your lane, isn't there?"

"There is."

"I can call and leave a message so Isaac and Martha won't worry about you and Grace."

Hannah joined Mike by the door and stared out at the downpour. Not only were the roads going to be treacherous to navigate, but the sky had turned overcast, bringing on an early dusk, further hindering visibility. A sudden flash of lightning followed by a clap of thunder loud enough to make her jump settled the matter.

They were right. It was too dangerous to drive in this.

It appeared she and Grace would be spending the night at Leah's house.

* * *

Mike went on the porch with his cell phone. He punched in the number Hannah had given him along with her family's extension and left the message on the answering machine.

He didn't go back inside right away. Instead he turned up the collar on his shirt and stared at the rain. But his thoughts were turned inward.

How deep did his feelings for Hannah really go? There was no doubt he admired her and was even attracted to her. That moment when he'd touched her cheek was proof of that. He still remembered the warmth and softness of her skin, the way her remarkable eyes had widened and the trust and something more reflected in her expression. In that moment he'd longed to protect her, to be his best self so he deserved her trust.

But there was more to her than that one moment. She was sweet but knew how to stand up for herself and others. She was generous with her time and talents and had a genuine caring heart, but she wasn't a doormat. She could be stubborn and push for what she wanted, but she was never mean.

She was the first person he thought of when he had news to share, and he sought her opinion when he had a decision to make.

Was that what love felt like? He wasn't sure. But he did know he'd never felt like this about anyone else.

When Mike stepped back in the house, he saw Hannah wrapping cellophane around the last of the prepared dough. "Does this mean we're done with baking for the day?"

"Done for now. I'm cleaning up so Leah can get supper on the table."

Mike nodded. "I'll check on the animals while you ladies take care of that. I imagine they'll all need a little extra feed tonight."

His mother frowned in concern. "I have a rain poncho and hat you can use, but I don't think my boots will fit you."

Her concern made him feel like a child again. But he didn't mind. Having her fuss over him was a really good feeling.

And he was certainly glad he'd donned her rain gear when he went outside. He didn't dawdle, but by the time he'd fed the animals and laid down extra bedding for them, nearly an hour had passed.

He stamped his shoes on the mat by door, then stepped inside, absorbing the cozy warmth of the kitchen.

"Sorry I made you wait. You should've just gone ahead and eaten without me."

"Nonsense, *familye* should eat together." Leah turned her smile on Hannah. "And for tonight Hannah is *familye* too."

And as they sat around the table, Mike realized that was exactly what it felt like—family. Longing stabbed though him with an unexpected fierceness akin to a physical pain. He wanted this, to have an actual family composed of these people who were so special to him.

But for tonight he'd have to settle for pretending.

* * *

"Back at it?" Hannah looked up as Mike entered the kitchen.

The kitchen had been cleaned and Grace put to bed.

Leah had turned in and she thought Mike had too. But apparently not.

"I thought I'd get started on an order of cupcakes."

"Care for some help?"

Was the storm keeping him awake? "The cookies we baked earlier should be cooled enough to decorate."

"I'm not sure my artistic skills are up to your standards."

"I saw your chalk drawing and the cookie you decorated at Whispering Oaks, so I know better. But all I need you to do is outline the edges of each with the blue icing I already have mixed and ready to go."

"I can do that."

She pointed to the frosting bag and tips on the table. "Do you remember how to use these?"

He nodded. "Thin, even line, I remember."

She smiled. "Still a quick learner, I see."

Mike went to work on his assigned task. "Does Grace normally sleep through the night?"

Hannah nodded. Regardless of her feelings on the matter, she supposed he needed to learn about Grace's bedtime routine, all her routines for that matter. It would make the transition easier for Grace.

So while she mixed her batter and filled the paper wrappers she explained their bedtime rituals, ending with "And then I lay her in her crib and tuck her in with her doll and her stuffed kitty."

He straightened at that. "She sleeps with the kitten I gave her?" He sounded both surprised and pleased.

Hannah nodded with an indulgent smile. "It's become one of her new favorite toys."

"And then she goes right to sleep?"

"Usually. Sometimes, when she has trouble settling

down, I'll sing to her again." Then she cut him a side-ways glance. "But of course you and Grace will develop your own routines over time."

Then she changed the subject with a question of her own. "If you don't mind speaking of it, would you tell me about your sister? I'd like to learn about Grace's *mamm*."

He didn't answer right away, and when he did his voice had a defensive quality. "I know you must think she was terrible for abandoning her baby. But she wasn't like that."

"I assure you, I don't think anything of the sort. One can't ever know what's in another person's heart. And if your *shveshtah* hadn't left Grace in our barn that night, I wouldn't have had this wonderful year with her, would have never known what it was to be a mother."

He stiffened. "Wait a minute. Are you telling me Madison left her baby in a barn in the middle of the night?"

"*Jah*. But she wrapped her up and made sure she was well protected from the elements. I'm also fairly certain she stayed nearby until we found Grace because I heard an *Englisch* vehicle start up shortly after."

He'd stopped working. "That only makes me feel slightly better. But I suppose in a lot of ways, Madison had still been a child." He met her gaze again. "To answer your question, my sister was a very bubbly, carefree sort of person. She was a phenomenal volleyball player but didn't have much interest in other sports. She liked to read and she especially loved fairy tales—she collected volumes of them from all over the world."

Then he smiled. "As a matter of fact, I'd planned to donate them to the local library but hadn't gotten around to it yet. I think now that I'll save them for Grace."

Hannah's smile softened. "She'll like that." Then she changed the subject slightly. "Do you think Grace looks like her?"

"She has Madison's eyes and her dimple." Then he snapped his fingers. "Wait a minute, I've got some pictures on my phone so you can see for yourself." He pulled out his cell phone and after scrolling a bit he held it up for her to see. "This is my favorite photo of her. But there are others."

Hannah accepted the phone and held it at an angle to bring the picture in focus. "She's very pretty, for sure and certain. And I see what you mean about the eyes." Then her forehead wrinkled. "I think I remember her."

"Remember her? You mean the two of you knew each other?"

"*Nee*, I mean *jah*." Several things were starting to make sense now.

"Which is it?"

"We met briefly the day before Grace came into my life." Hannah traced a circle on the table, not quite meeting his gaze. "She found me sobbing behind the marketplace. I'm not even sure why she was there, but she said she'd gotten lost looking for the fire station."

* * *

She'd been looking for the fire station? Could his sister have been planning to leave her baby there after all? What had changed her mind?

But Hannah was still speaking.

"It was shortly after I got the awful news from the doctor and Timothy broke up with me. Anyway, I was suddenly overwhelmed. Madison was very kind and asked if I needed help. Poor thing, I rewarded her kindness by dumping my whole story on her—it just all came tumbling out."

The idea of Hannah in such pain, even if it was emotional rather than physical, made Mike want to go out and do battle, to make it all better. But he knew she wouldn't appreciate him commenting on it, so he focused on the part his sister had played. "Madison was always a sympathetic listener."

"She also told me about all the dreams she had for her life—to get her degree in art history, to travel the world, experience other cultures and actually see some of that art in person. Then she said she'd made some big mistakes that threatened to take those dreams from her and that she'd been forced to make some impossible choices."

Mike tugged on his sleeve cuff. "Madison, for all her intelligence, could be very naïve and she had a tendency to think things would all work out just because she thought they should."

He met Hannah's gaze. "And she didn't have the baby with her when you saw her?"

Hannah shook her head. "That's something I'd remember. I might even have connected her to Grace."

"Why didn't you tell me all of this when I told you why I was here?"

"I just told you, I had no idea she even had a baby. And she told me her name was Sonny. It didn't occur to me it'd be short for Madison."

"That makes sense. She decided to go by Sonny when she started college. I think she thought it made her sound more free-spirited." He wished he'd made more time for her, been someone she felt she could turn to.

"Even so," Hannah continued, "she was so very *Englisch* I never imagined she had any family connection to the Plain Folk."

"What does her having Amish family ties have to do with it?"

"It was something she wrote—" Hannah stiffened. "I almost forgot. I'll be right back." She set down her spoon and wiped her hands as she hurried from the room.

While she was gone, Mike moved to the window, staring out at the night. The rain had slowed to a drizzle and the sky had cleared enough to reveal a three-quarter moon. He thought of Madison, of how much she'd been looking forward to all life had to offer her. He suspected that was why she'd given up her baby—she hadn't wanted to be weighed down.

He turned at the sound of Hannah's return and smiled as he saw she'd fetched her always-close-to-hand notebook. As she crossed the room to join him, she turned to the back where there was a pocket. She plucked out a folded sheet of paper and handed it to him. "This is the note that was left with Grace. I meant to give it to you earlier but forgot."

Madison had left a note? He studied it first and there was no doubt it was his sister's handwriting. Then he read it, twice.

There was no doubt she'd specifically selected Hannah to raise Grace.

When he looked back up to meet her gaze, he found her watching him closely.

He handed the note back to her, but Hannah shook her head. "I was saving it to give Grace when she got old enough to understand. Perhaps it's best you keep it for her now."

Mike nodded and slipped it into his wallet.

Hannah moved back to the table. "It was because of that reference to the *boppli* having Amish roots that I never even considered that the *mamm* was *Englisch*. I actually suspected it was someone who'd left the community, found herself with child and wanted her baby to be raised here."

He raised a hand. "I understand—you don't need to keep explaining." He raised a brow. "She says in the note that you did her a kindness."

Hannah shifted uncomfortably. "Your *shveshtah* was very distressed over whatever decision she had to make. I told her she should pray about it, that *Gotte* would offer her unconditional love and comfort. But she said she didn't know how to do that. So I prayed with her, and we discussed it for quite a while. Afterward I told her I would continue to pray for her. And she said she would try to do the same for me." She smiled. "I've actually prayed twice for her each night—once for the distressed young lady who had difficult decisions to make, and once for Grace's mother who gave me the incredible gift of entrusting me with her child."

Then she turned away. "I'm going to clean up my mess and then I believe I'll head for bed."

"I won't be up much later myself."

Mike tried to process this new information. He knew how his sister's mind worked. Madison hadn't left her baby with a random stranger. She'd learned of Hannah's hurting heart, had witnessed her deep devotion to God and, in a way that satisfied her love of fairy-tale happily-ever-afters, had decided it was meant to be.

And who was he to say she'd been wrong?

Chapter 22

This is our final stop, the home of Simeon and Mary Ruth Eshel."

The morning had dawned sunny and clear, though the water still filled the ditches and there were lots of puddles to remind Mike and Hannah of the previous night's storm. They'd left Grace behind with Leah and had stopped at the Eicher place to allow Hannah to pick up the food boxes for delivery.

After all that had transpired yesterday, Hannah felt edgy, her thoughts scattered. The fact that Mike didn't seem changed at all only added to her unsettled feeling.

But she did her best to carry on as normal. "Mary Ruth has bronchitis and Simeon, by his own admission, isn't much of a cook. We're making sure they have something besides sandwiches at least every other day."

Mike gave her a quick smile before turning his gaze back to the road. "There's some extra stew left. Since this is the last stop, why don't you give them what's left?"

"*Gut* idea."

When they arrived, Mike hitched the horse to the fence rail while Hannah boxed up the food. The two had developed an easy working rhythm that required little verbal communication.

Hannah knocked at the door and waited patiently for Simeon to answer. The elderly man moved slowly these days and he was likely taking care of something for Mary Ruth. But after several minutes and two more knocks and a hail, she exchanged worried looks with Mike.

He stepped forward and tried the door. When he found it unlocked, he frowned in concern. "Perhaps we should go on in and make sure everyone's okay?"

Hannah nodded agreement. As soon as they stepped inside the house, she heard Mary Ruth's wheezy cough and then a weak "Help us."

Alarmed, she and Mike rushed forward and found both Mary Ruth and Simeon on the kitchen floor. Simeon appeared to be unconscious and Mary Ruth sat with his head in her lap.

Hannah attempted to rush forward but Mike stopped her. "Please get my go bag from the buggy."

With a nod she turned to do as he asked. By the time she returned, Mike had Simeon stretched out flat and was speaking on his cell phone in crisp, authoritative tones.

He hung up and thanked her for the bag. "An ambulance is on its way," he said as he reached in the small duffel. Then he glanced at Mary Ruth. "Can you tell me exactly what happened?"

The elderly woman pushed a strand of hair away from her face with trembling hands. "Last night before coming to bed, Simeon came here in the kitchen for a glass of milk. But he fell—I heard him call out and then nothing.

When he didn't answer my call, I came in here to check on him."

Her hand went to her throat and Hannah saw her eyes water and chin quiver. "I found him on the floor. I tried to help him up, but I was too weak. And I knew I probably wouldn't make it to the phone shed with all the rain and thunder." She paused as a fit of racking coughs overtook her. Then her gaze met Mike's. "And what if I tried and couldn't make it back? Who would help Simeon then?" She looked down at her husband. "So I just fetched a quilt to help keep us warm and sat here with him, keeping him company and giving him drinks of water when he was awake enough."

"You did everything right." Then Mike turned to her. "Why don't you help Mary Ruth freshen up and maybe get something to eat?"

"I don't want to leave—" The woman's protest was interrupted by another bout of coughing.

Mike kept his gaze on Mary Ruth but subtly signaled Hannah forward. "I promise I'll take good care of him."

Hannah reached down to help the woman up. "Come on, Mary Ruth, let's make you more comfortable. Then I'll heat up some of this delicious chicken stew Micah here cooked for you."

"I want to stay with Simeon."

"I know you do," Hannah coaxed. "But we must give Micah room to do his job. And you can trust him to take good care of Simeon. He's a very skilled paramedic. Besides, you won't be any help to Simeon if you don't take care of yourself first."

The woman finally gave a reluctant nod, so Hannah helped her wash up and change out of her nightdress and robe and get into a fresh dress. Then she carefully brushed out her hair and pinned it up, covering it with a *kapp*, all the while keeping up a conversation to help distract Simeon's wife from her worry. She tried to convince Mary Ruth to get into bed and rest a bit, but when the woman refused, Hannah escorted her to the kitchen where Mike still knelt beside Simeon.

"How is he?"

"I've made him comfortable, but he needs more help than I can give him with just what's in my bag. The ambulance should be here soon to take him to the hospital."

Mary Ruth spoke up. "I want to go with him."

Before Hannah could reply, Mike spoke up. "Of course. You should get looked at as well, just to make sure your bronchitis hasn't progressed to pneumonia."

While they waited, Hannah fixed Mary Ruth a cup of hot tea and gave her one of the muffins from the food basket. She also washed the dirty dishes in the sink and just generally made herself useful. She also reassured Mary Ruth that she would close up the house for them and also get word to the bishop as well as their closest daughter.

When at last the ambulance arrived, Mike quickly and succinctly explained the situation and then Simeon and Mary Ruth were loaded into the ambulance and driven away.

Mike repacked his go bag without speaking.

"Do you think Simeon will be okay?" she asked.

"It's hard to tell. His chances would be a whole lot better if we'd gotten to him sooner."

Before she could respond, he closed his bag and headed for the door. "I'll check on the animals while you finish up with whatever you're doing in here."

"Do you know how to milk a cow?"

He nodded, continuing out the door without pausing.

Hannah went back to sweeping the kitchen floor, but her thoughts weren't on her work. Mike had looked troubled by something just now. Was it worry over Simeon and Mary Ruth, or was something else on his mind? Whatever it was, surely he would benefit from talking about it.

Hannah quickly finished the cleaning, put away the items from the food basket, then closed up the house and went in search of Mike.

She found him in the barn, just getting up from the milking stool.

"All the animals have been fed, but I'm not sure what to do with this pail of milk."

"The house is already closed up. You can either pour it out for the barn cats to enjoy or bring it home to Leah."

With a nod, Mike grabbed a few pans that were lying around and poured out the milk.

A few minutes later they were seated in the buggy and Mike set the horse in motion.

"If you don't mind, we need to stop by Asa Yutzy's place. As the bishop he should know that Simeon and Mary Ruth are in the hospital."

He nodded. "Just let me know how to get there."

Hannah gave him directions, then settled back. Silence settled on them and Hannah could almost feel the weight of it. Something was definitely bothering Mike.

She was still trying to decide if she should say something when he spoke up. "Who's going to take care of the livestock while the Eshels are in the hospital?"

"Don't worry, the bishop will get the word out—it'll be taken care of."

He nodded, his gaze on the road.

Silence again.

It's a *gut* thing you were with me today," she said. "If I'd been alone, I'm not sure I would have been much use."

"You could have at least gone to their phone shed and called for help." If anything, his expression turned more somber. "I didn't want to worry Mary, but Simeon's condition is serious." His jaw tightened. "If they'd had a phone in the house a lot of this pain could have been avoided."

She straightened. "You know that's not our way."

He cut her a look that was almost angry. "And you're okay with that? What if this had happened with my mother or with Grace? It's like digging a hole with your hands when a shovel is available. How can you live like this knowing there's a better way?"

Is this what had been on his mind? "Not better, just different."

"How can you say that after this? Surely you agree that if they'd been able to contact someone when Simeon first fell, it would've been better for both him and Mary Ruth."

She strove for a calm tone. "Perhaps. But you of all people should know technology doesn't solve all problems. Otherwise none of you *Englisch* would end up in the hospital."

"I'm not claiming it solves all problems, but technology can certainly help in a lot of areas. Such as what we just dealt with."

Hannah refrained from responding. She could tell he had his mind made up already. And since he'd lived with such technology most of his life, she could see why it might be difficult for him to understand.

When they arrived at Leah's, Hannah wanted to just gather Grace up and leave. But she had cookies to decorate, so she headed inside to get to work.

* * *

Mike took care of the horse and buggy but his thoughts were elsewhere. Today had been a wake-up call. His feelings for Hannah had made him lose sight of his goal to give Madison's child all the advantages of an English upbringing.

But there was too much at stake for him to let sentimentality sidetrack him. Yes, there were a lot of good things about the Amish lifestyle. But to be honest, while he hated what his father had done in abandoning his mother and in telling the lies that kept them apart, he wasn't sorry for the break they'd made with the Amish community. He'd benefited in so many ways—an extended education, lots of travel, the ability to drive a motorized vehicle, to become a paramedic. Not to mention his connection to the wider world and all the technology that had enriched his life and expanded his horizons.

And now it had been dramatically brought home to him that Grace's very health and safety were at stake. He wasn't sure now that he was comfortable leaving her here for weeks at a time. Even though he knew Hannah would give her the best care she could, the lifestyle she lived couldn't offer her the level of safety and security he could.

When he entered the kitchen, however, the scene that greeted him momentarily drove all other thoughts away.

Hannah had positioned herself behind a kitchen chair

that Grace stood on. Grace had her hands on the handles
of a rolling pin and Hannah had her hands on Grace's.

"That's it, sunshine, slow and steady."

Grace giggled in delight as she pushed the rolling pin
across the surface of the dough. Then she released the
implement and clapped her hands, sending little puffs of
flour bursting around her.

Leah sat at the table across from them, knitting. She
looked very grandmotherly as she watched Hannah and
Grace with an indulgent smile.

Family. That's what this image said to him, and it
tugged at him every bit as strongly as it had before. What
would it be like to come home to something like this
every day?

Then he shook the thought out of his head. That kind
of thinking wasn't productive. He greeted them all with a
quick hello and the information that he had some work to
do down in the basement and quickly made his exit.

As he headed down the stairs, though, it occurred to
him that he might just have the answer he'd been looking
for all this time.

He pondered that question for the next several hours
as he worked down in the basement, fixing loose boards
on the stairs.

By the time he returned to the kitchen, Hannah was
cleaning her work space, apparently done with her baking
for the day. His mom and Grace were nowhere in sight.
If he was going to speak to Hannah today, now was
the time.

"Looks like you could use a hand."

She glanced up and smiled. "Your timing is perfect.
Do you prefer to wash or dry?"

"I think I'll dry."

She handed him a dishcloth and wet bowl.

He decided to ease into the conversation. "Did you get everything finished that you needed for the graduation party?"

She nodded. "*Jah.* And I prepared another batch of dough that I'll bring to the bakery tomorrow just to make sure I don't get caught short."

He accepted another freshly washed bowl from her and took a deep breath. "I'd like to discuss something with you, something I've given a lot of thought to since we returned here this afternoon."

She looked up, meeting his gaze guardedly. "I'm listening."

"First off, you do know I love Grace, don't you, and that I only want what's best for her?"

"*Jah.* And I feel the same."

"That being said, I've come to the conclusion that I just can't leave her alone here for any significant length of time."

She stiffened but to her credit she didn't argue.

"What we walked in on with the Eshels reminded me of at least one reason I can't leave her here. I've seen so many deaths and crippling injuries that could've been avoided or lessened if the victim had received care sooner. I won't take the chance that Grace will be in that number."

"Are you saying now that you don't want her to visit here, under my charge, at all? That I won't see her again once you adopt her?" Her gaze no longer met his, and she was scrubbing the platter she held with an excessive amount of energy.

"Not exactly. I'm saying I want to raise Grace as English. Yes, I want her to know and respect her Amish ties, but I want her feet to be firmly rooted in my world. But that doesn't mean you won't see her anymore. I'll return often to visit my mother. You can spend all the time you want with her then. You can even take her into your home for the occasional overnight visit."

"I see. I'd be like an *aenti* to her."

She said that as if it was a bad thing. "Yes. But there's another option."

"And that is?"

"You can come to Missouri with us."

Her gaze flew to his in obvious surprise. "I don't underst—"

He took the soapy spatula from her and set it back in the dishpan. Then he took her hands and captured her gaze. "Hannah, will you marry me?"

* * *

Hannah was already reeling from Mike's declaration that he wanted to cut back on the time Grace spent in her home. And now this. He wanted to marry her all of a sudden. Was it because he felt guilty for taking Grace from her knowing her chances of having another family were slim? Or because it would make Grace's transition easier? Or maybe it was just so he would have a built-in sitter.

He certainly hadn't mentioned anything about love.

She studied his face. "Why?"

He frowned. "Why what?"

"Why do you want to marry me?"

"It just makes so much sense." He rubbed the back of his neck. "You and Grace could be together permanently. I wouldn't have to put myself and Grace through the ordeal of finding her a nanny. And we already know we get along well, so we could live together comfortably."

So, just as she'd thought, love didn't play a part in this.

Mike pressed on, apparently intent on convincing her. "Look, I know marrying someone who's not Amish is a big step for you, but isn't the chance to be a mother to Grace, to help me build a real family for her, worth it?"

"Much as having Grace in my life is important to me, I can't marry you." She was glad to hear her voice hold steady even though her heart was breaking.

"Can't? Or won't?"

Hannah tried to not take offense at that. "I don't think you really understand what you're asking me to do."

"Then explain it to me."

"I've been baptized, so I'm a full member of the church and responsible for following the *Ordnung* among other things. I made vows at that time, vows that I take very seriously and that the church takes seriously as well. If I were to marry someone who is not baptized in the church, I would break those vows. I would also face the strong probability of excommunication."

He grimaced. "Which means your church will force you to choose between having the daughter you yearn for and having contact with your family and friends."

She raised her head and unflinchingly met his gaze. "Sacrifices are a part of life, especially for those who submit themselves to *Gotte*'s will."

"Maybe that's true. But do you even know why those rules exist? Do you truly think you can only honor God and be obedient to Him if you stay here and follow the *Ordnung*?"

"I know what the teachings are and—"

He gestured impatiently. "That's not what I asked

you. It's one thing to know the rules of something. It's quite another to really understand and know why they're in place."

Was he questioning her beliefs? "And then there is faith." She eyed him sternly.

His expression hardened. "I agree that faith is important. But is it really faith if it hasn't ever been truly tested?"

She stiffened. How could he say such a thing to her? He knew her story, the tragedies she'd faced.

He must have read something of what she was feeling in her face, because his expression immediately shifted. "I'm sorry." He rubbed the back of his neck. "I didn't mean to attack you that way, you didn't deserve it."

She nodded, then shifted the conversation slightly. "Have you given any thought to returning to your own roots? After all, if your *daed* hadn't, well, hadn't done what he did, you would no doubt be a baptized member of the congregation yourself. And I know your *mamm* would take great joy in having you back in our midst."

He shook his head. "It's been too long. Yes, there's a simplicity and honesty to the life here that I find myself drawn to. But I've spent the last twenty-two years as a member of the English world and I'm very comfortable there. I have a life with a career I find fulfilling, and I also have outside interests I could never pursue here." He set the now-dry bowl aside and reached for the spatula she held. "At this point in my life returning to the Amish lifestyle would feel like a step back."

She stiffened. "A lot of people think of our community as backward, but I didn't expect you—"

He lifted his hands in protest. "Now you're putting

words in my mouth. I didn't say backward. I was thinking more of the modern-day conveniences. I just don't
understand this insistence on keeping technology at arm's
length when it has such strong potential to be helpful.
Didn't you see what happened to Simeon? And to my own
mother when she had that accident all those years ago.
Both could have avoided so much suffering if they'd had
access to help sooner."

"We've already discussed this. If technology was all
that was required, then there wouldn't be any health-
related pain in the world."

"I never said it was a cure-all, just that it's another tool
we can use to help us, like the items in my go bag."

"I'm not going to debate the merits of technology with
you right now." She grabbed another platter and rubbed
it with her soapy rag. "How did we get on that topic
anyway?"

"I was telling you why I think it best Grace lives in a
twenty-first-century world."

She heard the frustration in his voice and knew further
discussion wouldn't serve any purpose. "You will soon
be Grace's guardian and you must do what you think
best for her. You can rest assured I won't challenge
your decisions." She handed him the last of the dishes.
"Now, it'll be dark before long. I'd better get Grace and
head home."

* * *

She'd turned down his marriage proposal. He thought
he'd prepared himself for that outcome, but it stabbed at
him more than he'd expected.

So she loved her church more than she cared for

Grace. Or for him. Her church was not God, didn't she see that?

Abruptly making a decision on a call he'd gotten last night, he set the wet sheet pan on the counter and turned to her. "Speaking of heading home, I plan to head back to Missouri tomorrow."

Her head shot up and she met his gaze with a startled look. "For how long?"

"About a week. My supervisor contacted me last night and asked if I could come in and cover some shifts. He's got several men out sick right now and is running shorthanded." He shrugged. "It'll also give me time to get my place set up for when Grace moves in. But don't worry. I told you I wouldn't take Grace until the end of the month and I stand by that."

She nodded. "I appreciate having the extra time." Then she smiled. "Do you have any idea how to set up your home for a toddler?"

"I've done some research. And I have a few buddies with kids I can get pointers from."

"Your life is about to change in so many unexpected ways."

She was right. His life had already changed since his search began—some of those changes were small, some enormous.

He'd gained a mother and a daughter-to-be.

He'd fallen in love.

And he'd been rejected.

Chapter 23

Over the next several days, as Hannah went about her usual business, Mike's words kept echoing in her mind. Was she so committed to staying here, to remaining true to her Amish faith, because it was comfortable and familiar, because it was what was expected of her?

She even visited with the bishop, asking for his guidance. She'd been sorely tempted to accept Mike's proposal. And still was to a certain extent. After all, was it any more unreasonable for her to ask him to forsake his familiar world to enter hers than it was for him to ask it of her?

Hannah prayed for discernment and tried to keep a cheerful demeanor, but her heart remained heavy. Even though she and Mike had their disagreements, she missed seeing him, missed his smile that brightened her mornings, missed having him to talk to, missed seeing the way he interacted with Grace.

And when it came to Grace, she wanted by turns to cram as much time as possible with her into every available moment, and to responsibly prepare the toddler for the day when they wouldn't see each other at all for long stretches of time, if ever.

Saturday afternoon, when Hannah stopped by Leah's to pick up Grace, Leah invited her to sit down and have a cup of coffee and chat.

"I'm worried about you, Hannah. You look exhausted."

Hannah waved a hand, trying to discount her friend's concern. "The special orders are a bit overwhelming right now, but it'll return to normal soon."

"I certainly hope so." Leah sat up straighter. "But it makes what I have to say more difficult."

What was going on? "You can tell me anything."

"I've decided I'm leaving in the morning for Missouri. I want to see where my son spent the greater part of his life."

Hannah tamped down the little flare of jealousy. "How are you traveling?"

"I've hired a driver to take me there. I'll return with Micah on Wednesday."

So Mike planned to return on Wednesday—that was good to know.

"Your *daed* has generously agreed to take care of the livestock for me while I'm away. And you should feel free to come by and use the kitchen if you need to."

"*Danke.*" When had Leah had time to speak to *Daed*? Was Martha right about there being something happening between the two of them?

"But my leaving means you'll need to make other accommodations for Grace for three days next week."

"Don't worry about that. Between Martha, *Daed* and me, we'll work it out. You just enjoy your trip."

"I admit to being nervous. I've never been farther than twenty miles from Hope's Haven."

"Oh, but think of all the new things you'll see—it'll be an adventure." She studied her friend. "It's a long way to Missouri, ain't so?"

"Micah said it took him about eight hours to drive it. But I'll have my Bible and a novel with me to read and I'll take some knitting as well, so the time will pass agreeably enough." Then her gaze turned serious. "There's one other thing I wanted to speak to you about."

Hannah nodded. "Okay."

"I'm not sure what happened between you and Micah on Wednesday, but he looked very unhappy after you left. And he didn't look any better when he drove off the next morning." She leaned back. "I see that same lost, unhappy look in you."

Hannah stared down at her cup. "Did he tell you he proposed to me?"

Leah straightened. "*Nee*, he didn't."

"I turned him down."

"I see." A moment of silence, then, "So you don't love him."

Hannah looked up quickly, then back down again. "My feelings don't matter. He's *Englisch* and I'm Amish and neither of us is likely to change." She waved a hand. "Besides, he wasn't looking for love, he was thinking about what would be best for Grace."

"First, your feelings absolutely do matter. Because it will make a difference in whether or not you want to fight to make things work out for you and Micah." She placed a hand on one of Hannah's. "And what makes you think Micah doesn't love you?"

"When he proposed, he said it was to keep from having

to separate me and Grace and to make the transition to her new life easier on her. Love was never mentioned, either before or during."

"He may not have said it out loud, but it's there in his eyes whenever he looks at you."

Was that true? Why hadn't he ever said anything to her? Of course, to be fair, he had proposed . . .

"Besides, have you ever said those words to him?"

Leah's question brought Hannah up short. "*Nee.*" Then she shrugged. "What would be the use? He knows about my medical condition. And again, he's *Englisch* and I'm Amish."

Leah sighed. "Even if the two of you never marry, if Micah loves you, wouldn't you like to hear him say it?"

Hannah nodded.

"Of course you would. It's *gut* to know you're loved in that special way, ain't so?"

"For sure and for certain."

"And don't you think Micah would also like to know he's loved?"

"I suppose."

"You know he would. He's lost so many people in his life, he needs to know there are others who care deeply for him. It's something we all need."

"But again, there's no way we can overcome the Amish-*Englisch* divide between us."

"Where is your faith? Don't you believe that with *Gotte*, all things are possible?"

"*Jah.* But just because *Gotte* can do all things doesn't mean He will give us everything we want."

"But He *will* give us what we need."

Chapter 24

How was your trip?" Mike helped his mother from the car, then took the luggage from the driver and handed her a generous tip. He'd been surprised when his mother called yesterday to let him know she'd like to visit. Surprised but pleased.

His mother looked around with bright, curious eyes. "It was long, but interesting. There are so many people on the roads and everyone seems to be in a mighty rush."

Mike hid a smile as he led the way to the elevators. He was going to enjoy introducing her to his world. "My apartment is on the third floor. I have the guest room ready for you. I thought you might want to rest for a few hours this afternoon and then I can take you to supper at one of my favorite restaurants in Drifton."

If she enjoyed her visit, could he convince her to come on a regular basis? He'd love to have her as a strong influence in Grace's life. Especially since it looked like Hannah wouldn't be.

Best not think about that now, though.

"You don't have to fuss over me, Micah. And I'm not one for fancy restaurants."

"It's my favorite restaurant, but trust me, it's not fancy. In fact it's a humble barbecue joint. And if a guy can't make a fuss over his *mamm*, who can he make a fuss over?"

Later, as they drove into the parking lot of Tommy Lee's Barbecue Restaurant, he gave his mother a grin. "As I said, nothing fancy, but their food is great."

"I can smell the smoky aroma from here. It's making my mouth water."

"And I assure you, the food definitely lives up to that promise."

Once the server had taken their order and moved away, his mother leaned back in her seat. "This is nice."

"I'm glad you like it. But you'll like it even more when you get a taste of the food."

Her smile softened. "I wasn't speaking of the food, Micah. I meant this." Her gesture took him in. "Spending time with my son."

Mike nodded. He was getting used to her calling him Micah, was even starting to like it. "Dad stole so much time from us, time we can never get back, but I'd like to start making up for that lost time."

Her expression sobered. "Micah, you must forgive your *daed*, just as I have. It's not *gut* to hold on to anger and bitterness."

"How can you forgive him so easily? He abandoned you when you needed him most. Then he divorced you, which must have been difficult for you. And on top of all of that, he told each of us the other was dead. Any one of those things is despicable. Taken all together, it paints him as an outright villain."

She reached across the table and took his hands in hers. "Micah, we don't forgive people because the actions no longer hurt us or because we want the person who hurt us to feel better. We forgive them, first and foremost, because *Gotte*'s word tells us we should, that He alone has the right to judge. But we also do it because anger and hate are like acids that eat at us from the inside and keep us from feeling peace in our lives."

"I don't know how to do that, just let go of the anger."

"It helps if you read your Bible and pray for the willingness to lean only on Him."

Mike shifted in his seat. How long had it been since he'd opened his Bible? He considered himself a Christian and a believer, but he mostly ignored that part of his life.

She patted his hand and then drew hers back. "Your *daed* is gone now, so what purpose does holding on to your anger serve?"

Their food arrived just then, saving Mike the need to reply.

Once they'd spent a moment silently giving thanks, Mike decided a change in topic was in order. "So who's caring for the livestock while you're away?"

His mother picked up her fork. "Isaac promised to take care of things until I return."

That was a dead end. He tried again. "Is there anything in particular you want to do or see while you're here?"

She shook her head. "I just wanted to be able to picture you and Grace in your home when I think of you in the future. Perhaps you could show me where you work and some of your favorite places to go here in Drifton."

He smiled, pleased that she was taking such an interest in his day-to-day life. "We can do that." In fact, he'd come up with a list of places and activities that would hold a special appeal for her.

"How's Grace?" It had surprised him how much he missed her. Once he'd moved in with his mother in Hope's Haven, he'd been able to spend time with his niece every day.

"That sweet *lamm* is growing so fast and seems to learn something new every day. It's a joy to be a part of her life."

Mike met and held her gaze. "You know, once I adopt her, you will officially be her grandmother. I hope you plan to remain a big part of her life for a long time to come."

"For sure and certain." She gave him a pointed look. "And what about Hannah?"

Her question caught him by surprise since he'd been trying to come up with a casual way to ask about her himself. "What about her?"

"Will you allow her to be a part of Grace's life?"

Okay, this was not the question he'd been trying to ask. "To a certain extent," he responded, hoping he didn't sound defensive.

"What does that mean?"

He tried for a reasonable tone. "She can spend time with Grace whenever we visit Hope's Haven. And if she'd like to come down here for a visit, she would be welcome."

"You do know how much she cares for that little one? And how much Grace cares for her? A little girl needs a mother."

And if Hannah had agreed to his marriage proposal, Grace would have one. But he couldn't say that to his mother.

"What happened between you and Hannah before you left?"

"What makes you think something happened?"

"I have eyes. The two of you had grown very close and there was a glow about you when you were in each other's company. It gave this mother's heart hope to watch it grow."

Surely she hadn't believed this would end in marriage for him and Hannah?

"But something happened just before you left to change all of that."

He supposed they hadn't been very subtle about how things were going. "We had a disagreement over how Grace should be raised."

His mother shrugged. "Disagreements can be worked through."

"Not always. And I'm Grace's uncle, her closest relative. It's my responsibility to look out for her."

"It's *gut* that you want to take care of Grace, but I think Hannah wants what's best for her as well, ain't so?"

Mike grimaced. "That's what our disagreement was over—what's best for Grace."

"And you believe taking this child from the only *mamm* she's ever known is what's best for her?"

Her tone was gentle, but it carried a hint of rebuff. Or was it just his own guilt making him feel that way? "Hannah is not Grace's mother. She's not even her adoptive mother."

"Hannah is the closest thing to a mother Grace has had this past year. She was also the person your *shveshtah* handpicked to care for her."

He studied her a moment, trying to figure out what was behind her words. "Are you saying you think I should back away from my claim on Grace and leave her in Hannah's care?" Did she think so little of his ability to be a father? Or was it his worthiness she was questioning?

"Not at all. I just think the two of you should work harder to find a solution that will allow you both to be a part of Grace's life."

Easier said than done.

She made a dismissive gesture. "But I'm being a meddling grandmother. If it helps you to know, I had a similar conversation with Hannah before I left Hope's Haven."

"And how did she respond?" He was afraid he didn't entirely succeed in keeping the eager interest from his voice.

"She seemed just as miserable about the way things turned out as you do."

Mike didn't really have a response to that, so he merely made a noncommittal sound.

But her next words brought him up short. "She also told me you proposed."

Why would she discuss such a personal thing with anyone?

"Now, don't you get your back up. The poor girl just needed someone to talk to."

"I suppose she also told you she turned me down."

"She did." There was sympathy in her gaze if not in her matter-of-fact tone.

He stared down at his plate. "It seems she values her Amish traditions more than she does Grace or me."

"If you believe that, you really don't know Hannah."

Was his mother right? Was there really hope that he and Hannah could find a way to build a family together?

If she had the answer, he sure wished she'd share it.

But for the rest of their meal they talked about food and things they might do while she was in town.

Back at his apartment, Mike gave her the rundown on his schedule. "I'm working the ten p.m. to eight a.m. shift right now. So make yourself at home while I'm out. I've stocked the refrigerator and pantry. I'm sorry there's no front porch and rocker for you here, but there's a balcony with seating and a good view."

"I'll be fine. There's no need to worry about keeping me entertained."

"Sometime during your stay, I was hoping we could discuss how to set my place up to accommodate Grace."

"For sure and certain." She looked around. "So this is where you plan to raise Grace."

"Of course, it's my home." There had been no judgment in his mother's tone or demeanor, but Mike suddenly felt defensive. He looked around, trying to see his apartment through the eyes of a parent. It was sparsely furnished, but what furnishings were there weren't exactly child-friendly.

His coffee table had a glass top with square corners. His work desk, complete with laptop, tablet and charging station, sported a handful of dangling cords.

Those were just two problems he could see in a few seconds. What other issues were lurking here?

"I know this setup isn't ideal, but I'm sure whatever issues we uncover here will have an easy fix."

"I'm sure you're right." She smothered a yawn. "Now it's my bedtime. If you'll excuse me, I think I'll turn in."

"Of course." He grabbed a pad and pen. "I'll write down my number. If something comes up while I'm at work that you want to speak to me about, don't hesitate to call." Thank goodness he'd been too lazy to get rid of his landline.

After she went to her room, Mike plopped down on the sofa. He started to reach for the remote, then changed his mind. Out of deference to his mother he'd decided to keep his use of electronics to a minimum while she was here. Truth to tell, it wasn't difficult. After the weeks he'd spent living among the Amish, he'd grown out of the habit of checking in with social media or news reports on a regular basis.

Once he was alone, his thoughts turned to Hannah as they had every night since he'd left Hope's Haven. Was his mother right about her having feelings for him? Even so, he knew how firm Hannah's resolve could be, he couldn't imagine her choosing to break her baptismal vows.

So where did that leave them?

He grabbed a throw pillow and punched it in frustration.

* * *

When Mike returned from work the next morning, he found his mother at the stove, and from the aroma wafting his way she was apparently cooking lunch. "*Mamm*, you're a visitor here. You're supposed to let me feed you, not vice versa."

She waved his words away. "I'm your *mamm*, not a visitor. And you can't expect me to just sit around and do nothing all day." She made shooing motions. "Now you go on and get some sleep. I'll be here when you get up, and hopefully your meal will be as well."

He walked over and kissed her forehead, then moved

toward his bedroom to do as instructed. Having his mother here had turned his apartment into a home.

Wanting to spend as much of his off-duty time with her as possible, Mike kept his nap short.

Once they'd eaten her savory lunch, Mike took her to some of his favorite places.

Their first stop was Mayweather Park, a place with a playground for children as well as lots of open spaces for picnics and impromptu games of flag football, Frisbee golf and other activities.

Then he took her to visit Fontenot's Botanical Garden, complete with a greenhouse and butterfly house.

After an early supper at a seafood restaurant, he took her to an observatory where she was able to look through a telescope that gave her a view of constellations and another aimed at Saturn.

Her wide-eyed amazement brought him a quiet joy.

And all the while he thought about Hannah and how much he wished she and Grace were here as well. They would love these places.

How had Hannah's Monday afternoon visit to Whispering Oaks gone? Had she missed his presence? Had any of the residents noticed his absence?

As they returned to his apartment, his mother squeezed his arm. "Thank you for showing me around your town today."

Mike smiled. "You're quite welcome." Then he cut her a sideways glance. "But I have an ulterior motive. I'm hoping to entice you to come back to visit often."

Her smile took on a measure of regret. "I'm afraid that road trip is not one I plan to take very often. Besides, as nice as your town is, big cities are not for me."

He was disappointed but understood her reasons.

"I was just wondering," she continued, "don't people who live here like being with each other?"

"What do you mean? We've seen lots of people hanging out together in the places we visited today."

"But they're not really together, ain't so? They spend their time looking down at their phones rather than interacting with each other. It's as if they're lightning bugs each in their own jar. The jars are all gathered together, but they're also separate and alone. Even the *kinner*."

Was that what had her worried? Was she concerned that Grace would be raised this way?

Could he guarantee that she wouldn't?

Chapter 25

Monday evening Hannah was again in her kitchen, working on yet another large order. Even though Leah had invited her to use her kitchen while she was away, Hannah felt uncomfortable doing so. Besides, if she mixed the dough here at home, she could chill it overnight and bake it at Sweet Kneads tomorrow.

And waiting until after she put Grace to bed to take care of her baking had the added bonus of giving her more time to focus all her attention on Grace. She felt a sense of urgency in spending time with her precious child while she could.

How was Leah doing away from Hope's Haven? It was a long trip—it would have taken a great deal of courage for her to set out on her own. Mike was no doubt pleased to have her visit.

She tried to push thoughts of Mike out of her mind, but it was no use. Truth to tell, he hadn't been far from her thoughts since they parted last Wednesday. Her visit to Whispering Oaks without him this afternoon had driven home just how much she'd grown used to having him around.

Strange to think the day was coming when he'd return to Missouri and not come back except for occasional visits to see Leah.

She still couldn't quite believe he'd proposed to her. It had been so tempting to say yes, to leave everything behind and drive off with him and Grace to build a new life. Of course it had been done more out of convenience than any tender emotions or true feelings of love.

But one good thing had come out of their discussion, it had forced her to do some soul searching, not all of it comfortable, but all of it necessary.

She'd searched her heart and prayed deeply and now knew with certainty that she wanted to stay here among the Plain people not because it was familiar and comfortable, but because the beliefs and practices of her people rang true in her own heart.

However, making peace with her decision, knowing her choice was the right one for her, didn't make it any easier. The idea of having Grace think of her as a friend of the family rather than as her *mamm* was almost more than Hannah could bear. She just had to keep reminding herself that *Gotte* was *gut*, that He loved her and would be with her every step of the way.

Hannah turned her dough out on a floured surface and began to knead it.

The other issue Mike had raised during that last conversation was one she'd steadfastly avoided thinking about. Until this afternoon when it had refused to stay buried any longer.

She'd definitely faced some tragedies and hardships

in her life. But thinking about it objectively, she'd had a blessed life overall.

She had a *familye* who she knew loved her. She could even admit that, as the youngest, she'd been a bit spoiled.

True, her mother had died when she was still young, but almost immediately after, Leah had come into her life. And as a woman who'd lost her own child, Leah had been more than willing to focus her motherly energy on the grieving child Hannah had been, providing at least some of the maternal influence and affection Hannah yearned for.

Then came the shattering medical diagnosis that had destroyed her dreams of someday having a house full of children and caused her to lose the man she'd thought she would marry. And she had felt the tiniest of cracks in her belief that *Gotte* loved her. But again, almost immediately the blow had been softened by the wondrous miracle of having Grace left in her care, if only for a short season of her life. If that hadn't happened, would her faith have been strong enough to survive? She'd like to think so, but as Mike had said, faith wasn't faith until it was tested. It was a humbling thought.

Finally satisfied with the consistency of her dough, she rolled it up and wrapped it tightly. Then she placed it in the refrigerator next to the other dough she'd mixed earlier. Then she turned and began the cleanup.

* * *

Thursday morning, Hannah's gaze kept drifting to the bakery's doorway. After returning from his daily check on Leah's place yesterday afternoon, her *daed* had confirmed Leah and Mike had made it back to Hope's Haven and that Leah was ready to start watching Grace for her again. Hannah thought she spotted a flash of disappointment in Martha's countenance before she'd turned away. It appeared Martha, who'd acted as Grace's sitter the past three days, was going to miss having the toddler in her care.

Hannah and Mike had left things in such an unsettled place last time they talked. Would he still stop by every morning to get a cup of coffee and a whoopie pie? Or was he ready to wash his hands of her?

Eight o'clock came and went. Then eight thirty. When the clock showed nine Hannah decided Mike wasn't going to show up. And since the worst of the morning rush was over, she left Maisie and Ada to handle the front of the store while she went back to the kitchen to do some baking.

She worked mechanically, not finding the joy her work usually gave her. It was foolish to get her feelings hurt. This was actually for the best. Mike would be leaving soon, taking Grace with him, so it was a good idea for her to get used to him not being around.

And she had another decision to make today anyway.

Now that spending time with Grace was no longer going to be an option, what did she do about Maisie's work hours?

If she decided to leave them just as they were now, she'd be backing out on her agreement with Maisie, and the girl would be disappointed. But if she went ahead with the changes she'd planned without having Grace to spend her free time with, it would only drive home what she'd lost.

Maisie and Ada came in and out of the kitchen at

various times, but Hannah barely paused to acknowledge their presence. She glanced at the clock when she finally pulled the last batch out of the oven. Just past ten thirty.

While she waited for the last batch to cool completely, she figured she'd go through the order slips that had come in this morning and get them organized.

She'd just started on that task when someone stepped into the kitchen. As she looked up, her gaze collided with Mike's, and for just a heartbeat her breath caught in her throat and her chest tightened. She wanted to reach out to him but held herself back. She didn't have the right.

She managed to smile a welcome. "*Wilkom* back," she said, turning back to the order slips. "I trust your trip went well."

"It did. And it was a nice surprise having my mother join me for part of it."

This stilted, awkward talk was a far cry from the comfortable give-and-take of their normal conversation, but Hannah wasn't sure how to go back to the way it was before. It seemed like so much had changed since that last, awful conversation.

Then Mike stepped forward. "There's something I'd like to discuss with you. Do you have time to go to lunch with me?"

She hesitated. Did he want to tell her about other decisions he'd made regarding Grace? But to refuse him would be both cowardly and petulant. After all, nothing he'd done had been mean-spirited. He couldn't help it if he didn't love her and wanted to adopt Grace himself.

So she met his gaze with the best smile she could muster. "Of course. Let me finish this up and then we can go. I shouldn't be more than ten minutes if you want to go out front and get a cup of coffee."

He stepped closer, as if he hadn't heard her suggestion. "Is it something I can help you with?"

She waved a hand over the slips of paper. "I'm adding the current batch of orders to my order board."

"Why don't I read them out to you, and you can update the board?" He smiled. "If we work together, we can get it done and head to lunch quicker."

"All right." After all, how could she refuse?

As they worked together over the next few minutes, Hannah felt some of her tension ease. Mike definitely seemed to be in a good mood and it was contagious.

He made several teasing comments about how jam-packed her order board was getting and then talked about how he'd missed her whoopie pies while he was away.

Apparently he'd gotten over any dismay he'd felt over her rejection of his proposal.

Ten minutes later they'd taken care of the last order slip and Hannah declared herself ready to go.

As they exited the store Hannah felt unaccountably nervous. What did he want to speak to her about? Did it concern Grace or Leah? Surely he wasn't going to propose again. "I haven't seen Leah since your return," she blurted out. "I hope she made the trip well."

Mike nodded. "She was tired when we got in yesterday, but a good night's sleep in her own bed did wonders for her. She was looking forward to seeing Grace when I left."

He must have gotten out early this morning if he left before *Daed* arrived with Grace.

Mike held the door for her as they stepped out of the marketplace. "Based on what I saw on your order board, I'd guess you'll be using the ovens at Mom's this afternoon."

She nodded. "Probably tomorrow and Saturday as well."

"Good." Mike grimaced. "I don't mean good that you have so much work to do. I mean good because I'll have more time with you and Grace."

She wasn't sure how to take that, so she didn't comment. As they paused at the crosswalk, Mike frowned. "The parking lot looks pretty crowded. I hope they have a table available."

"If not, we could always go to the counter and order takeout."

"And where do you suggest we eat this take-out order?"

"The loft over at the marketplace."

He smiled and opened the diner door. "Good idea. Let's do it."

To expedite things, they both ordered the Thursday lunch special—shepherd's pie.

Mike filled the wait time by telling her some of the highlights of Leah's trip. Luckily their lunch was ready in five minutes. Five minutes after that they were climbing the stairs to the loft.

Noah was in his office when they passed by, but they merely exchanged waves as they passed. There were three other people already inside the former nursery, so Hannah bypassed that as well.

"Noah set up a few tables and chairs in this open area so folks could make better use of the space." Then she grinned. "I actually think it was Greta's idea."

They took their seats at one of the tables and Mike set out the Styrofoam containers that held their lunch. He looked around with an approving smile. "This is nice."

She nodded as she extracted her plastic fork from the cellophane wrap. "For sure and certain. I actually prefer eating out here in the open over using the meeting room."

Keeping her gaze focused straight ahead, she decided she had to speak up before she lost her nerve. "Before you bring up whatever it is you want to discuss, I have something to speak to you about."

He leaned back. "I'm listening."

"I think we should start getting Grace accustomed to the life she'll be leading once you assume custody."

He didn't say anything for a moment as he opened his Styrofoam container.

"And did you have a plan for how we do that?" he finally asked.

"I assume you'll live at Leah's house until you go back to Missouri." *And take my precious girl with you.*

"Of course."

"Then I suggest we start by letting Grace sleep over there a few nights a week." The thought of giving up even a small part of the precious time she had left with her sweet Grace was like a physical pain.

But it was the right thing to do.

* * *

Mike could see behind Hannah's serene expression just what this suggestion was costing her. But she was right. "I agree, Grace will need time to adjust."

He rubbed his jaw. "Since Mom keeps her during the day, she already has most of the things we'll need. But I think I'll go ahead and purchase a crib. A pallet on the floor is fine for a nap, but she needs a proper bed to sleep on at night."

"That will be nice."

"What else will I need?"

"I'll send some of her toys and books with her when the time comes." She spread her hands. "Leah already has everything else Grace will need, at least for now."

He reached across the table and placed a hand over hers. "I know this hasn't been easy for you." Her small, work-calloused hands were warm, her wrist surprisingly delicate.

"It's important to me that we make this as easy on Grace as possible." She slid her hand away and he felt its loss.

"Of course."

They sat in silence for a while, focusing on their meals. Finally, Hannah spoke up. "You said earlier you wanted to discuss something with me?"

Mike had had some second thoughts about that. "Actually, if you don't mind, can we put that on hold until I see you at Mom's place this afternoon."

Her forehead furrowed. "It's nothing serious, is it?"

"No, no, nothing to be anxious about. I'm considering some changes in my life and I'd like to get your opinion. But I just realized I need a little more time than what's left of your lunch break for that discussion. Besides, there's one or two additional things I want to look into."

"I suppose I'll just have to be patient." She shook a finger at him. "But I must say, it's not fair of you to build up my curiosity this way."

He grinned. "It adds to my air of being a man of mystery."

She rolled her eyes at that and then lifted her fork. "Well then, if we must wait on whatever your news is, why don't you tell me more about Leah's trip to your hometown?"

Mike followed her lead and scooped up a bite of his shepherd's pie as he recounted anecdotes of his mother's visit.

All the time his mind was on his companion. It continually surprised him how she could project so much grace even when she was hurting. Would he have been so accepting if the roles were reversed?

He'd hated to put her off, especially when he thought what he wanted to say would go a long way toward making her feel better about the future. But he needed to make sure he'd be able to answer her questions without having to rush through it all.

On the drive back with his mother yesterday he'd realized he wasn't okay with living so far from her.

He'd only just found her again and life was too short—he didn't want so much distance between them anymore. And not only his mother. He had a whole ark full of relatives—aunts, uncles, cousins—that he wanted to get to know better. And that he wanted Grace to grow up with.

And he also realized there was a simple solution for that. So simple, in fact, that he wasn't sure why he hadn't thought of it sooner. He'd move back to Hope's Haven.

Moving here didn't mean he'd return to the Amish way of life. There was a thriving English community that existed right alongside the Amish. He'd talk to Ford about getting a job with the Hope's Haven EMT crew and look for living quarters—another apartment or maybe even a small house with a yard for Grace to play in.

He and Grace could then build relationships with their Amish family while she could grow up with all the benefits the English lifestyle had to offer. And it would allow

Hannah to spend more time with Grace as well. It was the best of both worlds.

Just thinking about how Hannah would receive the news brought a smile to his face. If nothing else, he hoped it would bring back her ready-to-face-all-comers smile.

Chapter 26

Mike hung up the dishcloth and turned to Hannah. She'd been remarkably patient this evening, but he could tell she was dying to hear what he had to say. "I know it's getting late, but we still have an hour or so before the sun goes down. Why don't we take a walk? I'm sure Mom will keep an eye on Grace."

She nodded, her expression reflecting curiosity. Sure enough, as soon as they stepped on the porch, she cut him a sideways glance. "Don't keep me waiting. What's this decision you made that you want to discuss with me?"

He decided to throw it out there without further buildup. "I've decided to move to Hope's Haven."

Hannah, who'd been descending the porch steps, paused on the bottom tread. A heartbeat later her smile practically burst from her. "*Ach*, Mike, that's wonderful *gut* news."

"I'm glad you think so." Was her obvious joy brought

on because *he* was staying or was it all for Grace? He took her arm to help her down the final step, and the two of them headed toward the barn. "I can't believe I didn't think of it before," he continued. "Now Grace can grow up here, where you and my mother will be able to remain a big part of her life. And of course there's all the aunts and uncles and cousins she'll get to know."

"Being with *familye* is *gut*."

Did he detect some guardedness beneath her enthusiasm? "This really does give us the best of both worlds. Not only can Grace and I be close to family and friends in the Amish community, but there's a thriving English community here as well. I can live in town and enroll Grace in the public school. She can also have access to whatever technology is necessary for her comfort and well-being."

Some of Hannah's glow faded. "So you still intend to raise her *Englisch*?"

Surely she hadn't thought... "Yes. I'm sorry, I didn't mean to mislead you. I still feel strongly that that would be best for Grace. But even so, this will allow you to be part of her life, on a daily basis if that's what you want." He studied her face, trying to figure out what she was thinking. "I thought it would make you happy."

She waved a hand and gave him an understanding smile. "Of course I'm happy. Leah will have her son and granddaughter close to her, and you'll have lots of *familye* around to help you if you should need it."

"And she'll be able to maintain her relationship with you of course."

"*Jah*, I'll be a part of her life too, as much as I can."

"So again, why do I see more guardedness than happiness in you?"

"I'm worried about what trying to keep a foot in both worlds will do to Grace, especially as she gets older."

They entered the barn and took a moment to let their eyes adjust. She moved to one of the stalls and stroked the horse's nose.

Mike leaned against a nearby support post, gathering his thoughts. "I know it's not ideal, but kids are resilient and we'll both be right there with her to guide her. And there are any number of instances of people who were brought up in the Amish community but left for one reason or another and they're able to return to visit as often as they wish to. Like your friend Temperance's daughter, for instance."

"You mean the daughter who rarely returns, who obviously has put her Amish life and community behind her in favor of her very busy *Englisch* life?"

He grimaced. "That was a poor example, but you have to know that not all English put their careers above their families. And if that does happen with Grace, then that means we didn't do our job as parents properly. Besides, there are others who seem to be able to go back and forth between these two worlds easily, holding on to their family connections even though they've spread their wings and ventured outside the community. I, for one, intend to be among that number. So why do you think Grace won't be able to?"

"Because you're talking about those who, before they make that decision to join the *Englisch* world, have grown up living this Plain life and truly understand what they're giving up. Grace, on the other hand, will grow up more as an observer looking in on how we live our lives. It's not the same." She waved a hand. "I'm not saying she won't be able to make it work, just that it will be difficult."

Then Hannah seemed to shake off her somber mood and smiled. "But it's not my place to judge the *Englisch*. If she grows up to embrace that world then, as you said before, one can worship and honor *Gotte* from anywhere. And that's what's most important."

Did she mean that? Could she possibly be more open to his suit now?

She lifted her chin. "And I didn't mean to be negative, because you're right, this is wonderful *gut* news. Being able to see Grace on a regular basis will be right nice." Her smile turned sympathetic. "I imagine it won't be easy to leave your familiar life behind you."

This was going to work out. The more she said, the more confident he became. "Actually, it was easier than I would have thought a few weeks ago. And every minute that passes it feels more right than the minute before. It's as if, instead of moving away from home, I'm returning to my true home."

"What about your work as a paramedic? I know that's important to you."

He nodded. "That was a key piece to making this work. I spent the morning with Ford over at the fire station and he said that with my skill level he shouldn't have any trouble adding me to one of their crews, though I might have to wait a few weeks for the paperwork to go through. I've already spoken to their HR department and turned in my notice at my current job."

He spread his hands. "In just a month, I went from having no family to having more relatives than I can count on my fingers and toes. And of course there are friends here, both old and new, and...well, and dear friends that I'm happy I get to remain in close proximity to."

* * *

Hannah took a deep breath. The look he was giving her would have made her heart soar if she didn't know a marriage between them could never be.

He seemed so pleased with his decision, so certain everything would work out. "Your *mamm* must be happy. Though she did a *gut* job of keeping your secret."

"That's because she doesn't know yet. I wanted to tell you first."

Ach, Mike, you're making this so hard.

"Actually though, it was something Mom said that inspired me to do this. She challenged me to stop looking at this from how it affects me, but to look deeper for a way to make things work out for everyone."

Hannah nodded. "She said something similar to me." But in her case, that looking deeper translated in learning how to find peace in letting go.

Letting go of her dream of being a mother to Grace.

Letting go of her dream of finding a *mann* like Mike.

Letting go of her dream of having a home and *familye* of her own.

Perhaps this was a season of testing for her, a lesson in submission to *Gotte*'s will, even if she didn't understand the whys and wherefores.

There was another aspect of this that bothered her, one that was a bit selfish, one she was too embarrassed to mention out loud. She knew most of the *Englisch* thought of the Plain Folk more in terms of what they lacked than what they offered. And that really didn't bother her, because she was confident in her beliefs and in her place in the world. But the thought that Grace might someday see the Amish that way made her sad.

Mike cleared his throat, bringing her thoughts back to the present. "Forgive me, but you aren't as enthusiastic about this news as I expected."

She tried to shake off her melancholy mood. "I truly am happy. Happy you're coming back to us. Happy Leah's not only getting her son back but also getting a granddaughter in the process. And happy that I'll be able to observe and play a small part in your lives."

"It doesn't have to be a small part. Don't you know you're a big part of the reason I'm doing this?" He took her hands. "Hannah, I don't want to pressure you or belabor the point, but I'd still be honored to call you my wife."

"Oh, Mike, you asking me to marry you means more to me than you'll ever know. Especially since you know about my medical issues."

He made a dismissive motion. "That doesn't matter. We'll have Grace. And if we want a larger family, the foster care system is filled with children looking for a home and family."

Her heart was slowly breaking, shattering into tiny pieces. What he was offering her was so tempting, so much of what she yearned for. But... "I can't marry you."

Some of the light in his eyes went out. "Because I'm not Amish." His voice was flat, resigned.

She nodded. "My feelings haven't changed on that point. I've done a lot of thinking and praying about this since the last time we discussed it."

He raised a brow but didn't respond otherwise.

She pressed on. "Even though I didn't want to hear it, you were right. I needed to understand why holding tight to my baptismal vows is important other than it was how I was raised."

"And you feel that now you know."

"I do. It's true that I can honor and be obedient to *Gotte* from anywhere, just as you said. But how does it bring honor to *Gotte* if I break my baptismal vows to marry you? And if I do so, aren't I making a decision for the wrong reasons? Doesn't that start me down the slippery slope of thinking of myself and what I want in making decisions rather than putting *Gotte* first and seeking His will in all things?"

"Do you truly believe God is against this?"

She ignored his comment. Faith was not something you could argue or debate. "There's also the fact that if I turn my back on the Amish way of life and break the vows I made at baptism, I'll be turning my back on my *familye* and friends, and I'll no longer have those people in my life going forward. What lesson does that teach Grace?"

"Do you really think your own family would shun you?"

"They'd have no choice. And I would never test them by making them choose."

"Then that's it. Marriage between us is off the table."

She nodded, hating the hard expression on his face. She could tell she'd hurt him. "Unless you're willing to return to our way of life and submit to baptism."

If anything, that seemed to put more distance between them.

Before she could say more, Mike turned to the door. "The sun will be going down soon. You should probably get Grace bundled up and head home."

Hannah stepped away from the stall and brushed at her skirt. She couldn't leave things on such a strained note. Not again. "In case I didn't say it before, I do think it's wonderful *gut* that you've decided to relocate here so we can all remain close."

Mike jammed his hands in his pockets and stared through the open door. "It'll be good for Grace to have you and Mom in her life."

As Hannah moved to join him, she struggled to find something to say, something to ease this tension between them.

But even so, a part of her selfishly wondered if his moving here might make things more difficult for her. Because it was inevitable that a good-hearted, industrious, honorable man like Mike would eventually find a discerning *Englisch* woman to marry. And when that happened his future *fraa* would naturally assume the role of Grace's mother. And with a sweet but active toddler for Mike to raise it would likely happen sooner rather than later.

And she wasn't certain her heart could bear to witness that up close. Just the thought of it was almost enough to make her want to push him away now.

Then she remembered Leah's words about how, when you loved someone, you had to find the courage to say the words to them even when there was no expectation of having those feelings returned. And that you did it because everyone needs to know they are loved, regardless of the situation.

Did she have that kind of courage?

* * *

Mike was ready to get out of here, away from Hannah and her closed-off thinking. He'd really thought, once she saw him making the effort to stay, trying to meet her halfway as best he could, that she would meet him the rest of the way.

But it seemed it was all or nothing with her. And once again, he'd fallen short.

A heartbeat later he was startled by the touch of her hand on his sleeve. "Mike?"

The concern in her expression had him wondering if this wasn't the first time she'd tried to get his attention. Well, he certainly didn't want her feeling worried on his account. "I'll get your buggy ready while you fetch Grace."

"If you don't mind remaining here for just another couple of minutes, there's something I need to say."

"If you're thinking about apologizing, there's no—"

"Oh help, *nee*."

Something about her voice, about the emotion in her eyes caught his attention and he snapped his mouth shut. Crossing his arms over his chest, he nodded. "I'm listening."

She didn't speak immediately. Instead she fiddled with her *kapp* string as color climbed up into her cheeks. Whatever it was that she wanted to say certainly had her flustered.

Finally she straightened and met his gaze. "I love you."

Mike immediately came to attention. Had he heard right?

His heart thudded in his chest as he stepped forward and gently took hold of her upper arm with one hand and brushed her cheek with the other. "My sweet, honest, stubborn Hannah, those words are the most precious gift you could give to me."

She rested her hands against his chest, an ocean of *if onlys* pooling in her eyes. "You know this doesn't change my answer, don't you? I still can't break my vows. I just wanted you to know that you are truly loved."

"Awww, Hannah, sweetheart, what do you want me to do with that information?"

"I want you to bury it in your heart and let it become a part of who you are. If ever you doubt yourself or your worth, remember you are someone who is loved and believed in. Then get on with your life." She stepped back, breaking from the embrace. "As I must as well."

She met his gaze without blinking. "If you can't find it in yourself to return to the Plain life, then you must find a *fraa* among the *Englisch* who you can love and who will love you and Grace. Because you both deserve that. You need that."

Then she moved past him and headed back to the house.

And he stood rooted to the spot, not trying to stop her.

* * *

Mike didn't sleep well that night. Knowing Hannah loved him made everything so much better and so much worse. How could she say she loved him in one breath and tell him to look elsewhere for a wife in the next? It made no sense.

He was up before dawn the next morning and headed out almost before his mother was up and about. He did a few extra laps on his morning run, pounding the ground until he just couldn't anymore.

After he showered and changed at the fire station, he looked for Ford so he could pick up some paperwork he had to fill out in anticipation of starting work here soon.

He found him in the kitchen, pouring a cup of coffee and grabbing a donut, his expression pinched and drawn.

Mike grabbed a cup and joined him at the coffeemaker. "You look like you've had a rough morning already."

Ford nodded and leaned back against the counter, rotating his neck as if to get out the kinks. "Sometimes I think the Amish have the right of it with their attitude toward technology."

Surprised that his friend had hit on a subject so close to home, Mike almost spilled his coffee. "What do you mean?"

"Sorry, just got back from a tough call. An accident involving a seventeen-year-old girl who was apparently texting while driving on her way to school and ran off the road. She's in critical condition at Mercy General, and I understand that if she survives it'll be minus most of her left arm."

Mike grimaced. "Unfortunately, I've been on way too many calls of that sort myself."

But Ford wasn't done venting. "That's the third texting-related accident I've been called in on in the last two months. And last week, a twenty-one-year-old guy forgot about something he left simmering on the stove because he was down in the basement playing video games. He probably would've burned to death in the resultant fire if an alert neighbor hadn't spotted the flames and called nine-one-one."

Mike sipped on his coffee, sensing the man needed to get it all off his chest.

"Sadly those sorts of incidents are becoming common-place. And not just with our young people. A couple of weeks ago a middle-aged man was running along a trail down by the river. He had earphones in, listening to a podcast. He failed to hear an out-of-control four-wheeler coming toward him despite the driver yelling at him."

Ford cut him a sideways glance. "Sorry. Didn't mean to dump all that on you. It's just some days get to me more than others. That girl this morning is the same age as my own daughter."

"No need for apologies. We've all had those kind of days, those kind of calls."

After that, their conversation turned to paperwork and other hoops Mike had to jump through in order to be considered for a job here. A mere formality, Ford assured him.

When Mike left the fire station, he headed for the bakery out of habit. He sat in the parking lot for a few minutes, trying to decide if he should go in. Yesterday's conversation still played over and over in his mind. Would Hannah want to see him this morning? Could they go back to being just friends again?

Finally, he climbed out of the truck. He'd have to face her sometime, and it was better not to put off the inevitable.

As usual, there was a line of people waiting to place their orders. Hannah was handling the crowd with sweet smiles and her usual grace. He kept his gaze focused on her, waiting for the moment she would spot him.

When she finally did, there was that immediate spark of connection, that special smile he'd always looked forward to. But it was followed almost immediately by a shy, almost embarrassed expression as her cheeks pinkened and she ducked her head. She quickly turned back to her customer and finished his order.

When his turn came a few moments later she seemed to have regained her composure.

"Before you order the usual," she said with a raised index finger, "you should know that we have our chocolate whoopie pies with strawberry cream filling on sale for fifty cents off."

He smiled but shook his head. "I'll stick with the regular."

She rolled her eyes with an expression of long-suffering. "One of these days I'm going to find something that tempts you to try something different."

Good. She still cared enough to tease. He watched as she fetched his order, then he handed her his credit card.

"Do you have any special plans for today?" she asked as she rang him up.

"Actually I have an appointment to speak to Vivian Littman at eleven o'clock. We're meeting in one of the local library's study rooms." He signed his receipt. "If you can get away, I'd like for you to join us. After all, whatever plans we make will affect you as well."

He saw a spectrum of emotions flash across her expressive face—dismay, resignation, stoic determination—before she settled on acceptance. "Of course. It's *gut* of you to include me. I'll meet you there if I'm able." Then she looked past him to the next customer in line. "*Gut matin*, Angie, what can I get for you today?"

Taking the hint, Mike moved away from the counter and over to the coffee bar. As he filled his cup he thought over their conversation and, more to the point, their interaction. On the surface it had seemed like everything was fine between them, but he noticed she'd put a sliver of distance between them. Even when she agreed to attend his meeting with the caseworker there'd been a subtle detachment in her demeanor.

He supposed he couldn't blame her. If their positions had been reversed, would he have handled it with the same grace?

He wasn't so sure.

* * *

As Hannah served her customers, she watched Mike from the corner of her eye. He seemed so confident, so unruffled. Apparently her declaration yesterday hadn't changed anything.

But as Leah said, the important thing was that she'd told him how she felt. What he did with that information was now up to him.

The fact that he hadn't reciprocated, never so much as referred to it, however, told her all she needed to know. He was fond of her, she was confident of that much. But he didn't love her in the way a man looking for a *fraa* loved a woman.

True, the fact that she was Plain and he considered himself *Englisch* created a gulf between them that would be difficult to cross, but that was a separate issue from their feelings for each other.

So now she knew.

"I asked for an apple raisin muffin, not a cinnamon muffin."

Hannah looked at her customer, realizing she'd let her mind wander too far afield. "*Ach*, I'm so sorry, Angie. Let me get you the apple raisin muffin you ordered and you can keep the cinnamon one, on the house."

She signaled for Maisie to take her place at the counter and slipped into the kitchen. She had to pull herself together, to quit this yearning for something that could never be.

But just how did one do that?

Chapter 27

Hannah arrived at the library just as Mike stepped out of his truck. He spotted her and waited as she hitched her buggy to a stanchion at the edge of the parking lot.

"I'm glad you could make it," he said as she approached.

"Maisie's getting quite good at taking over for me. And anything that affects Grace is worth making time for."

He nodded and opened the library door, allowing her to precede him. When they reached the private study room, they found Vivian already there.

"I hope we didn't keep you waiting long," Mike said as they exchanged greetings.

"Not at all. I finished my other appointment earlier than anticipated and have been using the time to catch up on my email."

Then she turned to Hannah. "I wasn't expecting you, but perhaps it's good you're here. This way you'll know just what to expect as we transition guardianship."

Hannah merely nodded as she took a seat. After all, there was nothing to say.

Mike pulled out a chair. "Before we get started, I need to let you know I've decided to move to Hope's Haven permanently. My mother is here, as are a lot of other family members who can support me in my effort to raise Grace and give her the network of family she can grow close to."

Vivian smiled broadly. "Well now, that simplifies matters immensely. We don't have to worry about cross-district issues, and as you say, having a network of family nearby enhances your position."

She glanced Hannah's way, and her expression turned almost apologetic. "I want to caution you, though, once Grace officially moves in with you it might be best if Hannah stays away from her for a while."

Hannah went absolutely still as she absorbed that advice, but Mike immediately took exception. "Why? I mean, even if Hannah is no longer Grace's guardian, I still intend for her to be a part of her life."

"But it's a distinction Grace needs to learn. And I'm truly sorry, Hannah. I know this is difficult for you. But Grace will need time to adjust to her new situation." The caseworker turned back to Mike. "She needs to learn that your home is now her permanent home and that you are her caretaker. Once she bonds with you and gets accustomed to her new surroundings and new routines, then Hannah can gradually come back into her life, in the way a favorite aunt might."

Again Hannah nodded. She didn't trust herself to speak. None of what Vivian said was a surprise, but somehow hearing it out loud drove home how much she was losing.

But Vivian had already moved on to another topic. "I understand you don't want to make any changes immediately."

"That's correct." Mike still wore a frown. "We want to ease her into this change."

"I would caution you not to leave it too long. It's going to be a big change for her, no matter when you do it."

Hannah cleared her throat. "Mike currently lives with his mother, who is also Grace's sitter. We discussed letting Grace spend the night there a time or two, just to kind of ease her into the idea of being away from me at night."

Vivian nodded. "That's a good plan. In fact, why don't you schedule the first sleepover sometime in the next few days."

Hannah clasped her hands tightly in her lap. "If Leah and Mike are willing, I could leave Grace with them tonight."

Vivian gave her an approving smile while Mike's expression had a more are-you-sure-you-want-to-do-this quality.

"Excellent." Vivian jotted down a few notes. "This will let you know what level of resistance you'll be dealing with once the time comes to hand Grace off."

Then she opened a folder. "Next, we need to discuss the procedures we have to follow to make everything official. You're living in your mother's home, is that correct?" she asked Mike.

"For now, but I eventually plan to buy my own place."

"And how do you plan to support yourself and Grace?"

"I've applied to join the local fire department as a paramedic. All indications are that I'll be able to start early next month."

"Great."

Hannah barely listened to the rest of the conversation, vaguely aware of talk of home visits and court dates and paperwork. Instead her thoughts were all for Grace and the fact that this would be the final week when she could pretend the child was hers. How long would she have to stay away so the toddler could bond with Mike as her primary caretaker? A few weeks? A month? Longer?

Would Grace feel she'd abandoned her during those first weeks? Just the thought of that broke her heart.

And during that time would Grace forget her and the bond they currently shared? Toddlers were so amazingly adaptable, and their memories were so shallow.

Hannah finally brought her focus back to the present when Vivian handed over a packet of papers to Mike and stood. "Do either of you have questions? I'm afraid I'm due to meet someone in Heartwood Crossing in thirty minutes."

Mike stood as well and shook her hand. "I need to read over these documents and think about our discussion some more but for now I'm good."

"Well, you have my phone number if there's anything we need to go over again." She turned to Hannah with a sympathetic look as she gathered up her things. "I know you can't really replace Grace, and it's too soon to consider anything just yet, but there are many children in our system who need good foster homes. If you decide in the future that that's something you'd like to pursue, we can talk."

Hannah was taken off guard by the suggestion. "You're right, it's too soon to think of fostering another child."

Vivian patted her arm as she moved toward the door. "I understand. It's just something to keep in mind."

Once Vivian had made her exit, there was a moment of awkward silence.

Then Mike spoke up. "We don't have to let Grace sleep over tonight if you're not ready."

"*Nee*, there's no point delaying things. Vivian's right, waiting won't make it any easier."

"It's not like we'll move her out of your house right away. We can ease into it over the next several weeks."

Hannah decided it was best to change the subject. "Have you started looking at houses yet?"

He shook his head as he moved to the door. "No, although I'm already checking out listings. But I'll wait until I've started working again before I get serious about settling on a place."

"Do you have a large home in Missouri?"

"I have an apartment, so I won't have to worry about selling it. I'll have to talk to them about ending my lease early and figuring out what to do with my things until I find a place here."

"I'm sure between your *mamm*'s place and ours we can store your things until you're ready to move into your own home."

His brow shot up. "Just like that, you'd volunteer to store my things, sight unseen."

"Of course. We have several rooms that aren't being used. And the equipment shed is weathertight."

"Thank you." Then he glanced up at the sky. "Here I am keeping you standing here when it looks like it'll start raining any minute. Are you going to be okay in your open buggy?"

She smiled. "That's a normal occurrence around here.

I have a raincoat under the buggy seat. But you're right, I should be on my way. I'll pack a few things for Grace and see you at your *mamm*'s later this afternoon."

"About that. I think, at least this first time, you should spend the night at our home as well."

"But the whole point is for you to handle—"

"I know. But we're just talking about easing her into this and I think your presence will go a long way toward making her comfortable with the change of routine."

"It's not like your *mamm*'s home is strange to her. We even stayed over there the night of the big rainstorm, remember?"

"I do, but I'd hate to have her become inconsolable. You can sleep in a separate room this time and let me handle anything that comes up with her, but at least you'll be nearby if we should need you."

Hannah thought about that a moment and decided it made sense. "*Jah*, I can do that." Then she added "And I can put my time there to good use and do some extra baking. I'm getting a little behind on my special orders."

"Good, that's settled then. I'll let Mom know to expect you." He moved to his truck. "If you'll excuse me, I have quite a few things to take care of today, so I'd better get started." And with a wave he headed off.

She slowly made her way to her buggy, finally allowing herself to relax the control she'd held on her emotions. First the discussion in the barn with Mike yesterday, and now she faced estrangement from Grace. Why had such treasure been dangled in front of her only to be yanked away? How would she get through this without falling apart?

Gotte, I'm a frail human who can be selfish, impatient

and unwilling to let go. Please help me get through this in a manner that is pleasing to You.

* * *

When Hannah returned to the bakery, she asked Maisie if she'd stay and work the counter so she could bake. Hannah didn't feel she was ready to face customers just yet.

She hadn't really planned to have Grace sleep over at Leah's so soon. Not that it was a bad idea. After all, if they wanted to transition Grace gradually rather than change things all at once, this was as good a way to start as any. But already she was thinking about not tucking her little girl into bed tonight and her heart ached. Grace wasn't the only one who needed to be eased into this new arrangement.

When she arrived at Leah's later that afternoon, Hannah was surprised to see Mike's truck parked near the house. She'd assumed from his comments when he left the library that he'd be running errands all day. But perhaps part of his errands had to do with work around the place here.

As she took care of stabling Clover, she prepared herself to face him with politeness and nothing more. Just friends, that's all they were. This morning's meeting with Vivian had shown her it could be done. There was no reference to her declaration of love, no awkward exchanges. In fact, if they hadn't had a shared love for Leah and Grace, they probably wouldn't have had the need for much interaction in the future.

She entered the house through the kitchen and exchanged greetings with Leah, then looked around expectantly. "Where's Grace?" Would it be too forward to ask about Mike as well?

"She's napping in my room. It's about time for her to wake up, though, if you want to look in on her."

"Let's let her sleep a little longer." Hannah set down the carpetbag she'd brought with her. "I don't know if Mike explained this to you, but we decided to ease Grace into our new arrangement."

"He told me. And for what it's worth, I think it's a *gut* idea."

"Did he also tell you that I'd be staying here as well this first time?"

"*Jah.* You know you're welcome here anytime too." Leah smiled indulgently. "Micah bought a truckload of furnishings for the room we've set aside for Grace. He's up there now putting the crib together. He also bought a lot of other things he thought would make for a proper toddler's room."

So that's what he'd been up to. She shared a smile with Leah as she imagined what he might have considered necessities.

"You can sleep in the guest room downstairs," Leah continued. "That way you won't be as tempted to check in on Grace during the night."

As if that would stop her if she felt she was really needed.

Hannah picked up the carpetbag. "I'll just bring Grace's things up to her room and see if Mike needs any help while I'm there."

Leah nodded with a knowing smile. "Of course."

Feeling that Leah saw a little more than she intended her to, Hannah headed for the stairs. She'd rarely had reason to venture abovestairs in her friend's home, but she found Mike easily by following the sound of the construction.

She stepped across the threshold of the room at the end of the hallway. Someone had obviously been very busy. The room was littered with heaps of packaging debris—cardboard, plastic wrap, Styrofoam and paper.

Mike stood in the middle of the room, studying what appeared to be a set of instructions. He had that totally focused look he wore when he was problem solving. The furrow on his forehead, the vertical line between his eyebrows, the little twist of his lips that brought out the barely-there dimple on the left side of his mouth.

His mouth. What would it be like to be kissed by that mouth?

Mike looked up just then and spotted her. She apparently got her expression under control in time because his demeanor turned to one of welcome and self-deprecation.

He held out his palm, revealing several screws, a small spring and a few other parts she didn't recognize. "I'm trying to decide if these are extras or if I missed something important when I was assembling the crib."

Hannah was relieved to be able to turn her attention to his handiwork. The crib looked to be solidly put together. There was even a mobile of pastel-colored baby animal figures attached to the headboard.

The crib Grace used at home was one Hannah's *daed* had built for his daughters when they were *bopplin*, so leftover parts hadn't been an issue.

She smiled. "As precise as you are, I think it's safe to assume you put this together just as you should."

He placed the parts in a plastic bag with a crooked smile. "Let's hope you're right."

He waved a hand in a broad gesture that took in the entire room. "What do you think? I tried to include everything we might need when Grace stays here."

Hannah looked around the room. He'd certainly been busy. There was a set of shelves that held not only a dozen or so brand-new children's books but some stuffed animals and other toys as well. A simple wooden rocking chair that looked suspiciously like one from Noah's workshop sat in a corner and a large open storage crate held more toys. Next to the crate was a child-sized dresser topped with a changing table that held a basket of disposable wipes, lotions and towels. A large case of disposable diapers sat next to it along with a diaper pail.

A braided rug anchored the center of the room and there were several bright and cheery nursery-rhyme-themed prints on the wall. She also noticed some electronic items scattered about, such as a baby monitor, a towel warmer and a few others she couldn't identify without a closer look. Apparently whatever they were they worked on batteries.

He hadn't been exaggerating when he said he'd included everything he might need. There was so much stuff here it was almost overwhelming.

Overall there was more of an *Englisch* feel than an Amish one in this room.

"It's certainly well stocked," she said, looking for the silver lining.

"I know I might have gone a little overboard, but I'd rather have more than I need than less."

"Is Leah aware of all this?"

"She's given me carte blanche to furnish the room as I like. Besides, it's not permanent. Most of it will be going with me when I find my own place." He studied her and his expression shifted. "You don't approve."

Apparently she hadn't done a *gut* job of hiding her feelings. "I know your intentions were good. But it just seems…" She gestured with a wave of her hands. "Excessive."

He didn't appear to take offense. "Perhaps by Plain standards. But I assure you, I used restraint and kept Mom's sensibilities in mind. Once I have my own home with electricity, Wi-Fi and proper plumbing, I'll get it set up properly."

Would he be turning Grace into one of those children who valued things above personal interaction? Then she pushed that thought aside as unfair. She never doubted for an instant Mike loved Grace. He'd see that she grew up with proper values. Especially with Leah to help him raise her.

"I think Grace will be delighted with all the colorful toys and books you've provided." She thought about the things in the carpetbag she still held. Would Mike think them too old and worn to fit into this bright, colorful, modern room he'd furnished?

She set the bag on the rocking chair. "If you don't mind, I think it might be easier on Grace this first time if she had a few familiar things around her as well."

"What did you have in mind?"

She started pulling things from the bag. "Grace always takes her doll and the stuffed cat you gave her to bed with her. I brought her hairbrush. I don't see one here, so I'll just set it in the dresser along with her nightdress." She opened the drawer and found it already contained two frilly little nightdresses along with a pair of onesies.

"I wasn't sure what she already had," Mike explained.

"So I picked up a few items of clothing for her. This way you won't have to worry about transporting things back and forth."

"It seems you thought of just about everything." Would he be buying *Englisch* day clothing for her soon? Maybe even cut her hair?

But she no longer had any say in the matter, so she held her tongue and turned back to her bag. "And here's the baby quilt my sister Greta made for her." She pulled two well-worn storybooks out of the bag. "I know you just bought her some new books so these may not be necessary, but these are her two favorites."

Mike, who'd been bagging the trash while they talked, tied off the bag and tossed it out the window. "I'll add it to the trash pile later." He grinned. "The trash, not the books." Then he joined her at the rocking chair. "I think having familiar things around her is an excellent idea."

He set the two toys in a corner of the crib and laid the quilt over the foot rail. "And I totally forgot to get a hairbrush for her and probably any number of other things as well."

"It certainly looks like you've been busy in here." Hannah turned to see Leah standing in the doorway with Grace on her hip.

"It's all Mike's doing. He's certainly showing that he plans to provide well for Grace, ain't so?"

Grace looked around the room with wide eyes and a delighted smile. Then she saw Hannah and immediately held her arms out, saying, "Maa."

Hannah crossed the room and took Grace, treasuring the precious way the little girl hugged her neck and buried her head in her shoulder. Then she remembered they were trying to wean the child from the close attachment they had.

She turned Grace in her arms so the little girl could look at the room and all it contained. "Look, sunshine, Mike brought you lots of fun things to play with." Should she start referring to Mike as *Daed* so Grace could get used to it? Or would he prefer to be called *Onkel* Mike? One of the many things they hadn't discussed about the future.

Grace started squirming to get down and Hannah set her near the bin of toys. Grace grabbed the edge of the bin and many of the toys spilled out. She reached for a colorful plastic open-weave ball with a bell trapped inside. Grace shook it and giggled infectiously at the jingling sound it made.

"I knew she'd like that one." Mike looked so proud of himself, it was all Hannah could do not to tease him about it. But it was actually quite sweet how hard he was working to see that Grace was happy and safe, even if she didn't agree with his approach.

Mike stooped down so that he was on a level with Grace and rolled the ball back and forth with her.

Hannah decided she should leave. After all, the whole point of the overnight stay was to give Mike time on his own with Grace. She did her best to slip unobtrusively from the room. But Grace caught sight of her and tossed the ball in her direction.

Hannah cut a quick glance Mike's way, but he didn't seem unduly bothered by the fact that Grace had switched her attention. Hannah rolled the ball back to the toddler, but Grace had already lost interest. Instead, a large empty box caught her attention. She immediately headed for it as fast as she could crawl and didn't stop until she was inside. Then she turned and sat up, facing them with a grin.

Mike shook his head. "All these toys and she wants to play with an empty box."

Hannah laughed. "*Kinner* don't know the difference between expensive playthings and free ones. You ought to see how she plays with cardboard tubes from aluminum foil."

Then she turned to Leah. "Speaking of which, if you don't mind, I think I'll get started on the shoofly pies that are at the top of my special-order list."

"Of course. In fact I need to get supper started, so I'll join you." Leah turned to Mike. "Should I take Grace with me, or do you think you'll be okay with her here on your own?"

"You two ladies get on with whatever you need to do. I think Grace and I will be just fine."

"We'll be in the kitchen if you should need us." And with that, Hannah turned and left the room. As soon as she reached the kitchen, she went to the refrigerator and retrieved some of the pie dough she'd mixed earlier in the week. At first, she took out enough for the three pies Mrs. Clopton had ordered, then changed her mind and pulled out enough for a fourth. After all, she might as well take care of tonight's dessert as well.

While she was rolling out her first piecrust, Leah entered the kitchen and pulled out pots and dishes. "I thought I'd do something simple for supper tonight. If I can have access to just one of the ovens, I'll fix a meat loaf, and I can cook the vegetables on the stove. I made fresh bread earlier today so we're okay there."

"That sounds delicious. And of course I can make do with two of the ovens for now—I'll use one for my pies and the other for the cupcakes I plan to bake." She waved a hand. "And don't worry about dessert, one of those pies is to go with our supper."

Leah smiled. "There's nothing better to finish off a meal with than one of your pies."

"*Danke.* It's the least I can do to repay your hospitality."

Leah pulled the meat from the refrigerator. "*Ach*, Hannah, you know you are always welcome here."

Hannah made a noncommittal response. Leah's statement tightened the knot already twisting in Hannah's stomach. Based on what had been discussed with the caseworker this morning, there would come a time in the very near future when she wouldn't be welcome here.

At least not while Grace was around.

Chapter 28

Once the piecrusts were done, Hannah worked on the fillings. More than ever, she needed the ability to focus that always came with preparing her baked goods. And with it the ability to temporarily forget everything else.

But that wasn't to be today. She'd barely begun pouring the filling into the first pie plate when she heard a thump followed by Grace's wails. She'd already set down the bowl and taken a step toward the cries when she heard Leah softly say her name. A moment later Mike called down the stairs. "Everything's okay. We just took a little fall."

Already the crying had decreased to a hiccup. Picking up the bowl once more, Hannah tried not to be jealous that Mike had handled the minor tragedy without her help.

As soon as her pies were in the oven, she went to work on a batch of cookies. Getting those baked and out of the way now would give them time to cool so she could do the decorating before she retired for the evening.

But it seemed the harder she worked on her baking, the more thoughts of Mike and Grace intruded. Perhaps, when Grace was older and her relationship as Mike's adopted *dochder* was firmly set, Hannah could spend time with her, teaching her to bake. And maybe other things a mother traditionally taught her *dochder* as well.

If Mike didn't have another woman in his life by then to take on that role.

At supper that evening she had to work hard to keep her conversation and demeanor positive and cheerful. Grace's high chair was placed between Hannah and Mike, and earlier she'd given him a few tips on how to deal with mealtime.

Doing her best to let Mike be in charge, Hannah deliberately kept a running conversation going with Leah. She didn't completely ignore them of course. Whenever Mike asked her opinion on how to handle something or Grace insistently tried to get her attention, she responded. But she always did her best to immediately redirect Grace's attention back to Mike or provide some other bit of distraction and resume her interaction with Leah. It worked for the most part, though Hannah did have to keep reminding herself that this was what was best for Grace.

After they pushed back from the table, Hannah steadfastly helped Leah clean the kitchen while Mike grabbed a washrag and carried off Grace, who seemed to have more food on her than in her.

Leah dished up the leftover peas in a plastic bowl. "I'd say, despite a few rough spots, that went well."

Hannah nodded without looking up. "Mike did a *gut* job balancing between helping her and letting her feed herself. And Grace will get used to it in no time."

"I wasn't talking about either Mike or Grace."

This time Hannah did look up and meet her gaze. "It's hard, but I'll be okay."

Leah smiled sympathetically. "I know you will. But I also know it won't be easy."

Ach! How could she have forgotten? Hannah set down the dish she'd been scraping and gave Leah a hug. "Sometimes I forget just how much you lost all those years ago. I have no reason to complain—at least Grace will still be around and in my life to some extent."

"It wasn't my intent to make you feel bad. I was actually commending you for not fighting this or railing at *Gotte* for allowing this to come to pass, though I know how tempting that must be."

Is that how Leah had reacted when she thought her son was lost to her? And all the rest that had happened? Those must have been dark days for her.

* * *

Mike stepped into the kitchen, carrying Grace. His mother had shown up in the living room a few minutes ago, casually mentioning that the kitchen had been cleaned up and she thought Hannah was preparing to do some more baking.

Did Hannah really have so much work to do? Or did she feel she wouldn't be welcome around Grace after their conversation with the caseworker this morning?

She stood in the doorway of her baker's pantry but wasn't reaching for anything.

"Mom says you plan to do more baking tonight."

Hannah spun around with her hand on her heart. "*Ach du lieva.*"

Mike grimaced. "Sorry, I didn't mean to startle you."

She dropped her hand and smiled. "That's okay. I just didn't hear you come in."

Grace held her hands out. "Maa."

"Sounds like she wants to spend a bit of time with you."

"But—"

He didn't miss the yearning in her expression, and it stabbed at him. "I know we talked about you keeping your distance, but we also want to ease Grace into this new arrangement." He planted a light kiss on Grace's head. "Besides, I think it must be this little ladybug's bedtime and I could use your help with that."

He held her out and Hannah only hesitated a moment before she crossed the room and took Grace from him. She buried her face in Grace's neck, and Mike realized it was the first time she'd held the toddler since she they'd looked over the nursery.

She finally met his gaze again as she stroked Grace's back and the little girl played with Hannah's *kapp* strings. "I'll be happy to go over our nightly routine with you again." Her expression was unreadable. "Or you can forget all that and establish your own routines."

"How about we do a little of both this evening?"

Her expression changed to a puzzled frown. "What do you mean?"

"Just that she'd probably be more comfortable having you nearby, at least this first time."

"Are you sure?"

"Absolutely."

When they reached the foot of the stairs, Mike attempted to take Grace from Hannah, but the little girl was having none of it. She just held on to Hannah tighter and buried her face in her would-be mother's shoulder.

Hannah gave him an apologetic look. "I carry loads up the stairs at home all the time. I'm fine with carrying her up to her room."

Mike nodded and followed the two of them up the stairs.

When they reached the room, Hannah moved immediately to the changing table. "You aren't smelling very fresh, sunshine," she said with mock-sternness. "I think someone needs a change."

Mike stepped forward. "Allow me."

Hannah raised her brow. "Are you sure?"

He grinned. "Are you doubting my ability?"

"It's not for the faint of heart." Then she gave him a challenging grin. "Or I should say, the faint of stomach."

"Challenge accepted. I need to learn to handle the good, the bad *and* the stinky—you and Mom won't always be around."

Hannah laid Grace on the changing table and stepped back with raised hands. "She's all yours."

Mike managed to handle the task without gagging and with minimal direction from her.

When he'd finished, she nodded approval. "I'm impressed." She handed him Grace's nightdress.

"I'll admit it wasn't the most pleasant of tasks, but to be honest, it pales in comparison with some of the things I've had to do as a paramedic."

He saw the softening of her expression, the flash of sympathy in her eyes. But before she could try to apologize, he changed the subject. "So what's this nightly routine you've established?"

"Drop the side of the crib and then pull the rocking chair up right next to it."

As Mike worked, he noted that, even though Grace didn't have a lot of hair, she looked very different without her *kapp*, much more childlike.

How would Hannah look without her hair down? Were those honey-brown locks of hers straight or wavy, thick or fine? Would it feel as soft and silky as it appeared?

He forcefully pushed those thoughts away and concentrated on the task at hand. Once he'd complied with her requests, she nodded toward the rocker. "Have a seat."

That surprised him. He'd expected her to demonstrate so she could hold on to Grace a bit longer. But he did as she indicated, and once he was seated she handed Grace to him. Their hands touched as they made the exchange, and he felt that tingling awareness her touch always evoked.

Then she fetched the hairbrush. "Now you brush her hair, but gently so you don't hurt her scalp."

Worried he'd be too harsh, Mike gently slid the soft-bristled brush through Grace's corn-silk hair.

"Now, while you brush her hair you tell her a story." Hannah's voice was a near whisper. "It doesn't have to be much—a short fairy tale or nursery rhyme, or something you make up. The idea is to just speak to her and let her know she has your undivided attention."

Feeling self-conscious, Mike settled on Old King Cole. He went through it twice before Hannah indicated he'd brushed her hair long enough.

She took the brush from him and placed it back in the dresser. "You might want to set up a small bedside table to keep things like this, a few books and maybe a sippy cup close by."

She remained by the dresser. "I think you can take it from here. You simply set the rocker in motion, sing her a lullaby and then tuck her into bed with her doll and cat."

Her tone was matter-of-fact as was her expression, but he could sense the longing beneath the surface, the effort it took her to keep her hands at her side.

"I'm not sure I know any lullabies or appropriate bed-time songs."

"Surely your *mamm* sang 'Schloof, Bobbli, Schloof' to you when you were a *kinner*? I've heard her sing it to Grace on several occasions."

"That does sound a bit familiar, but it's been over twenty years." He stood, still holding Grace. "Why don't you sing it tonight and maybe I can relearn it?"

Hannah nodded and took Mike's place in the rocking chair. He handed Grace to her and she cradled the little girl tenderly as she set the rocker in motion. Then, her voice soft and sweet, she began to sing.

Schloof, Bobbli, schloof
Der Daadi hiet die Schoof
Die Mammi hiet die braune Kieh
Und kummt net heem bis Marriye frieh
Schloof, Bobbli, schloof!

As she sang, it brought back memories of his own mother singing that very lullaby to him, of being cuddled in her arms, of being safe and loved. Which was the same gift Hannah was giving Grace right now.

He tried to remember enough of his first language to mentally translate the lyrics. The first line, of course, was "Sleep, baby, sleep." The next had something to do with the father tending the sheep and then the mother tending the cows.

As she sang the next several verses, he didn't bother trying to translate. Rather he just listened to the poignant sound of her voice and the tender love it conveyed. For just a moment she looked up and met his gaze and that deep, longing love encompassed him too.

If he'd had any doubt before of just how much Grace meant to Hannah, and how true her love for him was, this settled the matter. With an ache that was almost physical, he felt a deep longing to have the three of them together as a true family.

Why wouldn't she marry him? They would make such a wonderful family. Didn't she see that too?

Finally, after three or four more verses—he'd lost count—she let her voice trail off.

"All right, *mein Liebchen*, time to tuck you in." Hannah stood and gave the now droopy-eyed toddler a light squeeze and kiss on her forehead. Then she laid her in the crib and turned to him, one hand still protectively on Grace. "Now you kiss her good night, make sure her doll and cat are where she can see them, tuck her in snugly and raise the side of the crib."

And with that she walked from the room without a backward glance.

While Mike slowly followed her instructions, he inhaled the sweet baby smell and smiled at the soft, sleepy sigh as he kissed the top of Grace's head. It only took a minute of nestling in before her eyes closed and her breathing evened out.

For a while he just stood by her crib, looking down at her as she slept. It was amazing how much he'd grown to love this little girl in the short time he'd known her. The way she giggled when she took delight in something, the way she snuggled trustingly against his chest when she was tired or needed soothing and reassurances. And he couldn't be prouder than a true father when she did something clever like stacking her blocks or pretending to read one of her books.

How could his sister have given up this precious child?

Hannah was right, Grace was changing almost daily— growing physically, learning new skills, connecting with people and things in new ways. It was a joy and a cautionary tale to watch. And he didn't want to miss a minute of it.

He could understand why Hannah felt the same way.

And speaking of Hannah, her pain tonight was obvious. Turning the three of them into a real family would ease that pain. She claimed to love him, and it was obvious she loved Grace. Why couldn't that be enough?

Raking his hand through his hair, he straightened and stepped away from the crib. Once he'd turned out the lamp and switched on the monitor, he quietly left the nursery.

What now? Would Hannah welcome his company? Or would she prefer not to see him right now?

Only one way to find out.

* * *

Hannah was carefully decorating the cookies she'd baked earlier. She was glad to see her hands were so steady. Tonight was really driving home how much her world was about to change. Yes, Mike was being kind and understanding, but that almost made it worse. They both knew how this would end.

And her heart was breaking.

Leah was still in the living room knitting an afghan.

No doubt she'd be retiring for the night soon. And Mike would probably do the same once he had Grace settled down. It gave Hannah some time alone to wallow in her misery.

Meanwhile she still had to frost the three dozen cookies with beach-themed images.

She was so focused on her work that she didn't notice she was no longer alone. It jarred her when she glanced up and spotted Mike leaning against the doorjamb, quietly watching her.

When their gazes met, he straightened and moved into the room. "Sorry, didn't want to startle you while you were in the middle of your decorating."

"*Danke*. Was there something you needed?"

Rather than answering, he studied the cookies she'd already started on. "I take it you have to wait a little while before you work with another color."

She nodded. "I'm laying all the backgrounds down first. I'll come back and add the design next. Most of these are only two or three colors of frosting. The other colors will come from candies and colored sugar."

Mike set the receiver for the baby monitor on the table. "Is there anything I can do to help?" Before she could form a polite refusal, he raised a hand. "I don't mean with the decorating—I haven't your steady hand and fine motor skills. But I can mix frostings or wash bowls or other less creative tasks."

She thought about it for a moment. While it was tempting to send him away so she could continue to wallow in her feelings, she knew that was neither healthy nor Christian. So instead she nodded. "I need to bake several dozen more of these cookies tomorrow. Do you think, if I wrote down the instructions, you could mix the dough for me? It's not the same dough we worked on together the last time. It involves toasting some pistachios, but otherwise it's similar."

"I think I can manage that."

"*Gut.* Let me write down some quick instructions and then I'll leave you to it." She grabbed her notebook and turned to an empty page. Trying to think about it from the viewpoint of someone who had never done it before and wasn't familiar with baking terms, her instructions nearly filled the page.

When she handed it over to Mike, he raised a brow and gave her a little half smile. "You're nothing if not thorough."

She detected a note of teasing in his voice but ignored it. "This is my business, and my customers expect the best I have to give."

He sobered immediately. "Of course. I'll do my best to live up to your standards." And with that he headed to the pantry with her list in hand.

Hannah immediately regretted her tone. He was only trying to help after all, and he'd already proven he could mix dough when he knew what was expected of him.

She went back to her decorating, watching him from the corner of her eye every time she finished with a cookie. They worked in silence for a while, until the sound of Grace fussing came over the monitor.

Mike immediately came to attention and reached for a nearby dishrag to wipe his hands.

"Give it a minute," she cautioned. "She's probably just babbling in her sleep. She does that sometimes. If she really needs a diaper change or drink of water, you'll know."

A few seconds later the monitor went silent again.

"Thanks," Mike said as he went back to working with the dough. "I guess I still have a lot to learn."

"Don't worry. You'll learn to interpret her cries and baby talk soon enough." She straightened, drawing her shoulders back to ease the muscles there. "Speaking of baby talk, have you thought about what you'd like her to call you?" At his puzzled look, she elaborated. "*Daed*, *Fater*, *Onkel* Mike? Or perhaps the *Englisch* version of one of these?"

Mike's brow furrowed in thought. "I guess I hadn't really considered that yet."

"I only ask because I'd like to know how to refer to you when I talk to her."

His eyes took on an unfocused look as he continued to work the dough. "Technically, I'm her uncle. Yet once the adoption is complete in the eyes of the law I'll be her father."

"There's also the issue of you marrying at some point." She tried to keep her voice casual. "If that woman becomes her *mamm*, I would think you'd want to be called *Daed* so as not to confuse matters."

She hadn't been able to interpret his look at her mention of his marrying, but he nodded slowly. "You're right. Daddy it is. After all, she almost feels like a daughter already."

"Then Daddy it will be. But I hope you'll forgive me if I slip up and say *Daed* every once in a while."

"Consider yourself forgiven in advance."

She smiled. Then decided she needed to make her own apology. "I'm sorry I snapped at you earlier. I truly appreciate your help. And the dough looks perfect."

Mike raised a brow at that. "*Perfect* is a strong word."

Why was he always so self-deprecating? Didn't he

understand his value? "If you ever need a break from your job as a paramedic, I'd hire you to work in the bakery."

"High praise indeed." He resumed his kneading. "I must say, smelling the roasted pistachios and orange zest in this batter is making my mouth water. You'll have to save me at least one when you bake them."

She smiled. "I'll consider it your payment. I may even save you two."

"I'll hold you to that." He reached for a towel. "I believe this is ready to chill."

Hannah pinched off a bit of the dough and tasted it. "Mmmm, you're right. This is wonderful *gut*. Just make sure to wrap it tightly before you set it in the refrigerator."

The monitor crackled to life again but though Mike immediately came to attention, he stood in place and listened. When Grace settled down after a few seconds he relaxed. "That's going to take some getting used to."

Once Mike had taken care of the dough, she fully expected him to retire for the evening. But instead he met her gaze. "What else can I do for you?"

"You've already done more—"

He held a hand up. "I'm not ready to turn in, and I like to keep busy."

"All right. I'm almost finished here and then there's the cleanup to do. If you could fill the sink and start gathering up the dirty dishes."

"I'm on it."

By the time she was finished, the dishes were piled by the sink, the counter had been wiped down, and the supplies had been stowed away.

She shook her head as she added her dishes to the pile. "Is there anything you can't do?"

"Don't ask me to mop the floors. It's my least favorite household job and it shows."

"I'll keep that in mind."

Once the table was cleared, Hannah started washing, remembering Mike had said he preferred to dry.

They worked side by side in silence for a few minutes. Then Mike spoke up. "I know how difficult this is for you, giving up on adopting Grace I mean. I want you to know how much I admire and appreciate your handling it with such grace."

Hannah felt a twinge of guilt. If he knew her thoughts he'd feel differently. "It's what's best for Grace and that's what we both want, ain't so?"

"Of course. And I give you my word, that when she's of age, if she chooses to join the Amish community, I won't try to talk her out of it."

"Except you'll explain to her the dangers of living without technology, ain't so? After all, that's your main concern with leaving her alone with us."

Frustration dimmed his smile. "Surely, after what you witnessed with the Eshels, even you can admit she'd be safer if she can easily communicate with others if she finds herself in a similar situation."

"Of course, but that's just one circumstance. There are others where our manner of living has advantages."

That tic at the corner of Mike's mouth made an appearance. "I guess this is something we'll never agree on."

"Since you brought the subject up, I'll tell you how I feel about this. I mourn that she won't be raised the Amish way. Not because I think her soul will be lost. I know that *Gotte* doesn't allow only those who live and worship as we do into heaven, but I do feel that the Plain life teaches children such important values and allows them a closer relationship with Him."

"But she'll be around the Amish a lot—my mother, you, my friends and relatives in the community. When she's of age, she could very well choose to leave the English world and rejoin the Amish community."

"We both know it's easier for a Plain person to join the *Englisch* than the other way around." She waved her hand in his direction. "You're a prime example. Every time I ask you to consider returning as a member of our community you brush it away as an impossibility. And you spent your first seven years as one of us."

* * *

Mike realized she was right about that at least. It was much easier for someone who'd never lived with modern conveniences to adapt to life with them than to give all that up once he had become accustomed to them.

Since that conversation was going nowhere, he moved on to something else. "There's one other thing I'd like to talk to you about, though."

She indicated he should go on.

"I know we spoke with Vivian Littman about you staying away from Grace for a while once we make the transition. But I don't think that's really necessary. In fact, I'm not sure it's even advisable."

She didn't immediately agree with him as he'd thought she would. Instead she gave him a probing look. "Do you mind if I ask what brought you to this conclusion?"

"I think things worked out well with Grace today. There were a few little blips, but Mom tells me all babies cry occasionally and I'll learn to deal with the rest. The thing is, I think it was your presence, the ability for her to hear your voice and see you nearby, that kept things from escalating." He spread his hands. "And since you'll remain a part of her life even after I adopt her, or I hope you will, then I don't see the need to separate you now." He frowned. "I have to say, I thought you'd be happier about this."

"I am. And as long as Grace does well with this, I'm all for it." She gave a little grin. "After all, my bakery kitchen is here."

That was something he hadn't considered. So he could expect to see quite a bit of Hannah and Grace in the next week at least.

"But?"

"But once you move to town things will probably be quite different."

"It doesn't have to be." Then he grabbed another dish to dry. "But we can cross that bridge when we get to it."

* * *

Hannah frowned. Wasn't that just moving the problem down the road? Then again, *Gotte*'s own word cautioned not to worry about tomorrow, that each day had enough troubles of its own.

So she met Mike's gaze and nodded. "Perhaps it *is* better to take this one day at a time."

"Good." Mike put the last of the dishes away as Hannah let the sudsy water drain from the sink.

Leah stepped in the doorway just then. "I'm about to turn in for the evening. Hannah, I know you'll have an early morning tomorrow."

Hannah felt her cheeks warm. Had Leah felt it necessary to stay up and act as chaperone? "I'm sorry if we kept you up. I'm heading to my room now." Then she turned to Mike. "*Danke* again for your help. And I should warn you, Grace wakes early most mornings." With that she turned and followed Leah from the room.

Leah had assigned Hannah a room on the first floor, no doubt so she'd be less likely to check on Grace during the night. As she got ready for bed, Hannah thought about all that had happened today.

She'd been so angry with *Gotte* for taking Grace from her so abruptly. And to be honest, she'd also been angry with Him for sending Mike into her life, a man she loved deeply, only to put them in an impossible situation.

But being reminded of what Leah herself had gone through when she was only a little older than Hannah herself, knowing of her acceptance of her burdens and loss without complaint had been humbling. Leah's decision to focus on her blessings rather than her losses was a beautiful reminder of what faith and trust really meant.

Hannah only hoped she had the courage and strength of faith to emulate that kind of submission to *Gotte*.

Chapter 29

The next morning Hannah had no trouble rising early since her sleep had been sporadic. After she got herself ready to face the day, she went upstairs to check on Grace. To her surprise, Mike was there ahead of her, changing the toddler's diaper.

He was fully dressed, other than being barefoot, but his hair was sleep-tousled and there was a drowsy droop to his eyes. Seeing him like that, especially while he was in the midst of changing a diaper, should have had her rolling her eyes. Instead it warmed her down to her toes and set butterflies fluttering in her stomach.

His gaze focused on her for a moment, and from the way his eyes darkened she thought he might be feeling something similar. But all he said was, "Looks like Grace isn't the only one up early this morning."

Of course. She had to keep reminding herself—he liked her, but not in the way she felt about him.

"It's Memorial Day weekend. I expect the entire marketplace will be very busy today."

He pressed down the tabs on Grace's diaper. "Do you think you'll need some help?"

"We have everyone working a full-day shift, so I think we'll be okay." She almost felt sorry for him. He obviously didn't know what to do with himself while he waited for his new job to come through.

While they talked about the weather and other inconsequential topics, Hannah helped him dress Grace in her day clothes and *kapp*. Once done, she gave the girl a kiss and a hug. "There now, sunshine, time for me to head to the bakery and for you to have your breakfast." She handed Grace over to Mike. "She has oatmeal for breakfast along with apple juice in her sippy cup. Leah knows how much to fix if you need help."

"We'll be fine, but aren't you going to eat something before you leave?"

Hannah shook her head. "I'll have a quick cup of coffee before I go, then grab something to eat when I arrive at the bakery."

"I'll get your buggy hitched for you while you get your coffee."

"That's not necessary. Grace is ready for her breakfast and you—"

"Mom can help with that." And without waiting for her response, he handed Grace back to her and headed to his room, presumably to put on some shoes.

By the time she'd finished her coffee and had her pies and cookies packed up, Mike had her buggy hitched and pulled up close to the door.

When he stepped inside, he eyed the stack of pastry boxes. "How early today are you going to need those?"

"Mrs. Clemmons is picking up her pies at nine thirty and Mrs. LaBord asked for the cookies to be ready by eleven."

"Leave them. I'll drop them off at the bakery for you after I do my morning run."

Before she could protest, he made shooing motions. "It's no trouble. You know I'll be coming by for my morning whoopie pie anyway."

He really was going to be a wonderful *mann* for some lucky woman.

* * *

Mike watched Hannah drive off, then turned back to the kitchen. His mother was already feeding Grace, who seemed to be enjoying her oatmeal tremendously.

"Your eggs and biscuits are keeping warm on the stove whenever you're ready for them," his mother said without looking up from feeding Grace. "And there's a jar of blackberry jam I put up last year here on the table."

"Thank you." Mike took modest portions and sat at the table across from his mother and Grace.

His mother wiped Grace's chin. "You've told me about your *shveshtah*, but not about Grace's father. Did you know him?"

Mike shook his head. "Unfortunately, no. And Madison never spoke of him so all I know was what she wrote in her diary. Apparently she met him through one of those online dating sites. As soon as Maddi told him she was pregnant, he just packed up and moved on." Mike dreaded the day Grace would ask about her parents.

"I'll pray for him." Then she changed the subject. "I take it you and Hannah weren't able to work things out?"

It was the last thing he wanted to talk about. "No. It's hopeless."

"*Hopeless* is a terrible word. Our *Gotte* is a *Gotte* of hope, and through Him all things are possible."

Rather than responding, he blurted out the thing that had been on his mind since it happened. "The other day she told me she loved me."

His mother nodded. "*Gut* for her. Not that it wasn't obvious." Then she gave him a searching look. "And you did tell her how you feel, didn't you?"

Mike waved a hand as if it was a given. But had he actually said the words? "She has to know. I proposed to her not once but twice." There was only so much rejection a man could take.

She slumped, obviously disappointed. "Just like you knew about her feelings without being told."

That was different. Wasn't it? "What does it matter?" Mike knew he sounded defensive. "We can't marry if she won't agree to wed someone who's not Amish."

"So you asked her to leave her people?"

"I asked her to marry me. I left my job, my friends, my home and moved back here to make it easier for her. It's Hannah who won't compromise."

"There's another option, of course."

"Mother, I mean you no disrespect. But I can't leave the English world. I have a college education and worldly experiences that give me a different perspective from folks in this community. And honestly, I see no value in giving up things like my cell phone and the internet when there's nothing inherently evil about them and they have the potential to do so much good."

His mother nodded as if she understood. "So these

things, these conveniences are more important to you than Hannah?"

Not ready to answer that question, he pulled up another point. "Besides, I'm a paramedic—it's not just a job for me, it's a calling. I'm not a farmer or carpenter or craftsman of any type. I'm a paramedic."

"And you're so sure that rejoining our community would close that door to you?"

"What do you mean?"

Grace started fussing and his mother turned her attention to the toddler. "There now, little one, you're done with breakfast, are you? Let's get you cleaned up and you can play with your bowls and spoons."

Before his mother left the room with Grace, she turned back to him. "Since you're going to town, there's a note on the counter with a list of a few things I need from the grocery store. Would you mind picking them up for me?"

"Of course." Mike grabbed the list and headed out.

All during his run, his mother's words kept playing in his head. Did she really think he could effectively do his job as a paramedic and still follow the tenets of the *Ordnung*? Did she even know what his job entailed?

Conscious of the delivery he needed to make at the bakery, Mike cut his run short and didn't linger at the fire station once he'd cleaned up. When he arrived at the marketplace, he saw that Hannah had been right about the crowds. He was only able to find a parking place because someone was leaving just as he showed up.

As he wended his way through the groups of shoppers with his arms full, Mike wondered if he should have carried the boxes in in two batches. But he finally arrived at Sweet Kneads with the boxes and their contents intact. He didn't see Hannah at the front of the store, so he figured she was back in the kitchen. Making his way there, he found her pulling a pair of aromatic loaves of bread from the oven.

The smile she gave him looked more genuine than any he'd seen from her in a while.

"That's quite a crowd you have out there."

She nodded as she wiped her forehead with the back of her wrist. "It's been a *verrict* kind of morning. I had to turn down two large orders this morning and I for sure and certain hate to do that." She pulled some pie dough out of the refrigerator and grabbed her rolling pin. "I'm probably going to stay until three or so today just to keep the ovens going so we can serve our walk-in customers." Then she gave him a smile. "But good news for you is it gives you more time with Grace."

"My offer of help still stands."

"*Danke.* But besides me and Ada, Maisie, Rhoda and Bernice are all working a full day. If we have any more help, we'll start walking on each other." Then she gave him a speculative glance. "However, if you really want to help, there is one thing…"

"Name it."

"Our coffee delivery is delayed this week and Maisie tells me we're getting low. Do you think you could pick up enough to get us through today?"

"I'll be glad to. In fact, Mom wants me to pick up a few groceries for her anyway, so it's a two birds, one stone kind of situation."

She grinned. "Want to make it three birds? I made a grocery list after you did the inventory for me last night."

"I can see I'm turning into your errand boy."

She shrugged, unoffended. "You offered."

He grinned. "So I did." He held out his hand. "Hand it over and I'll get going. I assume you're in a hurry for that coffee."

To be honest, Mike really didn't mind running errands for his mom and for Hannah. He didn't have much else to do until his new job started in two weeks. If he had his own place, he could get it ready for Grace. He imagined how much she'd love a swing set in the backyard and maybe even a tree house when she got a little older.

Maybe it was because it was on his mind after what Ford had said yesterday, or maybe it was what his mother had said this morning, but everywhere he looked Mike saw reinforcement of that downside to the pervasiveness of technology. Waiting at a stoplight, he noticed the woman in the car beside him checking her phone and then typing a response to something. When the light changed and he pulled away, she was still staring at her phone. A few blocks down the road, a couple of men wearing identically logoed shirts stood at the corner waiting for the light to change. They also had their gazes fixed on the devices in their hand rather than talking to each other.

Later, when lunchtime rolled around, he stopped at a fast-food place to grab a burger and found himself comparing two groups of diners. One table had five people in Amish garb. From the looks of them, they ranged in age from early adolescence to late teens. All were involved in an animated conversation as they munched on their burgers and fries. Across the room was a group of four English teens, all of whom were busy reading and typing on their phones or tablets. When the waitress stopped at their table to take their orders, it was several beats before any of them dragged their attention away from their devices to focus on her.

Is that how Grace would be a dozen years from now? Was that really what was best for her?

Surely it didn't have to be that way. He could teach her to use mobile devices responsibly. And she would have her interaction with the Amish community to counterbalance her experiences in the outside world.

His gaze landed on an English couple who seemed to be communicating just fine. They were about Maddi's age and from the way they were holding hands and gazing into each other's eyes, they seemed to be in love. Was it real? Or was it like the trap Maddi had fallen into, all smoke and mirrors?

Come to think of it, those social dating sites could be considered yet another siren trap of social media. Though to be fair, he did know of two couples who'd met that way and things had turned out well for them.

Still, did the Amish have the right of it as Ford had said? Were the deeper connections and interdependence on family and community a good trade-off for the loss of the convenience and added security of instant communication capabilities?

Chapter 30

Wednesday morning, Hannah sat on the floor playing with Grace for just a moment knowing her time for this sort of intimacy was running out. Next week Mike would turn in the paperwork that would start the wheels turning to appoint him Grace's legal guardian and eventually her adoptive *daed*.

The animals had all been cared for and breakfast was behind them, so it was time to do the Wednesday basket delivery to shut-ins. Mike was supposed to pick her up this morning, but he seemed to be running a little late.

She finally heard the buggy pull up outside. Giving Grace one last squeeze, Hannah stood and dusted off her skirt. She moved to the kitchen but paused when she saw both Leah and Mike step inside. Almost more surprising than seeing Leah was seeing Mike dressed in the Amish style. He'd done so on Sunday when he attended church service at the Bixlers' place, but Hannah had assumed he'd only done that out of respect for the solemnity of the occasion. Unsure what to say to him, she turned to Leah.

"*Gut matin* and *wilkom*. But there wasn't any need for you to come. Martha has already said she's happy to keep an eye on Grace for me."

Martha smiled from where she stood by the counter. "And I still am. I've gotten to see much too little of Grace these last few weeks."

"Actually, I'm not here to watch Grace. Your *daed* and I plan to deliver the baskets this morning."

What was going on? "But why? I don't—"

Mike turned to her *daed* as if he hadn't heard her speak. "I'll help you get the baskets loaded."

It took the men two trips to carry the nine baskets out. And while they did that, Leah asked Hannah to create a list of who they needed to visit.

By the time she had the names listed, all the baskets had been loaded and Isaac and Leah made their exit.

Hannah turned to Martha and Mike. Why did she get the feeling that everyone knew what was going on here except her?

Mike took her elbow. "Since Martha agreed to keep an eye on Grace, why don't you take a walk with me?"

Growing more curious by the moment, and very aware of his hand on her arm, Hannah merely nodded. They walked without speaking for a while. Hannah glanced at him from the corner of her eye and realized there was something different about him today. He appeared more open, more at peace with himself than before. Was this change brought about by his growing closeness to Grace? Or was it something else?

She finally had to break the silence. "I wonder why

your *mamm* and my *daed* volunteered to deliver the baskets this morning."

"I asked them to."

When he didn't elaborate, she tried prompting him. "Why?"

By this time, they'd reached the hay barn and Mike waved toward the entrance. "Let's get in out of the wind."

Once inside, Mike led the way to some bales that were stacked just high enough to form a bench of sorts. As they took a seat, Hannah pointed to her left. "Right over there is where we found Grace. I can't believe it's only been a little over a year since she came into my life."

Mike took her hand. "And she's still in your life."

Hannah looked down at their joined hands, trying not to read anything into it. "Of course she is." Just not in the way she'd hoped.

"But that's not what I brought you out here to discuss."

The way he looked at her set those butterflies stirring again.

"I spoke with the bishop on Sunday. And again on Monday and Tuesday."

"Oh?" He still held her hand, which, for some reason, made it difficult to concentrate on his words.

"Yes, we discussed my work as a paramedic. Did you know there's nothing in the *Ordnung* that expressly forbids a member from working as a paramedic?"

Suddenly she had absolutely no trouble focusing on his words.

"What's not allowed is pursuing the extended formal education that's required. Of course, if someone came along who, say, already had that training and wanted to apply for baptism, he might actually be able to do both."

Hannah's gaze searched his face. Was he really saying what she thought he was? "*Do* you want to be baptized?"

"I do. The more time I spend here the more I find myself remembering and longing for the simple but abiding faith of my youth."

She searched his face. "And you're doing this for yourself, no one else?"

"The bishop asked me the same question, though he was much more confrontational. We talked for quite some time on the subject, as a matter of fact. But the answer is yes." He raised a brow. "But I'll need someone to help me relearn the language."

"I don't think that will be a problem." She clasped her hands tightly together trying to hold back the question she was longing to ask.

"Of course, there would be things to work out. Like not driving a motor vehicle or carrying a cell phone so you can be contacted in case of emergency call-outs."

Hannah felt she was on an emotional seesaw, first up and then down. "Those sound like big roadblocks," she said.

"I thought so, too. But Ford said driving is not a requirement of the job and carrying a pager would be an acceptable substitute for a cell phone." His smile broadened. "And apparently the bishop is willing to have the community discuss the possibility of using a pager under very strict circumstances."

"What about the lack of other technologies? That was the main reason you wanted Grace raised *Englisch*, ain't so? Because you felt it offered her greater safety and security."

Mike rubbed his jaw with his free hand. "Actually, after much thought I've come to see there are different ways to look at that issue, different aspects of what safety truly means to consider."

Enough was enough. "Are you saying you want to return to our community, to raise Grace among the Plain Folk?" she blurted out.

"Sweet Hannah, I'm saying much more than that. It's occurred to me that I've never actually told you how I feel about you." He raised a hand to caress her cheek, and almost without thinking she leaned into it.

"I thought it was obvious how very much I love you from the fact that I've twice now proposed to you. But as someone once told me, the words should be said aloud, the declaration made in no uncertain terms. So Hannah Eicher, listen to me and listen well. I love you. I love you deeply and sincerely. I think I have loved you almost from the moment I saw you walk into the diner with your beautiful smile and captivating eyes. I want to cherish you and grow old with you and spend the rest of my days trying to become the man you deserve. So, for the third time, will you do me the great honor of agreeing to be my wife?"

Hannah's butterflies were now in full flight and she could hardly breathe for the pounding in her chest. It was what she'd dreamed of, prayed for, for so long.

But she had to be sure. "Don't forget that I can't give you children."

Mike's smile was achingly tender. "Oh, sweetheart, you're so wrong about that. If nothing else, you kept Grace safe for me, for us. And she proved that a child doesn't have to be physically born to you to be a loving part of your family. There are so many children out there who desperately need families to love them." He gently ran a finger down the side of her face. "But you still haven't answered my question."

Hannah felt as if her chest could no longer contain her heart, as if her feet no longer touched the ground. "*Jah*, oh *jah* I will most certainly marry you. I love you so much, I feel like I'm the most blessed woman on earth!"

Mike's smile broadened and he wrapped his arms around her in a tender hug. In the shelter of his arms she felt cherished and safe and right where she was supposed to be.

* * *

Mike held this sweet, generous woman in his arms and felt like he was finally home. How could he have been so lucky as to win her heart? Having her by his side made everything he was giving up seem as nothing.

Of course there was more to be worked out, more issues to settle, but that all could wait for a bit—and with Grace by his side and lots of earnest and humble prayer, he had confidence it would all work out as it should.

He'd heard her once describe Grace's arrival as her springtime miracle. But building a family with Hannah and Grace was a springtime miracle of his very own.

Epilogue

Six months later

Hannah slid a pan of gingerbread cookies from the oven. The warm, spicy scent of molasses, cloves and cinnamon filled her kitchen.

Her kitchen—Hannah still wasn't quite used to thinking of it in those terms. It had been seven weeks since she'd married Micah and moved in with him, Grace and Leah. Even though she and Leah worked well together it had taken some adjustment on both their parts to figure out their relative roles in the running of the house. But then Leah had married Hannah's *daed* a week ago and moved to the Eicher farm.

Humming, Hannah set the sheet pan on the cooling rack. The wind was howling outside but here in the house it was cozy. Grace was in bed and Micah was in the basement working on a doll cradle to give the little girl for Christmas. She had been right, Micah was a wonderful *daed*. The day after their wedding the two of them had completed the adoption of Grace. It was the best wedding gift she could have received—they were truly a *familye* now.

"All done?"

Hannah turned with a smile to see Micah in the basement doorway, watching her, wearing that tender expression that always warmed her through and through. "*Jah*. I just need to package them up after they cool, and the shut-in baskets will be ready to deliver in the morning."

Micah approached and put his arms around her from behind as she worked at the counter. She leaned back against him, enjoying the feeling of being loved, cherished and protected. Her heart was so full of love for this man that there were days when she thought it would burst from her chest.

He nuzzled the nape of her neck and she shivered in delight. His beard was coming in nicely now and she thought it made him look even more handsome than before.

"Mmmm, you smell nice," he said.

She laughed. "You're confusing me with the cookies."

"I beg to differ." He turned her around and kissed her tenderly. "I could never confuse you with a cookie. You're so much sweeter."

Hannah stroked his cheek with the back of her hand, studying anew the face that had become so very, very dear to her.

And just as she had every day since they'd pledged their love, she silently thanked *Gotte* that Grace and Micah had come into her life. Never had a person been so blessed. *Gotte* had answered the prayers she'd uttered in her darkest hour by giving her this precious, beautiful *familye* to love and be loved by.

And she planned to spend the rest of her life doing everything in her power to cherish this wondrous, miraculous gift.

Then she stepped on tiptoe and gave him a quick kiss before she pulled away. "You, Mr. Burkholder, are a distraction, and I still have a kitchen to clean up before I go to bed."

Micah tapped her nose then stepped back. "In that case, I'll dry while you wash." And with that he grabbed a dishcloth and smiled at her expectantly.

Yes, she was very blessed indeed.

Don't miss Martha Eicher's story in the next heartwarming
Hope's Haven novel coming Spring 2023

Her Amish Patchwork Family

About the Author

Winnie Griggs is the multi-published, award-winning author of romances that focus on small towns, big hearts, and amazing grace. Her work has won a number of regional and national awards, including the Romantic Times Reviewers' Choice Award. Winnie grew up in southeast Louisiana in an undeveloped area her friends thought of as the back of beyond. Eventually she found her own Prince Charming, and together they built a storybook happily-ever-after, one that includes four now-grown children who are all happily pursuing adventures of their own.

When not busy writing, she enjoys cooking, browsing estate sales and solving puzzles. She is also a list maker, a lover of exotic teas, and holds an advanced degree in the art of procrastination.

You can learn more at:
WinnieGriggs.com
Twitter @GriggsWinnie
Facebook.com/WinnieGriggs.Author
Pinterest.com/WDGriggs

Fall in love with these small-town romances full of tight-knit communities and heartwarming charm!

**THE BEACHSIDE
BED AND BREAKFAST**
by Hope Ramsay

Ashley Howland Scott has no time for romance while grieving for her husband, caring for her son, and running Magnolia Harbor's only bed and breakfast. But slowly, Rev. Micah St. Pierre has become a friend…and maybe something more. Micah cannot date a member of his congregation, so there's no point in sharing his feelings with Ashley, no matter how much he yearns to. But the more time they spend together, the more Micah wonders whether Ashley is his match made in heaven.

THE SUMMER SISTERS
by Sara Richardson

The Buchanan sisters share everything—even ownership of their beloved Juniper Inn. As children, they spent every holiday there, until a feud between their mother, Lillian, and Aunt Sassy kept them away. When the grand reopening of the inn coincides with Sassy's seventieth birthday, Rose, the youngest sister, decides it's time for a family reunion. Only she'll need help from a certain handsome hardware-store owner to pull off the celebration…

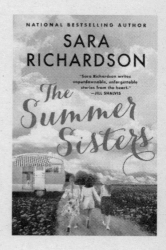

SOMETHING BLUE
by Heather McGovern

Wedding planner Beth Shipley has seen it all: bridezillas, monster-in-laws, and last-minute jitters at the altar. But this wedding is different—and the stakes are much, *much* higher. Not only is her best friend the bride, but bookings at her family's inn have been in free fall. Beth knows she can save her family's business—as long as she doesn't let best man Sawyer Silva's good looks and overprotective, overbearing, older-brother act distract her. Includes a bonus story by Annie Rains!

HOW SWEET IT IS
by Dylan Newton

Event planner Kate Sweet is famous for creating happily-ever-after moments for dream weddings. So how is it that her best friend has roped her into planning a best-selling horror writer's book launch extravaganza in a small town? The second Kate meets the drop-dead-hot Knight of Nightmares, Drake Matthews, her well-ordered life quickly transforms into an absolute nightmare. But neither are prepared for the sweet sting of attraction they feel for each other. Will the queen of romance fall for the king of horror?

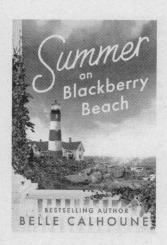

SUMMER ON BLACKBERRY BEACH
by Belle Calhoune

Navy SEAL Luke Keegan is back in his hometown for the summer, and the rumor mill can't stop whispering about him and teacher Stella Marshall. He never thought he'd propose a fake relationship, but it's the only way to stop the runaway speculation about their love lives. Pretending to date a woman as stunning as Stella is easy. Not falling for her is the hard part, especially with the real attraction buzzing between them. Could their faux summer romance lead to true love?

FALLING FOR YOU
by Barb Curtis

Just when recently evicted yoga instructor Faith Rotolo thinks her luck has run out, she inherits a historic mansion in quaint Sapphire Springs. But her new home needs fixing up and the handsome local contractor, Rob Milan, is spoiling her daydreams with the realities of the project . . . and his grouchy personality. While they work together, their spirited clashes wind up sparking a powerful attraction. As work nears completion, will she and Rob realize that they deserve a fresh start too?

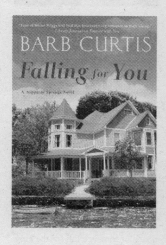

HER AMISH SPRINGTIME MIRACLE
by Winnie Griggs

Amish baker Hannah Eicher has always wanted a *familye* of her own, so finding sweet baby Grace in her barn seems like an answer to her prayers. Until *Englischer* paramedic Mike Colder shows up in Hope's Haven, hoping to find his late sister's baby. As Hannah and Mike contemplate what's best for Grace, they spend more and more time together while enjoying the warm community and simple life. Despite their wildly different worlds, will Mike and Hannah find the true meaning of "family"?

THE AMISH FARMER'S PROPOSAL
by Barbara Cameron

When Amish dairy farmer Abe Stoltzfus tumbles from his roof, he's lucky his longtime friend Lavinia Fisher is there to help. He secretly hoped to propose to her, but now, with his injuries, his dairy farm in danger, and his harvest at stake, Abe worries he'll only be a burden. Yet, as he heals with Lavinia's gentle support and unflagging optimism, the two grow even closer. But will she be able to convince him that real love doesn't need perfect timing?